120 June 5

# THE SISTERS OF SUMMIT AVENUE

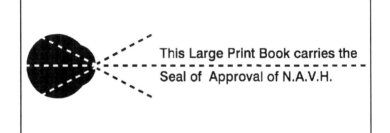

This Large Print Book carries the
Seal of Approval of N.A.V.H.

# THE SISTERS OF SUMMIT AVENUE

## LYNN CULLEN

**WHEELER PUBLISHING**
A part of Gale, a Cengage Company

LP FIC CULLEN

GALE
A Cengage Company

**LIBRARY OF CONGRESS CIP DATA ON FILE.
CATALOGUING IN PUBLICATION FOR THIS BOOK
IS AVAILABLE FROM THE LIBRARY OF CONGRESS**

ISBN-13: 978-1-4328-7246-5 (hardcover alk. paper)

Published in 2020 by arrangement with Gallery Books, an imprint of Simon & Schuster, Inc.

Printed in Mexico
1 2 3 4 5 6 7 24 23 22 21 20

*For my mother and her sisters,
my sisters, my daughters,
and their daughters,
and the good men in our lives.*

# How the story begins

*1908*

Little Ruth felt herself being shaken. She opened an eye. Six-year-old June leaned over her, the sleeves of her red robe dragging against Ruth's quilt.

"Get up! Santa's been here!"

Ruth sat up and rubbed her eyes, then blinked at the top of June's wavy gold hair as her big sister jammed slippers on her feet and buttoned her into her robe. She slid off their bed and let June lead her, slippers scuffing across the wood floor.

They crouched at the entrance to the front room. Empty pink sockets flashed where June's baby teeth had recently been. "Ready? One, two —"

Ruth joined in. "— Free!"

They burst into the room, where on a table, a scraggly pine, no taller than four-year-old Ruth, drooped under the weight of tinsel. The celluloid angel on top, a serene smile painted on her shiny face, dipped down as if to tell a secret. Mother and Dad, in their robes and nightcaps, stood off to the side, together, for once.

"Ho ho ho," said Dad. "Merry Christmas!"

Ruth and June mined their stockings for peppermint sticks and then, with the candy crooked in their cheeks, attended to the presents under the tree, one for each girl.

Ruth fingered a package wrapped in funny-papers as she eyed the larger one next to it.

"That one's for you, Ruthie," Mother called from under Dad's arm. When Ruth ripped it open, a rubber ball and metal jacks tumbled out. She looked over at her sister, freeing the bigger present from its sheet of newspaper — a doll the size of a sack of flour. Painted eyes stared out from its smooth cloth face.

Ruth watched the little red ball roll past the smattering of jacks and under a chair. Tears needled her eyes and nose.

June tilted her head at her, much in the manner of the tree angel. After a stroke of the doll's long brown yarn hair, she held it out to Ruth. "Trade."

Ruth snatched the doll, clutched it to her throat, then glared at June as if challenging her to take it back. But June wasn't watching. She was running her finger through the tinsel on the tree. If she gave her sister enough time, she would give it back. She always did.

# DOROTHY

Are you in there?

Good. I thought that you were.

As I was saying: That rain! It had turned from prickly sleet into a pitiless deluge. I can still feel it beating my hair from its pins and rapping my neck with cold knuckles before it snaked an icy rivulet down my back. Teeth chattering, I drummed down the steps and to the dead lawn, where I splashed past the bandstand, over a muddy flower bed, and through some little trees. I stopped short. Ten-foot iron spears loomed in the dark before me: the fence that kept in the residents. I grabbed onto one of the rusty palings to catch my breath, then hoisted up the baby. She looked up from inside my coat. Even with fat raindrops plunking on her eleven-month-old's fluff, her face was blank.

Ice shot through my veins.

I closed my collar over her head and

plunged on toward the gatehouse. There was nothing wrong with her, no matter what Mrs. Lamb said. And if there was, I didn't care.

The excuses I had cooked up for the guard were a waste. He wasn't in his little hut. I slipped out the gate and onto State Street, its bricks shining under a streetlamp.

I hadn't gotten far when I heard the sucking of shoe rubbers against brick. I turned away to let their owner pass.

The sucking stopped. Out of the corner of my eye, I saw soggy trouser legs about a body's length away. I tightened my grip on the baby. Caught!

"Are you all right?"

My sights crept up a long black coat to a dripping umbrella. The umbrella tipped to reveal a young man in a bowler and rain-fogged wire-rim glasses. He had a chin the size of a hand trowel.

"Ma'am?" he asked. "You need help?"

My teeth hurt from chattering. A horse pulling a buggy clopped by, leaving a weighty splat. I could smell the manure as the buggy juddered away.

The chinny fellow wouldn't leave. "Ma'am?" He cleared his throat. "You don't even have a hat."

I didn't. It had fallen off when I'd

snatched the baby out of the crib. *Go away,* I wanted to tell him, but couldn't move my mouth. People get lockjaw from stepping on rusty nails. This was what it must feel like.

"My sister Edna lives around the corner. On Parnell. I was just heading there from a wireless telegraphy meet-up." He stepped closer with a rubbery squish.

He had sensitive lips, sweet as a child's in that tremendous chin. I laughed. I wasn't quite right.

He pulled back his head. "Ma'am?"

From somewhere on the other side of the fence, a muffled groan escalated into a shriek, then dissolved in the spattering rain.

He sighed. "I don't know how Edna stands living by this place. I couldn't bear hearing this suffering all night and day."

The top of my coat gapped open as I turned away.

He leaned to look in. "Say, is that a baby in there?"

I shrank back.

My knees buckled. He reached out to steady me but stopped short of making contact. He seemed to know that if he touched me, I would run.

He spoke gently, as if to a skittish animal. "My name is William but I go by Bud. Bud Dowdy. Everyone calls me Rowdy Dowdy."

I rolled my gaze up at him. He looked as rowdy as a baby bunny.

He edged in the direction in which he wanted to coax me. "I'm going to my sister's now. Around the corner. See?" He pointed. "We can fetch a cab from there to take you wherever you need to go. But come get warm first." He saw my hesitation. "If you want."

He took a few steps away, then stopped, as if encouraging a stray cat.

The few times in my life that I'd trusted people had not worked out well. But there was something gentle about him, something good. And I had to get my baby out of the rain.

In his sister's home, a tidy frame cottage with a neat gingerbread-trimmed porch, I sat on the edge of a wooden chair, not wanting to get it wet, while I kept my grip on the baby on my lap and a cup of tea. Small as it was, it was a nice house, homey, smelling of furniture wax and fried potatoes. Clocks ticked on nearly every surface, brass clocks, wooden clocks, porcelain clocks, clocks with danglies dripping from them, each clock clicking to its own particular beat. On a pink-flowered chair, his sister Edna, no-necked, graying, as stout as a fireplug and blessed with the family chin, stared at me, stirring her own tea. She offered the baby her spoon. She glanced at me when the baby didn't reach for it. The baby couldn't even sit up right.

She laid her spoon on her saucer with a clink. "Who are you? What were you doing by the State School with a baby on such an awful night?" When I didn't answer quickly enough, she asked her brother, "Who is she?"

What could I tell them?

"Can't you see that she's in trouble?" William exclaimed.

The clocks chittered away.

"How old is the child?" she asked.

I told her eleven months.

Her chin rubbed her chest as she shook her head. "Bud has always brought home baby birds and rabbits and such. I have fed more little creatures with eyedroppers because of this man." She bounced her elbow on the arm of her chair in emphasis as she pointed at him. "But this is the first time that he's brought home an actual human baby and her mother."

He blushed so violently that it seemed to light up the fine black hair combed back from his forehead.

" 'Bud, Bud, Stick in the Mud.' He's always been shy. Knows more about wireless transmitters than he does about women. If you ever need to learn the Morse code, you're in luck." The clocks tapped as Edna twirled a curl at the base of her sagging yellow pompadour. "But you look like a good enough little girl."

I didn't know what to say about that.

She put down her cup and got up. "I'm not going to send you back out into the rain with a child. Come on. You can't stay in those wet clothes. You must be frozen."

When I didn't move, she snapped her fingers. "Let's go. Hop to."

William spread his hands as if there was nothing he could do about his sister. He beamed when I put down my cup and followed her.

■ ■ ■ ■

# PART ONE

■ ■ ■ ■

# ONE

*Minneapolis, Minnesota, 1934*

June had been working for Betty Crocker for two of her thirty-two years. Yet each morning when she arrived at the Minneapolis Grain Exchange Building with its wheat sheaves carved around the door and its imposing wall of elevators, and she clicked across the cavernous green marble lobby in her chunky-heeled nurse's shoes, her purse swinging on her arm above her gloves and the skirt of her white uniform swishing against her hosiery, she felt as if she were on the verge of discovery. Of what, she didn't know. As she rode up in the elevator thick with the smell of brass polish, she imagined herself to be like the heavy brown cicada larvae that lumbered up the trunks of the trees of her Summit Avenue estate in St. Paul. Her body was swelling, her too-tight shell was splitting, and her wings were unfurling to fly her up to the treetops — or

19

in her case, to the ninth floor — where she might sing, or soar . . . or fall down to the ground to buzz clumsily on her back.

None of the other women in the Betty Crocker test kitchen would guess her fear of failure; at least she hoped not. All twenty-one of them had an area of expertise. Karen from Hastings, Nebraska, was the go-to girl on naming foods; "Pigs in Blankets" were "Wiener Turnovers" until she came along. Carolyn of Angola, Indiana, was the Queen of Stretching a Dime, a handy skill when most people had so few of them these days. Eager little Darlene from Endeavor, Wisconsin, whose hunger for more than Bundt cakes was belied by her wholesome, well-scrubbed face, was their expert on pleasing men, proof that you should never judge a book by the cover.

June's role around the Crocker kitchen was to be the Sophisticated One. The other girls called upon her to create menus for "smart luncheons" and "elegant suppers," and to show how "distinguished social leaders" set their lovely tables in advertisements and cooking publications like last year's *Betty Crocker's 101 Delicious Bisquick Creations as Made and Served by Well-Known Gracious Hostesses, Famous Chefs, Distinguished Epicures, and Smart Luminaries of*

*Movieland.* (Advertising's title, not hers.) She was the Girl Friday to whom the others came when describing how to put on a proper plate luncheon, yachting party, or hunt club breakfast, activities the ad men imagined that Betty Crocker's fans dreamed of.

While a campaign that featured the man-trapping properties of flour always played well, increasingly Advertising was turning its attention to the everyday housewife. Once they got her married, what did they imagine that the American Woman wanted? More, that's what, of everything! She wanted, no, she *deserved* the High Life and all that came with it: furs and maids and Cadillacs, and most importantly, the burning envy of her peers. And once the ember of that desire was fanned and stoked into a raging fire of need, how might the American Woman attain it? How might your plain penny-squeezing Jane, at home frying cabbage for her unemployed husband and letting down the cuffs of her growing children's coat sleeves, transform herself into the elegant, popular, tiara-wearing hostess portrayed in publications? By listening to that oracle of success (who happened to use a lot of flour) Betty Crocker — that's how!

And so June had been hired. She was the

only girl on staff without a home ec degree. Her husband had been her qualifier. Not only was Richard a prominent surgeon in town, but his family came from money. Buckets of it. No one at the company had asked her who her own family was when they'd hired her. They still hadn't.

"Here we are, Betty!" The elevator operator, Mr. Gustafson, an elfin, elderly gentleman with a long upper lip and bright gray eyes, folded back the brass restraining gate with the same zeal that he'd shown since hiring on a few months ago — grateful to have employment in these difficult times, June assumed. He called all the women who worked in the Betty Crocker kitchen "Betty."

He pulled the heavy lever to open the doors. "Go make someone happy!"

June replied to him as she did every day. "I will, Mr. Gustafson, I will."

She stepped across a mat bristling with the word welcome. Even the floor was friendly in Betty Crocker's world. A push through glass doors brought June into the Tasting Room, a yellow-papered space bright with stylish caramel-colored Early American tables and chairs, ruffled curtains, and the smell of warm spice cake, frying bacon, and Lysol. The girls were already at work. You had to get up early to get ahead in the Crocker kitchen.

At her cubby, June peeled off her gloves, purse, and hat, stashed them on the shelf, checked her mirror (small blemish by her nose — who knew that you still got pimples at her age?), and readjusted her trademark pearl choker. She was the only Crockette to wear such an expensive accessory. She would have rather left it at home out of respect to the others, most of whom were the only breadwinners in their families and wore the same plain white dress every day to work, but her bosses complimented her on the necklace and encouraged her to wear it. For now, it stayed.

She took out her binder, and then went through an additional set of glass doors to enter what appeared to be a cross between a scientific laboratory and an appliance store. To the left gleamed a white-enameled bank of the latest in electric refrigerators, ovens, and ranges, upon one of which the previously detected bacon sizzled. To the right, a dozen women in white, down to their shoes, tapped purposefully around the rows of white porcelain-topped tables, measuring concoctions, pouring mixtures into pans, or writing notes, even at this early hour. White sinks stood along the back wall, ready to sanitize.

But this was not your typical dull research facility. Pains had been taken to give the test kitchen the feel of a lady cook's playground. Orange and navy plates marched across the cornice above the stoves. A tomato-red watering can and a copper teapot winked from the corner shelves. Blue checked curtains waved from windows open to the springtime breeze and a view of the nearby flour mill, atop which scrolling letters spelled out in lights: *"Eventually."*

*Eventually — Why Not Now?* was the company's original slogan. June supposed that "You're going to want our flour sooner or later, so you might as well buy it now," was probably not the most compelling argument to make a sale. But the forefathers had made a leap in figuring out how to net buyers in 1921, when one of them realized that a likable female character might sell goods better than even a catchy motto ever could. Hello, Betty Crocker!

June laid her notebook on one of the tables, then peered into the bowl that her neighbor, Darlene from Endeavor, hugged to her white lapels. Man-loving little Darlene, squeaky-clean, honey-blond, white-lashed, and every bit as energetic as you'd imagine someone from a town called Endeavor might be, was fresh out of the home economics department of the university in Madison. She wouldn't last long. She'd gotten married last year and a baby would surely follow. They always did. Unless you were June.

"What are you making today?"

"Cheese and bacon waffles!" Darlene sang.

"Interesting. Do you put the bacon in the mix?"

"No, just the grated American, half a cup per recipe. I'm thinking I'll lay cooked strips directly on the waffle iron, then *sssss* —" Darlene acted out clamping a lid down on a waffle iron, sending a glop of batter from her spoon into her bowl. "— I'll seal them in. I got the idea in a dream last night. I woke up Gary when I wrote it down. He was quite the grump — until I made it worth his while."

When they glanced at one another, Darlene laughed. Wife humor.

She ironed the grin out of her voice. "What do you think of using cheese and bacon waffles on a breakfast menu for Clark Gable?"

June raised her chin as if she and Richard, too, were going wild under the covers, although anyone with a touch of class might consider it just a wee bit gauche to boast about it. "Hmm. Sounds promising. I'll think about it. Thank you."

It was genius.

And there was nothing happening in her and Richard's bedroom for her to brag about these days, even if she'd wanted to.

Anyhow, she had her own new recipe for *Let the Stars Show You How to Take a Trick a Day with Bisquick,* the booklet they were currently developing. Until twenty seconds ago, she'd been pleased with it. She'd gotten it last evening while being walked by the dog, a rambunctious German shepherd named Stella that Richard had chosen and she took care of.

It had been a glorious evening in May, with the air full of the scent of new leaves and blooming lilacs, the kind of evening that makes one feel inexplicably hopeful. Stella had been yanking her past a ragged man shooting a slingshot at pigeons on a telephone line (dinner, apparently) and some youths tossing a football on the lawn of the college down the street. Suddenly the boys' calls to one another got louder and their dives for the ball more exaggerated. They were looking in her direction. June responded to the college idiots as did the peahens to the peacocks shaking open their tail feathers in the Como Park Zoo: she ignored them.

She was studiously doing just that as Stella wrenched her arm from its socket, when a football skidded on the sidewalk in front of her. The dog lunged for it, nails scrabbling on cement.

A boy slicked back the blond lock that was flapping in rhythm with the wide legs of his flannel trousers as he trotted up — a rich kid, or at least his family had been, before The Crash. He grinned. "Hey, gorgeous, has anyone ever told you you're beautiful?"

The knee-jerk burst of relief that came from hearing that as a matron of thirty-two, she had not yet totally lost "it," evaporated. The heat of shame leaped up in its place, her fig leaf of status snatched away. Her Chicago-bought clothes, her Bes-Ben hat, her diamond ring were for naught. She was back to being a nobody, just a good-looking broad, unworthy of respect. How did he know?

Aware of the ragged man watching them as he stuffed a fallen bird into his gunny sack, she pried the ball from Stella's mouth to make her escape. And then, even as the sweat of embarrassment sprang into the dress shields under her arms, it came to her: she could do a football-shaped chocolate cake for *Take a Trick,* playing up Clark Gable's image as an athlete.

Already scheming how this might be achieved — she could cut the layers and re-assemble them! — the milk chocolate frosting could be dappled to resemble leather! — she had absentmindedly heaved back the ball to the startled youth. Here, shake your tail feathers, sonny!

Now, as she smelled the bacon Darlene was cooking, she realized a cake that looked like a football would never excite men as much as something with bacon in it. Although she wouldn't eat the stuff — she felt too sorry for the pigs — she knew that her bosses thought recipes with fatty meats, and any other foods that men particularly liked, sold flour well, even though women were the ones usually buying the product. Maybe if she used bacon as a seam on a football-shaped waffle . . .

She took a stool. As sophisticated as she and her pearls were supposed to be, she wasn't the best at developing recipes, one of every girl's duties on the job. They were expected to follow their products from the time the items were hatched in the research lab, through the famous Betty Crocker "Kitchen-testing," then through market testing and on to promotion on Betty's radio show and in publications. They all chipped in to answer Betty's fan mail, too — four thousand letters on some days, nothing to sniff at. They spent a portion of each day doling out their expert advice on cooking, homemaking, and, often, men. (Those letters were handed to Darlene.) They signed their responses in Betty's rounded, uniform, maybe a tad childish signature. One of the fellows in Advertising had chosen it.

The glass doors to the test kitchen crashed open. In barged a substantial woman, hair-netted, wire-spectacled, and sprigged-cotton-clad. A large patent leather purse hung from one fleshy arm and a picnic basket from the other.

"We've come to see Betty Crocker!"

The girls stopped in their work, alert as a herd of deer.

Advertising had been stepping up their encouragement of Betty Crocker's radio fans to visit her in her kitchen in Minneapolis. June worried about the wisdom of this. The country was oozing with lonely, desperate, destitute women, women anxious for something to cling to with so many of their men cut adrift. Over the last four years, America had become a nation of hoboes and Hoovervilles, bank robbers and soup lines, home foreclosures and sky-scraper leaps. In Minneapolis, men walked around the Gateway District with a stunned, sheepish expression on their faces. Jobless single women lived in the stacks in the libraries or in the train station, speaking to no one, as elusive as ghosts. Packs of children snuck into the comforting darkness of the movie shows, where Frankenstein and King Kong scared them less than their own sleepwalking parents.

Even the weather had gone haywire, breaking heat and drought records across the country. In some parts of the West, waves of jackrabbits, grasshoppers, and spiders had descended, all of them hungry for the crops that had already been lost. Millions of families courted disaster of some sort each day, and they were starved for relief and diversion. Betty Crocker gave it to them. Oh, sometimes Betty's radio shows sounded trivial, with her finicky football players looking for wives, her infantile bachelor doctors, and her no-roll pie crusts. She spent entirely too much time showcasing the thoughts, desires, and recipes of movie stars. Who gave two figs what Bing Crosby ate for supper?

But often what Betty Crocker did was heroic. She was at her best when she cheered on everyday women, making them feel proud of holding their families together. She gave them the strength to dry their eyes on their aprons and get cooking for their paralyzed men and frightened kids, no matter what disaster was on their doorstep. She gave women hope. She gave them advice. She gave them cookies. She was America's mother. June wished, fervently, that she were hers.

It was a shame that Betty didn't exist.

At the visitor's hip wavered her thin, younger version down to the same flowered print, as if Mama had been cranked through some sort of grinder that took off years and pounds. She ducked her head at the girls. "We don't know if she's here, Mother. She might be on the radio now."

The mother's small steel-edged teeth shone along with her glasses in the artificial light. "Can't be. It's not showtime."

Over bowls and clipboards, the girls exchanged glances. Would she go easily or hard? You couldn't tell by looking. Sometimes the sweetest old ladies fought like bobcats.

"Nonsense. She said to come visit her in her kitchen and here we are!" The mother lifted her arms, bashing her basket against a refrigerator. Out from under the lid popped the flop-eared head of a beagle pup.

Darlene from Endeavor went first. "Good morning!" She kept stirring as she approached the visitors. "I'm sorry, ma'am, but we don't allow animals in here. Health department orders."

The dog dropped back inside the basket as if he understood.

"There was nobody at home to watch him." The mother placed a protective hand over the basket lid. "We've come all the way from Topeka. At great expense."

June eased to her feet, a green feeling rising in her throat. In her peripheral vision, she could see the other girls cautiously leaving their bowls and pans and cookie sheets. She picked up one of the boxes of tissues placed around the kitchen just for these occasions.

"We'd better go, Mother."

"No, Enid. Betty and I are friends! We've exchanged letters. I've got them right here." The mother released her purse clasp with clumsy gloved fingers. When it gaped open, carefully slit envelopes, a handkerchief, a coin purse, a box of Milk Duds, a hand-colored portrait of a young man, and a copy of Betty's *15 Ways to a Man's Heart* tumbled out in a colorful shower. The little booklet fell open to a photo of Betty Crocker. "It's easy to have 'A WAY WITH MEN,' " it crowed, "just try these recipes!"

The other girls were scooping up the items and stuffing them in the woman's purse when June stepped up, smiling in spite of the nausea that always flared before a confrontation. "May I help you?"

The mother gasped. "You're . . . Betty." She grabbed June's wrist. Her voice broke. "Betty! It's me. Blanche from Topeka!"

"I'm so sorry, dear, but I'm not Betty."

The mother thrust her face close, her gloved fingers digging into June's wrist. "Look at those blue eyes, that sweet smile, that slim neck, just like in your pictures. Though you're blonder than I thought." She squinted at June's hair. "Did you peroxide?"

June actually did somewhat resemble the painting of Betty used by Advertising, although it was just a coincidence. The forefathers had had Betty drawn up years before June was hired. "I'm afraid I'm not Betty Crocker, ma'am."

"I guess you don't really sound like her." Reluctantly, the mother let go. "Then where is she?"

June swallowed back another green wave. Her head was starting to pound. Her whole life, conflict had undone her. She didn't know why. You'd think that her life as a society wife would have eased her discomfort, but it hadn't. If anything, it had made it worse.

"I am sorry to tell you this," she said, "but there is no one, single Betty."

"What? What do you mean? I don't understand." The mother looked from June to the other girls, forming a semicircle around her. "Who's that on the radio, the friend of all the movie stars and society folk, the peach who's always helping gals to land men? She's got those nephews who have that terrible habit of gobbling up all her goodies, the rascals. You know — Betty!"

"I think you might mean Agnes White," June said gently. "Agnes performs on the national show. That's her lovely voice that you hear."

"Agnes who? Are those her nephews?"

June massaged her pearl choker. "You also might be interested to learn about Marjorie Husted. She writes all our marvelous radio scripts."

The mother shook her head. "So *she's* the aunt of those boys?"

"Wait a minute." The daughter's face had gone tight. "We know that Betty has a lot of helpers testing out her recipes and such. She says so on the radio and in her letters. Is that who you are?"

"Yes!" exclaimed Karen from Nebraska, perhaps too quickly.

"Well," said the daughter, "we didn't come all this way to meet them."

The mother opened her purse again and drew out the portrait. "Here's my boy Alvin who I wrote Betty about." She displayed the picture with the edges between her palms so as not to fingerprint it. "I know that Betty says she's having too much fun baking cakes to marry, but she's got to be lonely." She shifted as if irritated by her girdle. "I promise you, my Alvin will make Miss Crocker a bang-up husband. He's a wonderful son and he's got good work — he's a brakeman on the railroad. Tell Betty that! She might be interested."

"Mother," the daughter said grimly, "don't you see? What they are saying is that there is no Betty. I think they made her up."

Still holding up the portrait, the mother gazed around the circle. "Why would they lie?"

"You're getting double your money's worth with all of us!" Darlene exclaimed. "We are all Bettys."

"No, you're not."

The charade was over. Time to cut their losses. June held out the box of tissues, the sight of which released the woman's tears.

It always did.

The daughter's voice was thick. "You should be ashamed of yourselves."

June offered her a Kleenex, too, the pearls around her neck suddenly heavy. It was the third marriage proposal that Betty had received in the mail this week but the first delivered in person by a parent. She drew an exhausted breath. "They need water. Could somebody please bring these tired women a glass of water?"

She felt her way back to her stool and dropped down as the other Bettys helped the visitors.

Ten minutes later, mother and daughter were at a table in the tasting room, sipping water and eating Cheese and Bacon Waffles, a stack of autographed Betty publications next to their plates. Judy from Duluth, the most junior Betty, smiled and chatted with them as she signed another booklet in the slightly juvenile Crocker signature. Under the table, the beagle puppy lapped water from a china soup bowl that someone had produced.

Darlene settled next to June at their table in the test kitchen. "I'm all thumbs when we get caught, but you are so good at soothing people. How'd you ever learn that?"

The sleeves of June's white dress swished

as she crossed her arms. She drew in a breath, then let it out with a smile. "What other recipes do you have for Clark Gable?"

# Two

*Indiana-Michigan Line, 1934*

The wooden head of the clothespin dug into Ruth's palm as she clipped John's under-shirt to the rope line. She was surprised by how much it hurt. She didn't think she had a tender place left on her body, what with all the milking, hoeing, hoisting, and hauling that she had to do with a husband permanently laid up in bed, not to mention having to ride herd over four kids. Work boots weren't as tough. She was only thirty.

She glanced at the barn then walked along, swiping her forehead with the sleeve of her faded dress as she pinned. She must have been nuts to have told Mother she'd finish hanging up the wash for her in this heat. Today at dawn the thermometer outside the kitchen window said eighty-seven degrees. Who ever heard of such weather on May 8th in northern Indiana? 1933 held the record for the hottest year ever, but already 1934 was breaking it. Look at the grass, prostrate in the wake of her Sunday shoes, too juiceless to lift itself. It needed rain, the crumbling empty furrows of the field behind her needed rain, everything needed rain. There hadn't been a drop since March.

Another glance at the barn, then she plucked a wet dress from her basket. A picture she'd seen in the paper last year reared up in her mind. *Black blizzard sweeps plains,* the caption said. In the grainy newsprint photo, a black billowing earth-to-sky cloud of dirt was devouring a town of white frame houses. She imagined frenzied deer and their fawns leaping over fences to escape, rabbits, foxes running, while earth-bound cattle, trapped in their blocky bodies, huddled against the barbed wire while dust slowly filled their lungs. She saw women, children, old folks, hiding behind closed doors as dust spilled around the edges like sand through fingers. She heard children coughing.

She rammed a pin on the clothesline. *Oh, quit scaring yourself. Black blizzards never made it past Oklahoma. One is never going to hit here.* Her real worry was in finding what little hay there was left in the Tri-State area due to the drought. She needed to supplement her whisk-broom of a pasture, not that *she* had the money. Yet, at a time when so many people were losing their farms, *she* was never going to go under. Lucky, lucky, her. *She* was getting a handout from the most humbling of all sources: her own sister, June.

She threw another glance toward the barn. The scent of bleach in her daughter's undershirt stung her nose as she clipped it to the line — her mother was way too heavy-handed with the stuff. Anyhow, she shouldn't resent June. June was just trying to help. It had been Ruth's own choice to marry a farmer, a risky line of work even in the best of times. She'd had other suitors back in Fort Wayne, where she'd grown up. While she might not have been the homecoming queen, the Pep Club secretary, or the girl voted Most Popular in high school as June had been, boys liked her well enough; at least the ones she wanted did.

When she had been a senior in high school, she had chosen John. No one had made her. She couldn't say exactly why now. That she loved how he smelled didn't seem like a good enough reason, or that he had fine brown hair that was almost black, just like her dad's, or that he was tall. There had to be more to her attraction to him than that. Although it probably hardly counted as a reason — it probably did not matter at all — her sister, June, had wanted him, too.

Ruth had been surprised when June had first brought him home, back when June was in art school in Chicago. He wasn't June's type. He didn't dress sharply, or talk a lot, or try to stand out. He wasn't rich. Even back in high school, June's usual boyfriends were sons of lawyers and doctors. Bigwigs. One had even been the son of a senator, if you could believe that. John was just a farmer. All he had going for him were those eyes that seemed to notice everything, and his calm. He was almost scarily calm. She could tell that June really liked him. Any little sister would have looked twice.

Now see how Ruth's life had turned out. Then look at June's. Was there anyone who knew them who would not have predicted this outcome?

Fury boiled up behind her breastbone. She stashed the extra clothespins into their bag hanging from the line, frisked her hair for bobby pins, then shouldered her way through the wet sheets Mother had hung earlier.

The farmhand, Nick, was leading her mother's horse, JoJo, from the barn. "Thank

41

you!" Ruth called out.

"You're welcome," Nick told her when she reached him.

Poor old JoJo started, her drooping whiskered lips flaring as if she'd been surprised that her leader had come to a stop. Nick gave her a reassuring stroke. Beneath his slouchy brown fedora with its salt-streaked band, his whole face, lean and tanned, gathered into an easy smile.

"Thank you for what?"

He had a slight accent, having come over from Italy as a boy, his native tongue showing up only occasionally, like in the pronunciation of her name. He was from the northern part of that country, where they had light blue eyes, the same clear light blue as the aquamarine ring June had overgenerously sent Ruth's oldest daughter, Margaret, for her birthday. How did people even have eyes that color? Such see-through blue irises didn't seem possible to someone as coweyed as she was.

"Thank you for taking over when my sister comes. I feel terrible leaving you with everything." The rage squeezing her lungs effervesced into butterflies. It was those aquamarine eyes.

After Dad had died last May, Mother had moved in with Ruth "to help with the girls," but it was Nick who had saved Ruth. He'd shown up at the farm right before Mother had come, the day after Ruth had let go of the last of the farmhands who'd worked for her after John had fallen ill. It had taken him a few minutes to convince her that he was not just another hobo at the back door, looking for a sandwich — there were a surprising lot of them these days, even out here in the sticks. Or that he wasn't a bank robber running from the law. Plenty of them were out here, too, another product of hard times, although she had yet to meet one and hoped that she never would.

He'd said he was looking for work, any work. She avoided those eyes that were already too much to look at as she told him that while she had plenty of work around the farm, she couldn't pay him. That was the reason the last hand had left. Anyhow, she was selling the place; not that she'd get much for it in these rotten times. She was tired of holding everything together like human baling wire.

He said that until she sold out, he was fine with hiring on for room and board. He'd be happy just to have a job, as scarce as they were.

Later, he spoke of going down in the mines of West Virginia. He told of watching his pals get crushed in cave-ins, and of being owned by the mining company store. He hinted that he'd done something terrible to get away. That a man would go to extremes to get ahead thrilled Ruth a little. Whatever it was that he had done to arrive at her farm, she was glad that he'd done it. At least he was taking control of his life.

The clank of cowbells lazed from the pasture. Nick rubbed strands of JoJo's dull mane between his fingers. "I am happy to help. You should have a nice visit. Have a good time with Betty Crocker."

She felt the familiar zing that followed the meeting of their eyes. She was not going to let mention of her sister ruin it. "She's only one of a bunch of women playing Betty."

"I know, Root. You told me. Please tell her thank you from an admirer."

Ruth frowned at the windmill clattering next to the barn. Thanks for what? On the radio, America's beloved and completely made-up (though "Betty" never bothered to tell you that) expert on baking was the patron saint of women on a manhunt. In between giving out recipes, Betty tipped off her followers on how to win a husband and keep him, not only by taking the proverbial shortcut through his stomach, but by keeping themselves attractive and interesting.

Betty, with her on-air interviews with bachelors about what they looked for in a wife and her ten-cent booklets full of man-pleasing recipes, implied that men were like dumb beasts running free on the plains, unaware that they were being stalked, until, bang! they were shot down by "Apricot Topsy-Turvy" or "Peeps and Squeals Sandwiches" served by a perky huntress in an apron. She wondered how her sister could live with herself, contributing to this nonsense. Of course, Sister June had always been a big game hunter.

Nick laid the mare's mane flat then stroked it. "Anyhow, I told John that I'd take care of everything while she was here."

The buoyancy leaked out of her. She was aware that John was in the house, essentially paralyzed in bed, and that she was despicable for yearning for another man while her husband was in such a state. She knew that John had only been trying to be a successful farmer, with the best stock and the best equipment and using the best methods, an ambition that took him to St. Louis eight years ago to purchase an especially fine bull. He had not tried to contract a case of sleeping sickness while he was there. It had not been in his plans to be one of the victims of the worldwide epidemic of what her sister's show-off husband called *encephalitis lethargica* or "von Economo disease."

Call it what you wanted, it killed millions of people, but those millions who survived often had an even worse fate than death. They became living statues, doomed to fall asleep before they could finish actions as simple as answering a question, raising a hand in greeting, or taking a bite to eat. When John awoke from a five-day coma during which Ruth had barely clung to her pregnancy with the twins, he could rarely do more than open his eyes. He would remain like that, largely helpless, these eight nightmarish years.

"You 'told John,' " she said flatly. She didn't know which infuriated her most, Nick talking to John, pretending that John was whole though he lay there like a haybale, or Nick reporting to John like John was the boss when she was the one actually running the place.

She suspected that she was going out of her mind.

A hot breeze, oiled with the scent of cattle, kicked up the dirt. "I had a hard time starting the tractor yesterday." She couldn't keep the irritation out of her voice. "You might want to look into that." She turned on her heel. She could feel him watching her walk away.

"Root."

She hesitated, then turned.

Below his worn chambray shirtsleeves, thick veins snaked under the fine taut skin of his crossed forearms. "Get Betty Crocker to bake me a cake, okay?"

She was tired. She was lonely. She hurt so bad that she could howl.

She wiped at her brow, then walked back. "What kind?"

She was only thirty.

# THREE

*Indiana-Michigan Line, 1934*

In a stuffy upstairs bedroom in Ruth's house, her mother braced herself against the striped ticking mattress of the stripped bed and got up from the floor, one sore knee at a time. She still wasn't used to her knees betraying her. They had swelled up and gone bad for no good reason the day after she'd turned sixty last July. And she had just been thinking then how young sixty felt when you actually got there. Felt just like forty only with no sleep. And cracked teeth. And a neck like a used paper sack. And the sinking realization that there really was an end to all this.

Once upright, she blinked away the tadpoles writhing across her vision to contemplate her quarry: a shoebox from Montgomery Ward's. Although she had important work to do, she could not resist scraping the dented cardboard lid from the box and then rustling the small brass coffer from the browning tissue paper. The bumps and curves of the cherubs embossed on its surface were as familiar to her fingertips as the bones of her own face. She wound the key on the bottom then pushed the delicate brass knob.

The oval lid popped open; up sprang a little bird. It twitched back and forth on its stem, jerking turquoise feathered wings and snapping its beak as it whistled metallically.

A door slammed downstairs.

She palmed down the lid and shoved the little box under her saggy pillow, instantly regretting how roughly she'd handled it. The automaton was very valuable, the most expensive gift she had ever gotten — her secret nest egg, if she could bring herself to sell it.

"Hello?" she called.

When no one answered, she sucked in a long breath, then let it out. Back to work. Junie was coming the day after tomorrow and Dorothy had to move out of the room. She'd already washed the bed, bleaching the sheets then soaking them in bluing, and not stinting on either, just like Mrs. Lamb had insisted upon when Dorothy worked for her. She'd crisp them tomorrow with a set of hot irons. June and her doctor-husband were used to living in a mansion, so everything needed to be nice. She herself would sleep on the davenport.

Brushing under her chin with her thumb — she was engaged in a running battle with the single stiff hair that had recently begun staking its ground there — she accounted for her nightie, her church dress, her "play" dress (she had her old play dress on to save her newer one), her spare slip, and her bed cap, all folded and in a row on her bed next to her good pair of shoes and the empty Montgomery Ward box. She needed a sack to put them all in. Ruth kept a stack of sacks, an inheritance from her dad's grocery store back in Fort Wayne, downstairs in the pantry.

It had been a nice grocery store, although Dorothy thought it should be called "William's" instead of the more common-sounding "Bud's" — *she* never called her husband that, any more than she called him "Rowdy Dowdy," the ridiculous nickname only he ever called himself.

How the store worked was how all the good stores did: his customers placed their orders by telephone. The "credit and delivery system" (the official term for it) was the most up-to-date way of doing business in the twenties. William had always kept his eye out for improvements since taking over the business from his sister Edna when she died of a bleeding ulcer the first year of their marriage. It wasn't a job that William had ever wanted, but it was there when they had needed it and he had made a go of it.

Dorothy could still see their employee Ned scrambling up the ladder, his jug-ears nearly grazing the rails on either side, as William read off the order. Then away Ned would race in the wagon behind JoJo, or later, in the Ford panel truck. He took payment upon delivery — or not, if customers took advantage of "Rowdy Dowdy's" tender heart. William would have given credit to Al Capone, if he'd told William that his child was ailing. Few customers felt the need to come into the store and buy their own goods. It just wasn't done that way.

Then Piggly Wiggly came to town. It spread like a cancer, first to Broadway, then to Columbia Avenue, then Calhoun Street, until a spoor took root at Crescent and State — just two blocks away from Bud's. Piggly Wiggly placed ads in the newspapers and city directory, bragging that they could save you "bushels of money" if you came in yourself and shopped. Self-service, they called it. The modern way to buy.

Piggly Wiggly claimed that not only was

choosing one's own goods smart, but it was fun. They invited people to come in and find all the foods they had heard about on the radios that were suddenly in everyone's parlors: Good-to-the-Last-Drop Maxwell House Coffee, Breakfast-of-Champions Wheaties, Carnation From-Contented-Cows Condensed Milk. There was Bing Crosby crooning about the glories of Woodbury Soap. Rudy Vallee swearing by Fleischmann's Yeast. Even on June's program, *Betty Crocker Cooking School of the Air,* Betty warned that you'd better use Gold Medal "Kitchen-Tested" Flour if you wanted her recipes to taste right. All of the radio stars were telling you what you just had to have, even before you knew you needed it.

Already strained from watching customer after customer, neighbor after neighbor, and friend after friend turn their back on him and go to the Piggly Wiggly in search of those recommended brands — even good old Ned with his big jug ears — William'd had a heart attack while installing a checkout counter in his store. People said that Piggly Wiggly killed William, but that wasn't who. It was the radio.

Movement outside the bedroom window caught her eye. Ruth was out in the barnyard with that Nick. Dorothy had been reluctant to let Ruth talk her into taking over hanging up the wash, and for good reason. Look at her, smiling as she talked to him, and in her Sunday shoes, too. Dorothy recognized that kind of smile. She'd seen it in her own reflection in the Lambs' silver teapot as she was polishing it, those thirty-some years ago, when Edward had slid up to her in the dining room and blown in her ear, before slipping away when he heard his mother coming. She knew how this would end, unless it was stopped right now.

Dorothy bustled downstairs as fast as her bum knees and the heat would allow, rubbing her chest to ease the crabbing inside. Lunch, she could make lunch, get Ruth back in the house that way.

In the parlor she switched on the radio and turned the volume clear to the right. She didn't wait for it to finish warming up before trundling out to the kitchen, where she banged the pan repeatedly on the stovetop, making the loudest racket possible — a din Ruth was sure to hear through the screened window.

Then Dorothy realized that she might be awakening John, who had a view of the barn from his bed. Everyone seemed to think he was too sleepy to see things, but she knew better. He saw.

Moaning, she cranked open a can of Campbell's Tomato Soup and then plopped the orange glob into the pitted aluminum pan. She scraped out the remainder with a wooden spoon, irritated by how long it took her to do the simple task, then yanked the pitcher of milk from the icebox. Unlike her daughter June with her "Frigidaire '34" with its miracle "Ice Cube Trays That Don't Stick," Ruth had no refrigerator. The house wasn't even wired for electricity.

Dorothy glugged milk into the soup can. When some splashed onto the white enameled tabletop, she plunked down the pitcher and groaned. How could she tell her daughter that relations with a man who can't promise himself to you could alter your life, when she had never been able to tell her girls even the simplest things? She had never even told them that she loved them.

The back screen door banged. Dorothy pushed upright as Ruth not so much walked but drifted through the back porch and into the kitchen. Ruth's radiance dimmed when she noticed Dorothy.

"Mother, why's the radio up so loud?" Her frown deepened. "And why are you just standing there?"

Dorothy dabbed her eye with the bib of

her apron. "Got milk in my eye."

Ruth didn't question this. She sighed, then floated from the kitchen.

Dorothy followed, her cat, Venus, trailing behind her. "Ruth!"

Ruth stopped at the stairs.

Dorothy had seen that Nick-person looking down at her daughter. He hadn't touched Ruth. He hadn't needed to.

"Lunch will be ready in a minute!"

In the parlor, "When the red, red robin comes bob, bob bobbin' along" chugged from the radio. Ruth pushed away from the stairs, flounced over to the radio set, and snapped it off.

"I hate that song."

"I'll get John's tray!" Dorothy exclaimed, hustling behind her to the radio and back. "You can take it to him!"

"You always feed him lunch, Mother. I always feed him dinner." She put a foot on a riser and bent down to rub under the strap of her dress pump. "I can't bear these shoes another minute."

"I think it would be nice if you took him lunch today."

"Please." Ruth gripped the cracked wooden ball topping the newel post. "Will you."

A strangled yodel slipped from Dorothy's

mouth as Ruth started back upstairs. "Ruthie!"

Ruth stopped.

Words jammed in Dorothy's mouth. *Warn her! Tell her!*

"You've got to take John his lunch!"

Ruth drew in a breath. "I can't." She hiked on up.

"Ruthie!" Dorothy sagged against the banister. She had no power over the girl. She never had.

She straightened slowly, feeling it in her knees.

But she knew who did.

# FOUR

*Minneapolis, Minnesota, 1934*

Several hours after the mother and daughter had left with dried eyes and a picnic basket containing a dozen signed Betty Crocker publications and a beagle pup, the Bettys went to lunch. Pushing through the brass doors of the Grain Exchange, they emerged into the clear Minneapolis sunlight with their lunch tins and baskets. They set off in chatty twos or threes, their white heels scraping the sidewalk as they aimed toward the benches in the shadow of the pink granite clock tower of City Hall, just across the street. This part of downtown had been swept clean of hoboes and homeless families by the police; now an officer in jodhpurs and polished boots held up the Buicks, Fords, and Hudsons whining down Fourth Street for the Bettys to pass. The girls crossed, waving at him with white-gloved hands and calling their thank-yous.

June kept walking as they claimed their places.

"Where are you going?" called Sue from Missouri.

Janet from Hector, Minnesota, spread her white skirt over the planks of her bench. "Aren't you going to join us?"

"Oh, let her go." Darlene took a sandwich wrapped in wax paper from her tin. "She's probably going to meet her dreamy husband at the hospital and lock herself in his office with him. I know that I would if he were mine."

June laughed as if that were actually a possibility. She continued in the direction of the hospital, her purse and lunch basket hanging neatly from her arm.

Her car was parked on a side street a few blocks away. Richard had gotten her the Hupmobile for Christmas. None of the other Bettys knew about it. With their husbands not working, most of them could barely afford streetcar fare to and from work, let alone their own automobile. There was no need to rub it in.

At the car, she heaved herself up from the running board, slid beneath the mahogany steering wheel, and then paused to look out over the enormous black coffin of the hood. What on earth was Odd Dorothy's daughter doing in such a flashy barge?

*Well, enjoy it.* Wasn't this what she'd always wanted? To be a cut above?

She started the car then maneuvered the fat whitewalls from the curb. Sealed within the comfort of her glassed-in case, she glided past sign-carrying workers calling for a strike; past the railyards, where a watchman flogged a bony fellow who was trying to hop a train; past a stand of weeds along the river, where a woman killed a turtle with a butcher knife, soup for her family tonight.

June turned onto a dirt road, then bumped along through brush until she reached the shadowy, hard-packed shore beneath the Lake Street bridge. As cars rumbled across the steel Erector Set expanse overhead, two dirty little girls milled around a lean-to cobbled together from a rusty Model T and corrugated tin. Their mother hunched on a folding chair outside of it, nursing a baby.

June stopped her car. Dust swirled around the fenders as she rolled down the window. She nodded at the mother as the girls trotted up.

"Hi, ladies!" she exclaimed. "Maeve! Did you lose a tooth?"

The younger child bared her empty socket to show her.

"I've already lost six," bragged the bigger girl.

June handed the younger girl the lunch basket. The lid was thrown open and wax paper torn off before June could pull back into the car. The girls peeled the strips of bacon from the waffles and stuffed them in their mouths.

June's chest ached as she watched them eat. "Do you girls like bacon?"

They nodded, chewing.

"Apparently so do a lot of men."

The older girl wrinkled her nose. "Who cares about men?"

Little Maeve puffed out the front of her dress. "I don't care about men."

"Well," June said lightly, "you might care about them, sometimes. Some are very nice. My dad was very nice."

"So was mine." The older one, Ethel, spoke around her bacon. "He bounced me on his legs. He said 'Heebie, Jeebie, Heebie-Jeebie-Jeebie!' and then he bounced me off."

"He was funny," Maeve agreed.

"Girls," called their mother, "are you bothering Miss Whiteleather?"

"Nooooo," they called back.

"Better leave some for your mother," said June.

"Okay," they chimed in unison.

She backed the car down the rutted road, plotting how she might take the girls shopping for clothes without offending their mother, who bristled at a whiff of charity. She had noticed the family on her way home from work two weeks earlier, and now visiting the girls was a highlight of her day. Their cheerfulness — and their pride — in the face of their precarious situation was both touching and familiar. She saw herself and Ruth at their age, pretending to speak a foreign language to each other while prancing through the nicest department store in town, hilariously pulling the wool over everyone's eyes, or so they thought. Was there a pluckier creature alive than a seven-year-old girl?

A few minutes later, she was home. Anxiety descended, squeezing her like a too-small coat as she guided the Hupmobile up the drive. She couldn't shake the sense that her own house was examining her, peering down through its circular porch window like an aristocrat with a monocle. *I have pillars, a library, and seven plush bedrooms,* it seemed to sniff. *Who, in heaven's name, are you?*

Defiantly, she parked the car under its lattice bower. *You're just a house! Bricks and wood! Sticks and stones! You can't hurt me.*

She went indoors, where she settled at the breakfast nook table, sketchpad in hand and Stella alert at her feet.

Over at the counter, the maid, Adela, filled a pie crust. Sunshine poured through the window over the sink, soaking the celadon green cupboards and yellow floors in buttery light. June noted the gleam the sunlight cast on Adela's forehead, on the bone of her cheek, and on the red ceramic bowl in her hands. Vermeer couldn't have painted a prettier picture.

Through the window at the table, she watched the five-year-old neighbor boy, Ernie, pedaling up her drive on his tricycle, Band-Aids flashing on his knees. She wondered how she might convey the energy in the child's greenstick bones with just the strokes of her pencil. Her heroes, Neysa McMein and Rose O'Neill, could have done it. Rose O'Neill infused so much character into her drawings of Kewpies that they made her one of just a handful of self-made female millionaires. Neysa McMein's portraits of women and children had cinched her popularity with the fast crowd in New York, earning her a place at the Algonquin Round Table with Dorothy Parker and Noël Coward. June bet their houses didn't look down on them.

Richard's car growled up the drive. June flinched with the screech of the emergency brake. As Richard walked around to enter through the distant sunroom — he liked to go through the garden and snap off a bloom — Stella sprang to her feet, then bolted out of the kitchen and through the dining room and back in a frenzied circuit, yipping as if scalded. Stella did not go berserk like that for June, although she fed and walked the dog.

A few minutes later, Richard strode into the kitchen. A pink tulip fell on the table in front of June with a lush flop.

"A beauty for a beauty." Richard rested his hands, still damp from the downstairs powder room, on June's shoulders, giving off the sweet, medicinal scent of ether. "What do you have," he called to Adela, "besides this awful tomato jelly that my wife is eating?"

" 'This awful tomato jelly' is called 'Chilled Tomato Salad' in Betty's *$25,000 Recipe Set,*" June said mildly. "The chef of the Hotel Croydon in New York commended it."

"How much did you have to pay him to get him to do that?" He dropped down across from her with a grin.

With his springy pompadour of light

brown hair, gray eyes shining from under their bony shelf, and wedge of straight nose, many thought Richard handsome. Thin from always being on the move, he rattled around inside his well-made suits, cut to make him look bigger. He moved with the cheery swagger of someone used to giving orders and having them followed, whether it be on the football field, in the operating theater, or in the bedroom, a slight man with a big personality. A man happy in his own skin.

Acquaintances thought he was a stitch when he boasted that his house was built by Frank Lloyd Wright (it clearly wasn't), or that he once plunged into Lake Michigan on New Year's Day with the Polar Bear Club in Milwaukee (the only diving he did was off the side of his mahogany speedboat in July), or that in college he'd sat on top of a flagpole outside his fraternity house until a thunderstorm forced him down (oh, please!). His patients adored him and his tall tales, and when he spoke of miracle cures, they believed him, their raised hopes aiding in their recovery. June had been married to him for eleven years. They were childless.

He tilted back his beige puff of hair as Adela laid a plate with a ham-salad sandwich before him. "Adela, has anyone told you that you have the sixth sense? How'd you know this was just what I wanted?"

Adela twitched unsmiling lips. She had come from Spain and with highest recommendation from Elizabeth Headford at the country club. Besides doing good work, Adela's bearing hinted of a highborn past. She held her back and shoulders so straight that you could almost see queenly robes draped upon them; her maid's starched white cap circled her black hair like a crown. June yearned to ask her about her exotic history, but Adela's reserve invited no questions. In truth, June was afraid of her, although they were close in age. She suspected that Adela knew she was a sham. For the same reason, June was uncomfortable around waiters and shopgirls.

"It's not magic," June said. "Ham salad is your favorite. She makes it every day, in case you come home."

Richard nodded at June's sketching pad. "What are you doodling at now?"

June drew a breath. She was one of a handful of women who had won a scholarship to the School of the Art Institute of Chicago based on her talent and, well, need. Dad, with his pity for widows and veterans, was owed more money than he made. When she had met Richard, she had been chipping away at her studies while clerking evenings in the housewares department in the basement of Carson Pirie Scott. He'd come along on the lowest night of her life and had beamed his searchlight upon her, and then he kept it there, until he'd won her with his interest, his exuberance, and his ability to rip her from her sorry roots for good. She had also adored his mother.

She held up the drawing tablet.

Richard scowled before sinking his teeth into the soft white bread. She knew that he hated when she drew children. It was a reminder of the thing she wouldn't give him.

He swallowed his bite. "Listen, about your trip to see your sister —"

June heard water blasting on the metal fender of a car outside the screened window. Adela's fifteen-year-old son, Angel, who did odd jobs around the house, had brought out a hose and was washing Richard's black Cadillac. When June looked out, Ernie had gotten off his trike and was begging Angel for a turn with the water. What was it about a child's skin that made it glow from the inside like a candle through wax, and how did she capture that on paper?

She had been good at drawing, once, good enough that her drawing instructor at the

Art Institute, Matilda Vanderpoel, had told her that she'd seen similar potential in another student she'd had, Georgia O'Keeffe. June had held that compliment next to her heart to this day, taking it out and holding it up to the light in time of need.

"I'd like to go with you," Richard said.

"What? To Ruth's?"

"I've got a little surprise."

"You want to go with me? You're able to leave your work?"

Nothing took precedence over Richard's practice. How many nights had she spent alone after the hospital called? How many events had she had to attend by herself? He hadn't been there to witness her winning "Most Valuable, Betty Crocker Division" at her company awards banquet, although she was always sure to go to his galas, hospital picnics, and charity balls.

But his work was more important than hers. She mustn't forget that for a moment. All she did was to show women how "luminaries" set their tables for brunch. He saved lives.

She had been warned by her mother-in-law that it would be this way. Linda White-leather was everything June's Dream Mother would have been: elegant but simple, kind but wise, wealthy but modest — everything the American Woman aspired to, or at least that June aspired to. Everything her real mother wasn't. Mrs. Whiteleather, short-waisted, chesty, with silvery blond hair caught in a sophisticated twist, had taken June under her wing, gently starting her education in manners by teaching her how a bed should be made, how to speak on a telephone, and table etiquette. (June realized on her own that she should drop the nonexistent "r" in "wash" when she spoke.) Refinements branched from there.

June aped Mrs. Whiteleather's behavior at parties, going so far as to imitate her tony accent and laugh. She wore her own hair in a twist (swimming against the current, with everyone wearing a bob since the twenties), bought hats with her at Bes-Ben on Michigan Avenue in Chicago, went to the same manicurist on Grand Avenue here in town. Mrs. Whiteleather seemed to genuinely like June, showering her with gloves, scarves, and sweaters, speeding June's assimilation into the upper crust with her kindness. She wasn't put off by June's gaffes, of which there were many, like not waiting to be the last in line at a buffet luncheon (the higher one's status, the longer one waited), or admitting what one paid for something (not even to celebrate getting a bargain), or letting more than twenty-four hours pass before writing a bread and butter note. Mrs. Whiteleather's tolerance was not matched by her husband, the elder Dr. Whiteleather, whose pursed smile told June all she needed to know about his opinion of her.

June recalled sitting with Mrs. Whiteleather in the tranquility of the Whiteleather den, soon after her engagement. Mrs. Whiteleather had put down her cup with a click of bone china.

"June, much will be expected of you as a Whiteleather. It will exhaust you. Especially if you weren't brought up in this milieu." She saw June's face. "I'm not trying to make you feel bad, dear. I wasn't brought up in this environment, either. That's how I know how difficult it will be. Oh, you'll be able to keep up, but . . ." She grimaced, then reached for the polished coffeepot.

"I have my art," June said. "I will never abandon it."

"I hope not, dear. But that's not how it usually goes."

June hadn't been really listening. She'd been so desperate that summer, with Ruth and John . . . doing whatever it was that they were doing.

"We'll leave tonight," Richard was now

saying. "We can return on Tuesday. Jim will cover my patients for me."

"What? Tonight! Your plan hardly gives us any time there — the train won't get there until tomorrow and we'd have to leave to come back home Monday. Driving would take even longer." She knew that he preferred driving. He liked to be in control.

"I realize that, darling. That's why I booked passage on a plane."

"A plane!"

"I thought that you'd like the idea of flying."

"I don't!"

"It's about time that we give it a try. These are the thirties, you know. Everyone's doing it."

"No one's doing it, except movie stars and tycoons."

"Well, in that case, one of us fits the bill. You're a star, you know, Betty."

"If only Betty existed."

"A quibble. Anyhow, you know I'm not a fan of trains and driving isn't safe these days, not as long as the countryside is rife with those ridiculously named fellows who are robbing banks and then making their getaways. 'Baby Face Nelson,' 'Machine Gun Kelly,' 'Pretty Boy Floyd' — where did these devils come from?"

She took up her fork. "They came from being poor, I would guess."

"It was a rhetorical question, darling."

June glanced outside. The countryside wasn't the only place filled with those fellows. John Dillinger, the subject of a nationwide manhunt by the Bureau of Investigation, was known to lurk around St. Paul. Just recently, he'd escaped in a shootout from the apartment in which he lived with his girlfriend, only a mile or two from there. The girl had been caught in Chicago and brought back here for a trial.

"Do you think Dillinger will come back here to break her out?" June asked.

"Who?"

"Dillinger's girl."

"I didn't know you were so interested in Dillinger, darling."

"I'm not." June had seen the pictures of the robber's woman in the paper. Her name stuck with June: Evelyn Frechette. She'd grown up on the Menominee Indian Reservation just outside of town, which had saddened June upon reading that fact. She could understand why the girl, deprived and scorned for being an Indian, would fall for a flashy man who could buy her things. Had she been all that different herself?

Adela poured Richard's tea. "Thank you,"

he told her. To June he said, "Did you see the article about him in this week's *Time*?"

She had. She'd pored over it. Evidently Dillinger had been crisscrossing the countryside between here and her sister's farm on the Indiana-Michigan line, on the run from the band of machine-gun-carrying detectives on a mission to take him "dead or alive." June had been struck by the picture of the outlaw, smirking from the glossy page of the magazine. Under a mustache as threadbare as a child's much-loved security blanket, his lopsided grin gave him the appearance of someone trying to be tough, even though he was bone-weary from the effort.

She'd felt curiously sorry for him, as she had for the fox at a hunt at the Hardings' to which Richard had taken her years ago. When Harry Harding had seen her expression as she watched the small black-footed animal flee across a field with a pack of baying hounds at its heels, he put his hand forwardly on her waist and assured her that the fox was a clever, calculating animal who controlled the chase by various ruses and deceptions. The creature enjoyed the sport of it, Harry told her with an overly familiar squeeze, and simply went home when he tired.

Harry hadn't answered when she asked what happened if the fox was caught.

She nudged the rubbery red pile on her plate. Outside, Angel, slightly taller than the Cadillac, was rubbing down the car, each thin arm muscle articulated under his smooth brown skin as he worked — an artist's delight. She hadn't realized how much she had been looking forward to going back home alone. She didn't know why that would be, as rudely as Ruth would treat her, when she was the one who should be rude. They both knew what Ruth had done.

Richard swallowed another bite of sandwich. "Listen, if you wanted, we could stretch out the trip another day in Chicago — we already have to fly in and stay the night there for the morning flight. I have a friend there I'd like you to meet."

Her antennae went up. "What friend?"

"Bert Hayes. We went to medical school together. He's an expert in problems like ours."

She didn't have to ask which problem.

How many examination tables had she had to lie upon over the last ten years of their eleven-year marriage? She'd been shucked open like an ear of corn as her most private self was studied and discussed by Richard's medical friends, many of whom they socialized with. When nothing could be found, the treatments began. She'd had carbon dioxide pumped through her fallopian tubes. (They were not blocked, it turned out — the resulting agony in her shoulders as the gas filled her body cavity proved that.) She'd swallowed fat capsules filled with ground-up animal pituitary glands. (And felt green for days.) She'd been dutifully stimulated by Richard in ways recommended to bring on the orgasm thought helpful for conception. (The surest way *not* to have a climax.) No special diet, no exploratory surgery, no having sex when she didn't want it, nor not having it when she did, could fix her. She was defective, it seemed, a poor bargain as the elder Dr. Whiteleather had suspected, an inferior specimen who didn't even have the grace to produce a baby.

When it became obvious, after nine years, that even with the benefit of the best of modern medicine there would be no little Whiteleathers, she'd switched gears. Her idea was that if she stopped trying to have a baby, one would magically come. She had heard of this working for friends who had adopted. Sue Browning had gotten pregnant the minute she brought home her baby.

With this in mind, June had applied to

the biggest employer in town. She had hoped that the company might take her on, part-time, for her to do a little illustrating for the advertising department while she waited for the stork. She had not expected to be offered a full-time position as a Betty. She'd not even known that being a Betty was a job.

Richard tipped back his glass. "Bert might find a new wrinkle in our case."

She laid down her fork. "But we've done everything." She left unspoken, *I've* done everything.

He stared at her, then swallowed his mouthful of tea. "What if there really were a new angle?"

She could not bear to get her hopes up again. "What new angle?" she said bitterly. The disappointment in her in his eyes crushed her. "Just give me time. All I need is rest."

"Then stop working!" he exclaimed.

"I will."

"You don't need the work, June. You're taking the money from someone who needs it. You're being selfish."

In fact, she sent all of her salary to Ruth, which he knew and approved of, but there was no winning an argument with Richard. "I'm going to quit, Richard."

"Isn't all this enough for you? Don't I give you everything that you want?"

"Of course you do." She had every intention of quitting, and yet she hadn't. She couldn't. It was the only place where she felt smart and admirable, most of the time. It was the only job in the world where everyone else was in on being a counterfeit. As someone who had never had anything to hide, he would have no idea what a relief that was.

Outside, Angel had given Ernie the hose and was helping the child to train a blast onto one of the wide whitewall tires, to Ernie's milk-toothed delight.

"How is your sister's husband, by the way?" Richard asked. "Any improvement? Or is he still essentially bedbound?"

June stared out the window. It was ridiculous how Richard would never speak John's name. He was always "your sister's husband." Anyhow, she hadn't seen John since he'd fallen ill. He couldn't come to Dad's funeral, and she wouldn't go out to their farm.

"I guess so, yes. I wouldn't know." The odds might be better for their having a child if they actually had sex more than once a month. He obviously didn't want her, turning away from her so often that now she seldom tried. At least when they'd been try-ing to make a baby, they were a team. Now they seemed to have come to a crossroads, or more accurately, to the edge of a cliff. She didn't want to jump, but she was cling-ing to the rock with the wind snatching at her clothes and there was nowhere left to go but into the abyss.

Richard pushed away his plate. When Adela strode to the table, he drew in a long breath, then grinned up at her. "What are you making over there?"

"Mincemeat pie, sir."

Richard shook his head in admiration. "Adela, where have you been all my life?" He caught June looking at him. "What?"

*Do you feel it, Richard? Are you on the cliff, too?* She tried to smile. "Nothing."

# FIVE

*Indiana-Michigan Line, 1934*

Dorothy was picking up the tray with John's bowl of tomato soup when she felt a touch on her leg. She jerked with a bleat and a slop of tangerine. Venus glared up at her, as if it were Dorothy's fault that the cat was hanging from Dorothy's stocking by a claw.

"Don't scare me like that." Her heart still pumping, Dorothy put down the tray, bent her balky knees, unhooked the cat, then lifted the animal to her face. She forgave Venus for putting a hole in her cotton stocking, just as she then forgave her for immediately twisting around and sinking her talons into the meat of Dorothy's shoulder.

There was little for which Dorothy wouldn't forgive the animal — maybe walking across a photo that Dorothy had just tinted for Cryder's Photography Studio in Fort Wayne. For good reason Mr. Cryder gave Dorothy all his important brides. She spent whole days painstakingly perfecting each picture and you didn't get those days back. Yet, she did not mind buckling down at her little desk with her Marlene solution, tubes of paint, and cotton swabs each day. Making her tinting money was important. That, and doing the family laundry, cooking the meals, washing the dishes, mending the clothes, canning tomatoes, carrying bathwater, picking up lint from the floor, sweeping the porch, and all the other things that made her yearn for rest, kept Ruth from throwing her out. She had a contribution to make.

Dorothy kissed the cat's cross face as she extracted her claws from her shoulder. She prized the kitty, and not just for her remarkably long tail, which Venus laid across her front paws like a passenger settling on a ship deck with a lap rug. She treasured how the cat so clearly favored her, flitting off at the sight of anyone else, the white tip of her outrageous tail bobbing over her head. Yet each night in bed, she put her arms around Dorothy's neck like a real live baby and curry-combed Dorothy's cheek with her tongue. Nobody knew what a good cat she was. That pained Dorothy.

Truth was, Dorothy was more comfortable in the company of her cat than anyone else. She seemed to have lost the ability to be around her own species, save for her son-in-law John, who only tolerated her because he was paralyzed in bed. Maybe she'd never had it. Ruth's little girls would be home from school soon. They'd skip right past her, chattering and making plans, as if she were no more significant than the pole propping up the clothesline. Her own girls had been the same, only interested in each other. They had their own secret jokes and their own little language, and though they squabbled, they would pull together to side up against Dorothy more often than not, which tickled her to no end even when they were looking up defiantly at her.

Truth was, she wanted them to band together. She could not have them be dependent on her. What if she got caught for what she'd done? She had looked it up in the library soon after marrying William — her crime carried a sentence of fifteen years to life.

Back when the girls were little, a single knock on the door would send her sailing through her skin. How her heart would roar as she squinted through the keyhole! It took all of her nerve to call out, "Who sent you?"

Once she knew she was safe and finally opened up, and the Fuller Brush man, the

California Perfume Company woman, or the neighbor selling raffle tickets showed her what they had to offer, she'd hop up on the piano bench to retrieve the framed photos of her daughters from atop the twangy old upright that no one ever played.

As if a dam had broken, she'd flash her girls' pictures and gush about their accomplishments. She told herself as the visitors retreated with their wares that she was weeding out the truly interested from mere entrepreneurs. She was separating the wheat from the chaff.

Problem was, all her visitors were chaff. By the time she dared to venture out, when the girls were well into elementary school, she had no friends. She became part of no group except for the Methodist church, where they had to let her in because William tithed. There she'd laid permanent claim to the last row, the better into which to slide her habitually late-arriving family unnoticed every Sunday morning. (The Gloria Patri, a quarter of the way through the service, seemed to be their personal entrance song.) She never gathered with the rest of the congregation on the sidewalk in front of the church after the service, but left during the last hymn, hurrying home in her typical head-down fashion, avoiding interaction. Her daughters and William walked home together when everyone else did.

As the girls got older, and her fear of being found continued to ease, William managed to coax her out of the house for the weekly Wednesday Night Supper in the Fellowship Hall in the church basement. To those, she brought her pink pressed-glass dish of fruit cocktail in Jell-O, her ticket to eat the good food that others had cooked. While William talked to friends and store customers over baked chicken and scalloped potatoes, she tucked into her meal undisturbed. Nor would she be disturbed for the rest of the evening, through the Cherryingtons' travelogue from their visit to the Holy Land, or a program about a mission trip. Often she'd doze off, weary from the day's laundering and tinting — perfection took its toll, even back then. William would touch her on the arm to wake her.

She would go through the roof. "Don't scare me like that!"

He'd pull in that chin and smile apologetically. "Sorry, Dorothy. But what do you expect from a fellow called 'Rowdy Dowdy'?"

Eavesdroppers would chuckle as they gathered their empty serving dishes. Everyone knew he was as rowdy as a fuzzy duckling. He was liked. And by their forced smiles and turned backs, she knew that she was not. Though she'd brought herself up on her own and so had missed out on learning the secret unsaid code people used to get along with one another, even she could see that.

Now, in Ruth's kitchen, as Venus struggled in her arms, a wave of homesickness for William surged over her. She hugged the wriggling cat until the longing ebbed away, leaving behind a hollowness that felt an awful lot like guilt. She'd never appreciated William enough. She'd been too busy thinking about someone else.

Holding John's lunch tray, Dorothy winged the doorjamb with her elbow. "Knock, knock."

He was asleep, as usual. Eight years hadn't lessened Dorothy's shock in seeing him, a tall man, flat on his back, felled across the twin bed like one of those giant trees out in California. He slept with his head thrown back as if he'd just been shot.

"John? I got your lunch."

She let her gaze travel over his face. It had sunken slightly from all his years on his back, making his strong cheekbones even more prominent. His head tipped back with his mouth ajar only added to the effect. His skin had gone as translucent as a slice of onion, but his hair had held on to its color and was still as black as her husband's had been. She had always liked William's hair. It was just like her father's, fine as a baby's and so brown it was black. All three men were kind. She liked to tell herself that.

"John?"

Rubbing the single stubborn hair under her chin, she watched her son-in-law for a sign of consciousness. He kept on sleeping.

"John, I'm going to feed you now." She sat down and picked up the spoon, a genuine silver-plate piece in the Friendship pattern, courtesy of a bag of Gold Medal Flour. She wondered if June, as an employee of the flour company, could get Ruth a complete set. Ruth had so little, compared to her sister, which always hurt Dorothy. Dorothy didn't like to think that she might have contributed to that.

She dipped the spoon in the soup. "Okay, John, open up."

He obeyed, although his eyes were closed. Funny how he could open up just like a baby bird at her command, yet appear to be out cold.

Well, looks could be deceiving. John was listening, even when he seemed to be sleeping. She could tell by the quieter way he breathed when she talked. She knew that he appreciated her talking to him. She knew this in the way that lonely people understood other lonely people.

She doled out a spoonful the color of muskmelon. As John swallowed, she told him more.

# DOROTHY

You are making good progress on this bowl. Halfway done! Campbell's makes a very good soup, don't you think? Though I wrote to the Campbell twins once and they didn't write back. Well, I guess they're just kids and can't be held accountable.

Anyhow, as I was saying, I was used to Edward leaving me, back when we were tots. Oh, we might have spent all day playing hide-and-seek in the Lambs' garden, or throwing sticks in the Lambs' goldfish pond, or showing each other our tummies in the stables, but evening always put an end to it. Off Edward would go, to change into his velvet short pants and floppy bow, and then to his dinner in the mahogany-paneled dining room, served by my parents. Off I went, up to the attic, where I would eat my bread and butter alone and then put myself to bed. There, in my cot, as my parents worked downstairs, I would gaze up at the stars out my little round window and imagine what Edward was doing. Was he building a ship in a bottle in the library with his father? Being bathed by his mother in his claw-foot tub? Sleeping on a satin pillow in his four-poster bed?

Still, it cut me deep when he was sent off to boarding school, then to college in the East, and then on long tours of England and Europe. When he came home on holidays during those years, he'd be friendly to me, inquiring about my activities, though I had a feeling that he wasn't really listening for my answer. His father had always treated me in the same vaguely pleasant way when I crossed his path, asking jovial questions and then not waiting for a reply. I had little experience with his mother. Mother warned me to stay out of her sight.

Dad would make a joke of it when she did. "Watch out for Mrs. Lamb!" He'd gnash his teeth. "She'll eat you up!"

Mother's face would go sour. "Shut up, Bill."

How old was I when Edward returned from the last European tour? Twenty-seven? I had given up on marrying by then. I had been working full-time for the Lambs since I left eighth grade, doing their laundry, and you don't meet husbands while running sheets through a mangle in the basement.

It was on a warm sunny day in late June, a Sunday afternoon, the only day of the week that my parents, as the butler and housekeeper, had a half day off. I was alone in the Lambs' garden, enjoying the scent of the blooming roses as I pushed a needle with chapped fingers through stretched gauze, when a gentleman wearing a straw boater stepped inside the gate.

I could only give him a quick glance, being in the middle of a stitch. I applied the same care to my needlework that I gave to the laundry and later to my photo tinting. "The Lambs are at the seashore."

"How have you been, Dode?"

I pricked myself. "Dorothy" had been too much for Edward to pronounce as a little child, when he would come to stand at the base of the service stairs. His shout of "Dode!" would send me flying down three flights.

How had I not recognized at first sight his golden skin, the color of the inside of a plum? As children, we would hold our arms next to the other's and compare their color: they were a surprisingly similar ivory-gold in winter but his got an enviable richer gold in the summer. How I loved his clear green eyes shaped just like a cat's — "leonine" is the actual word for them. And that golden hair that grew backward from its platinum roots in the whorl on his hairline, his mane magnificent on his large head. I often wondered how anyone could be so beautiful.

"Looks like life has treated you well," he said.

My heart felt too big for my chest. "Not particularly."

He laughed. "Just as blunt as ever. How refreshing you are."

I didn't know what to say about that.

"How is it that you aren't married," he asked, "as pretty as you are?"

"I'm not that pretty."

"And there you are mistaken." He took my hand and kissed the back of it. I could still feel the pressure of his lips as he strolled away.

The next day, he stopped me on the back stairs and asked me to accompany him to the art museum.

How would it look for the heir to a Cincinnati beer fortune to be strolling the galleries of a museum with his housekeeper's daughter? "We can't do that."

"Whyever not?"

I noticed that he had an English accent since coming home from his tour.

"I'm —"

"— beautiful," he said. When I frowned at his flattery, he added, "Just a little beautiful, if that makes you feel better." He winked. "And only in your heart."

Oh, I loved the art museum. I have always admired the smart use of color. I could have strolled through those echoing rooms forever, grit crunching on the marble floor under my Sunday-best shoes. But it is hard to focus on the Old Masters when a young man has his hand on the small of your back.

# Six

*Indiana-Michigan Line, 1934*

Mother's voice floated from John's bedroom out to the kitchen to where Ruth jacked the pump at the sink. How could anyone gab so much to a man who was fast asleep? She spoke so little to everyone else, just tinted, tinted, tinted all day. That's all Ruth could remember Mother doing since she was a kid, just tinting. And washing clothes. Not being much of a parent.

Ruth caught a jelly-jarful of water and, plucking her dress from her sweaty skin, drank it. A fly rammed against the rusty window screen, each furious buzz a protest at being denied the freedom that seemed so clearly at hand. Outside, chickens muttered as they strolled under the clothes on the line. Black and white cats slept on the sunny dirt by the barn, serenaded by the clank of cowbells and the groans of the cattle grazing in the pasture on the other side of the wire fence. Crickets chirped from the weeds at the base of the outbuildings, from one of which could be heard the chime of tools in use, and Nick whistling.

Ruth swelled with anticipation — until she remembered that her sister, June, was coming. She unhooked the screen one-handed and swept out the fly.

She refilled her glass. She did not understand the urgency of June's visit. Why did she insist upon coming now? It wasn't as if they kept up with each other. When was the last time Ruth had visited June, four years ago? June had paid to have her and the kids take the train to St. Paul. Ruth had been miserable the whole time, skulking through June's marble mansion, the hayseed mouse visiting her sophisticated relations.

The kids had thought the place was a fairyland. They didn't mean to, but they drove a dagger into Ruth's heart each time they packed into June's big peach-colored bathtub and scooted up and back on their bellies, singing and laughing, their bare bottoms shining in the water like porpoises. It killed her to see them crowd around the toilet, four dark heads watching the water gush into the bowl when they took turns flushing, and when they gathered around the refrigerator just to open the door and see the light come on.

She felt even worse when June last visited her, before John got sick, the gracious queen pretending that the peasant's lowly sticks of furniture were lovely. They weren't lovely. They were worn, hideous, and not at all representative of Ruth's taste. What she would buy if only she had the money! But no one would ever know her excellent taste. She was doomed to be the poor sister, lesser in all things.

It had always been this way. Even back when Ruth was six and June was eight, Mother had entered them in a beauty pageant held by the Sunbeam Bakery in Fort Wayne. All the contestants had to do was eat a slice of bread. Of course, June and her yellow ringlets won. She even ate cute. All Ruth got was a loaf of Sunbeam bread and a long stare from her mother followed by the pronouncement: *I never worry about you.*

Ruth thought that Mother should.

June topped her at everything. June had wavy blond hair; Ruth's was brown and straight. June had golden skin; Ruth's skimmed-milk flesh was shot through with veins. June developed curves in her early teens; Ruth was still waiting for hers at thirty. June was popular and busy and held the only high school class officer position available to a girl — secretary; Ruth could only manage one best friend, the ever-loyal Barbara. Ruth saw the way boys looked at her sister when she and June were walking downtown or went to a theater together. The boys would get loud and act silly, but June would ignore them. Meanwhile, Ruth stared right at them, daring them to see *her,* though she might as well have been a fire hydrant.

Yet, away from June, Ruth had her male admirers. Before she had been married and cloistered on the farm, she had known how to get the attention of the boys in high school, if she really truly wanted it. Mainly, she just had to act like she was interested in what they thought. Sometimes it wasn't too much of a ruse. She *was* interested at times, if they were smart. She liked clever boys who made her laugh. John had made her laugh. She could make him laugh, too. And other important things.

She remembered some years back, in the early days of their marriage, when on a hot afternoon in late May, she'd insisted that John dig in the lilac cutting she'd gotten from a neighbor. He'd already spent hours putting in new fence posts and was filthy and exhausted.

Oh, the sight of him when he had come back inside the house after planting the lilac, stripped to the waist, unselfconsciously muscular, dirt streaked, and grumpy. She had been swamped with desire. Her mother was visiting, so Ruth lured him out to the milking shed by saying the cream separator needed fixing. He groused all the way out there, complaining that she should have told him that morning, but once he started fiddling with the separator, she seized his face and kissed him mid-grumble. His bad mood soon improved.

After that, saying that the cream separator needed repair was their secret code for intimacy. Eventually just the word "cream" was enough to make them smile. Even someone innocently asking to pass it produced a knowing look between them.

Now, standing at the sink with her empty jelly jar, the memory of the life they'd shared drove a pain through her heart that hurt all the way to her fingertips. They had been good together, no matter that he'd loved June first. She had worked the farm with him in a way that June never could have, pitching in with the milking, taking care of the calves, the chickens, the horses, anything living, while doing the best job she could of mothering her daughters. Working with animals was something that she was better at than June, something she loved, and John knew it and appreciated it. Those years they had been a team, working hard, laughing hard, lovemaking hard. She had been her best with him. Finally, finally, she had actually been proud of herself. And then he had left her, not by choice, but he'd left her, just the same.

She furiously pumped another glass of water. She was putting it to her lips when she heard the tractor rumble and sputter and then roar to life in the machine shed.

Nick rode out on the stuttering beast, looked for her, then waved when he saw her, the shirt under his arm wet. She could imagine how he smelled. Like a man.

She pulled back from the window, hesitated, then waved. Let June come. Ruth wasn't ashamed. What was wrong with wanting more than her sad and lonely life? June, with her cornucopia of plenty, had no right to begrudge her at least a smidgeon of happiness. Hadn't Ruth paid enough already for what she'd done?

She dumped her glass and went out.

# SEVEN

*St. Paul, Minnesota, 1934*

Chunks of sunlight fell through June's windshield as she drove under the newly leafing trees of Summit Avenue. Spring green lawns, flowering bushes, and substantial homes spun by to her right. The grassy median of the boulevard was an emerald flash between tree trunks out her window to the left. Eleven years after moving here, and there wasn't a day that she took for granted living on this beautiful street, the finest in St. Paul. She knew that she should have been happy. Maybe she would be, if she could just have a baby.

As she wheeled the car around a corner, she glanced in her rearview mirror. In it, a girl in a long gray coat was heaving away on a rusty swing. The rhythmic squeak of metal against metal swelled into the interior of the car.

June swerved, hitting the curb.

The girl disappeared as abruptly as a soap bubble.

June tightened her gloved grip on the steering wheel, the jolt from striking the curb still radiating through her body. She hadn't lived across the street from the State School since graduating from high school. Her husband was a surgeon, she lived in a mansion, she was respected at work, she had an interesting job. She was safe.

She piloted the car onto Marshall Avenue, where a line of vehicles crept along the boundary of the Town and Country Club, slowed by some kind of obstruction on the bridge ahead. She was sure to be late now, and she had to hurry back to work if she was going to leave early. She thought of the little family who lived in the shadow of the spans, and hoped that they were okay.

Ignoring the pit greening in her stomach, she lifted her chin to see which of her friends were at the club as she passed. There were still plenty of members who had not lost everything in the Crash and sunken from sight, still plenty of nice-enough people to socialize with, although she wasn't particularly close to any of them — her shortcomings, not theirs. She squinted through the barrier of trees and shrubs that limited, though did not completely obstruct, the view of the club from the street. Perhaps by design, gaps had been left in the greenery, the better for regular folk to imagine the elegant events taking place on the other side.

When Ruth and she had been children, they would go joy-riding with Dad on a Sunday afternoon. On one such occasion she had been sitting tall, on top of the world, as they puttered through downtown Fort Wayne with its domed courthouse and awninged storefronts: Dad had a new (at least to her family) truck, a Ford, hardly dented, with "Bud's" scrolled on the sides. They had swung back past the house (no, Mother still did not want to come) and along the river, past the Centlivre brewery and its stink of cooking hops, to Johnny Appleseed's grave, where, after marking the headstone of the barefoot pioneer with three shriveled apples from the trees he had planted (Dad's idea of paying their respects), they had climbed back in the truck and joggled on their happy way. At last they came to the glorious summit of their journey — Forest Park Boulevard, home of some of the newest mansions in town.

There, they slowed to gape at the serene palaces lounging behind their trimmed green hedges. Who lived in such places?

They must be almost gods.

She looked at her dad, idling his delivery truck, the same brown hat he'd worn her whole life plunked down straight on his head as he craned his neck for a better view. The shirt cuffs above his hands gripping the wooden steering wheel were frayed. Then she looked at her little sister, her red hand-me-down dress barely covering her rear as she leaned out the truck window, wiping her runny nose on her arm as she gawked. June's favorite two people in the world.

In that instant, it was as if magic glasses had been dropped before June's eyes. With horrifying clarity, she saw her dearest ones — her own self — as who they really were: everyday people, maybe even poor ones, snot-nosed and fraying at the edges. How lowly they must seem to the near-gods on the other side of the hedges. And she had always thought that they were special.

Unconsciously, she wiped at her nose as she inched the Hupmobile forward. She belonged on the right side of the hedges now. She knew the fun of dining on the wraparound veranda of the Town and Country clubhouse, waited on by young men in starched white jackets. She was familiar with the intoxication of fox-trotting in a shimmering gown under the sparkling lights of the ballroom. She was privy to the exhilaration of climbing the winding stairs to the observation deck, with its queen's view of the Mississippi.

Yet, she admitted to herself now as she warded off the glare from the bumper of the auto in front of her, life at the club wasn't always a dream. Too often one of her fellow members would follow her out to the veranda or up to the deck, where he would offer her sips from his silver flask before lunging in for a stolen kiss. This attention confused and depressed her. Surely her "admirer" wouldn't have tried to so baldly seduce someone born into his circle.

How did she give herself away? Her accent? The way she dressed? Which inadvertent slip showed her ignorance of how to behave, of the knowledge that the cradle-rich imbibed along with their infant formula? She tried so hard. Maybe that in itself was the problem.

The line of automobiles inched forward. She patted through her purse on the seat next to her for her dark glasses, then unsnapped their case one-handed. She was too eager to please, that much she knew. She emboldened her would-be seducers with the knowledge that she would be too sweet, too nice, to reveal them. She had always been that way.

The aroma of coffee beans in the cast-iron grinder suddenly filled her nose, as did the wheaty scent of Wonder Bread in white paper wrappers, lined up in a row. She was seventeen and in Dad's store. It was a Saturday afternoon and she was the only one there. A fly buzzed around shelves neatly stacked with canned goods. She was refilling the pickle barrel with a new batch put up by old Mrs. Thigpen, the tang of vinegar rising up and slapping away the other cozy smells, when Mr. Horn entered.

They nodded. Nerves fluttered in the back of her throat. She'd always thought Mr. Horn especially handsome in a dark, sharp-featured way. Under his fedora, his hair was shiny black and his face thin and cool. He and his wife were some of the few customers who actually came into the store. He rarely spoke to anyone when they did. He let his wife, holding their baby, tell Ned what she wanted from the shelves as he stared at June with his Rudolph Valentino eyes.

Now the mysterious Mr. Horn was strolling through the store. She was listening for him as her heart pounded and pickles plopped into the barrel, when rough hands grabbed her.

In one movement, he pinned her arms behind her back, spun her toward him, and forced her backward against the counter. The edge of Mrs. Thigpen's galvanized bucket hit the arch of her foot when she dropped it. Pickle juice splashed up her leg.

His mouth, his sandpapery chin, raked her face and neck as she struggled. He bit the words into her ear: "I want to fuck you."

Vomit flashed to her throat.

Wherever he touched burned. His brutal kisses cut her to her soul.

The bell over the back door jingled.

He pushed her away. She was wiping her cheek, too shocked, too sick, to cry, when Ruth trotted in.

"Say, June —" Ruth stopped. She looked from June to Mr. Horn, who was pulling down his hat.

She snatched up the broom Dad kept by the counter and stabbed at him. "Get out!" She drove him backward. "Get out! Get out!"

He protected his face with his hands. "What are you so sore about?"

"Get! You monster!"

"What's your dad going to say? I'm a paying customer! No, wait — Rowdy Dowdy wouldn't say shit."

She landed one on his shoulder.

"Hey! That hurt!"

"Good!" Ruth hit him again.

"You little bitch! I'm telling the police!" Spit whitened the corners of his mouth. "I'm telling them Rowdy Dowdy's slut daughter attacked me."

"You do that!"

He backed his way out the door. "Whores!"

June's vision was blue with shock as the bell tinkled behind him. "Ruth! I didn't do anything wrong!"

Ruth put down the broom. "I know that."

"How'd you know I needed help?"

"You were smiling. He wasn't."

"Smiling? But I wasn't happy!"

"I know!"

White gloves flagged June into the present. From beside a police car parked against the traffic, the officer directing the crawling line of autos indicated for her to stop. She put on her dark glasses. He swaggered over in tall boots.

In spite of his erect posture, his lightly padded torso and the slightly reddened gooseflesh on the back of his neck suggested early forties in age. The stubble on his chin glinted in the sun when he tipped the patent leather bill of his cap. "Afternoon."

June kept on her dark glasses. "Good afternoon. Is there a problem?"

He bent down to look inside the car. "Oh, another man jumped from the bridge."

She felt a jolt, as if a shard of the broken man had been sent through her. Her heart took another blast: Had little Ethel and Maeve seen the man jump?

"Did you see a family living under the bridge?"

Her tone made him squint at her in assessment, as if he might have a hysteric on hand. "I have not been down there, ma'am. But don't you worry, they'll round up any bums they find. We won't let anyone bother you."

"That's not what I meant."

The policeman put both hands atop her open window, then leaned in. "White dress, white shoes. So am I right? Are you a nurse?" He grinned. "You must have married a doctor to drive a vehicle like this."

"Actually, no. I'm Betty Crocker."

She took advantage of his surprise to drive away.

On the other side of the bridge, she pulled the car to the shoulder of the street, panting as if she'd run there. She strained to see the dirt road below. Police cars were parked scattershot in the weeds near the rusty lean-to. Several officers were gathered around a white ambulance, the rear doors of which had been opened toward the riverbank. The girls and their mother were gone.

June scrunched back against the upholstery, flattened by the ache in her chest.

Ruth! How she wanted Ruth! And Dad! *Dad, I want you back. I'm lost.*

A Lamb Beer truck piled with steel barrels rumbled by, shaking June's car.

She fumbled for the radio, her hand trembling on the dial, and turned it on. After a moment, she was able to pull out into traffic.

"Here we are, Betty. Ninth floor!" Mr. Gustafson pulled back the shiny brass inner accordion-gate and then the elevator door. With a wink to June, he delivered his line with no less cheer than he had that morning. "Go make someone happy!"

His eager, wizened face fell when she didn't quickly return his grin. She felt instant remorse. *He* had not pushed that poor jumper over the bridge by the country club. *He* had not hounded off little Ethel and Maeve. *He* had not caused her infertility. *He* had not betrayed her by taking the only man she had ever loved.

She balled her cheeks into a smile. "I will,

I promise, Mr. Gustafson."

"Good!" he called after her happily. "You do that, Betty!"

She pushed her way through the glass doors of the reception area, unburdened herself of her purse and hat in the cloakroom, then entered the kitchen, loud with the clinking and clanking of spoons against bowls, pots onto burners, and pans into ovens. The air simmered with the rich scent of sugared fruit baking in lard and flour.

Darlene stopped nipping at her pencil when June joined her at their table. "I'm trying to be creative with menus for the other page of the Clark Gable spread. But honestly, just how much Bisquick can I make the man down?"

June pulled her white skirt over her knees as she sat. "You have him eating pancakes for his breakfast, yes?"

"Griddle cakes, yes."

"What if for the other page, you thought of all the other meals one can center around pancakes."

"I can do that." Darlene fluffed her hair in thought. "What about 'North Woods Breakfast'? Or 'Camp Breakfast'?"

"You don't have to do just breakfasts. How about some kind of woodsy supper?"

"I see what you mean. Then how about a

'Log Cabin Supper'? Or an 'End of the Trail Dinner'? 'Hunting Lodge Luncheon.' "

"That's the spirit."

Darlene wrote a moment then paused. "What do they eat in log cabins for supper, do you suppose?"

Before June could answer, Doris Hunter, tall, square-shouldered, dark-haired, and direct as a blast from a fire hose, was surging toward them with such authority that the very tables seemed to part. Her drive could have powered the *"Eventually"* sign outside — it sparked and crackled from her like electricity from a Tesla coil. For good reason, she was the head Betty. June was slightly terrified of her.

"Smells like pie!" she sang, loud enough to rattle cookie sheets. "DARLENE."

Darlene went rigid.

"Darlene, sweetie." Mrs. Hunter landed in front of them. "What are you forgetting?"

Darlene knew better than to speak.

"Are you forgetting *who you are*? You are Betty Crocker! You don't *suppose* anything. You *tell* those people in log cabins what to eat. And they will. They *want* to. And they will *thank you* for telling them what to think."

"Yes, ma'am."

Mrs. Hunter was just warming up. "People

these days are tired, Darlene. Worn out. Bushed. They don't want to think for themselves, whether it be about finding work or knowing how to behave or just making a pickle sandwich. So help them! Make it easy for them! Give them the relief of thinking *What would Betty do* whenever they're in a jam. Do them this little service. For their own good. The poor lambs no more want to think for themselves than to mine for rocks on the moon."

Her words settled over the room. Darlene gathered her courage.

"Well, then, Mrs. Hunter —"

"Kitty! You know my nickname is Kitty!" She had a gap between her teeth when she smiled.

"Kitty." Darlene cleared her throat. "I say *Betty* thinks that they should have Fried Ham and Eggs for their supper. With Green Tomato Pickles."

"That's the spirit!" Kitty thunked Darlene's arm, flipping the pencil from her hand. "And don't forget the pancakes. Sell that flour!"

The hem of Darlene's white uniform brushed the floor as she scooped up the pencil. Kitty trained her floodlights on June.

"June, sweetie."

June braced herself.

"I have some new copy for you for the Joan Crawford spread."

"You do?" June had finished the spread weeks ago. "I've sent it to Production."

"I just now spoke to Joan over her breakfast. It's morning, California time, you know. I asked if she were having some Bisquicks with her coffee, and she said, 'Betty, I certainly am!' "

Darlene lowered her head in a conspiratorial smile. "Does she really think that she's talking to Betty Crocker?"

Kitty laughed heartily. "Sweetie, if Joan Crawford wants to believe that, heaven forbid that I should be the one to stop her. Anyhow, I think she'll forgive me if she ever finds out. Surely the former Lucille LeSueur would appreciate the value of assuming an agreeable name." She unclipped a typed card from her board and thrust it at June. "She wants to use this for her Smart Dinner."

June scanned the card. The menu was especially unappealing, featuring lettuce soup and a mutton chop grilled with kidneys. At least it included bacon.

"She likes this picture, too." Kitty unfastened a glossy photograph from her board. "She had these airmailed."

June inspected the photo. A set of heavily

110

painted brows, eyes, and lips stared back at her. Any traces of the real woman behind them had been airbrushed into the satin backdrop.

"She told me this morning," said Kitty, "that she'll only appear in the *Take a Trick a Day* if I use them. Be a dear and fill in the rest of the spread with the riveting copy that you write so elegantly and get it back to me in a snappy."

Kitty was waiting when June looked up from the photo. "I know, I know. Betty is supposed to be the one calling the shots. But that doesn't mean it isn't wise for her to be under advisement from time to time." She winked. "Joan Crawford will never realize that she was the rare person to get Betty to back down. The fact is, people are usually too concerned about their own vulnerabilities to notice yours."

# EIGHT

*Indiana-Michigan line, 1934*

Ruth dried her face on a towel that June had sent her from some big-shot store in Minnesota. Ignoring the anxiety that rose in her lungs every day at this time, she tramped downstairs to where the girls were gathered around Margaret, who was at the dining room table, balancing a cardboard box of kittens on her knobby knees. Jeanne, the second oldest, called to Ruth as she petted an escaping kitten.

"Come see, Mommy!"

The middle child, she had a second sense about Ruth's moods, which made Ruth both proud and uneasy. Jeanne also bit her nails until her fingertips were fleshy stumps and suffered with headaches that forced her to lie motionless on the davenport for hours.

"I'll be there in a minute."

Ruth went on to the kitchen. She picked

up John's tray, aware of her mother watching her.

"What?" Ruth asked.

Mother shook her head.

Mother was acting even more strangely than usual of late. Hardening of the arteries? Ruth turned toward the downstairs bedroom with her load.

"Wait!" Mother ran outside into the dull evening light.

The spoon clinked against the bowl on the tray as Ruth pushed back her damp bangs with her arm. She listened to her daughters at the table. They were shouting their names for the kittens over each other, claiming ownership, much like June and she used to fight over the animals that Dad would bring home. Ruth usually won, which meant she had to care for them, which suited her fine. At one time she was juggling the mothering of a turtle, a bunny, a baby robin, a mouse, and their cat, Tom, a full-time job that involved eyedroppers, milk, and bits of hamburg, if she could get it. June would be off somewhere, drawing. That was okay. Ruth needed her little patients as much as they needed her. Taking care of them was one thing she was better at than her sister.

Mother reappeared with a branch of

brown-tinged lilac blossoms, the screen door slapping shut behind her. Panting, she stuck it in a Ball jar, plunked it on the tray, then stood back.

Ruth frowned at it. "What's this about?"

Mother waved at her with the handkerchief she'd pulled from her bosom. "Hurry! He's waiting."

*Dear Lord, do not let her arteries solidify quickly. I really cannot manage two invalids.*

"Go on! Don't make him wait!"

The back-room door was always left open so that John would not feel cut off from his family. Now, from the doorway, with the daylight lowering, the room looked to Ruth like an old-time photograph. The bed, with its headboard made from slabs of oak from trees that John's father had chopped down on their land and planed himself, the old wardrobe, the spread of the small bed that she'd been forced to use since Mother had come to live with her and driven her from her room, even the cracked plaster walls with a few lathes showing above the washstand, were various shades of brown.

After eight years, Ruth knew to wait to see if this was one of the days that he could talk. And to not expect that it would be. So often when she sat with him, he couldn't even open his eyes. They would quiver under his lids while his mouth and fingers twitched, like a long-dead monster coming back to life. No wonder the kids were afraid of him.

She took a deep breath and entered.

His eyes were open.

She cocked her head with surprise. "Hello."

His gaze inched along her body. "New — dress."

"You like it?" She lifted her brows. He *was* having a good day. Years ago, such a level of alertness would excite her. She knew better, now.

She pulled at the red-dotted Swiss of her skirt. "Mother gave it to me. I had to take it in on the sides." She didn't mention that June had sent it to Mother for her birthday, and Mother, being Mother and preferring her old, weird clothes, had given it to her.

He stared at the dress.

"Well, here's your supper." She picked up the spoon to feed him.

"Nick."

She felt a stinging ping. "What?"

"Nick."

"What about him?" Guilt rolled off her like steam.

"At dinner."

"Do you mean, will Nick be at dinner? Yes. Of course he will be. He always is. Did you want to talk to him?"

"No."

She hid her hand under her arm, then shot it out to touch the browning lilac branch tilted in its jar. She could smell its sweetness, even in this shriveled state.

"Look, John — lilacs, from the bush you put in. I made you plant it on the hottest day of the year. Remember?" She forced a laugh. "I thought you were going to kill me." She almost said it: *Until I got you to fix the cream separator.*

She didn't need to. The unspoken words hung between them, as real as breath.

He closed his eyes.

She glared at the spoon in her hand. A rock seemed to have been sewn inside her chest.

"Don't," he said.

When she looked up, his eyes were open again.

The hair rose on the back of her neck.

"Don't what?"

Sweat beaded his forehead. Keeping his eyes open cost him.

She glanced away. She didn't know what he meant. She didn't want to know.

She put the spoon back on the tray and

then stood up. Fists balled at her sides, she walked carefully from the room and down the hall. Nothing was left of her self-respect when she got to the dining room table.

"That was fast," Mother said.

Nick grinned from his chair at the table, the comb lines still visible in his wet dark hair. His turquoise eyes were even more disconcerting without his hat to shade them. He must have just come in from the barn, where he'd made a place for himself by hanging a curtain to wall off a corner and installing a bed and washstand. It was the same corner in which John had curled when he had come down with sleeping sickness and was delirious, but Ruth had never told Nick that.

She sat at the table. "I didn't finish."

"You didn't finish feeding him?" Mother exclaimed.

The kids looked over at her.

"No." As evenly as possible, she said, "You do it."

"Me?" Mother's eyes widened behind her glasses.

"You do such a good job. You should go talk to him about —" She shrugged. "— whatever it is that you talk to him about. He likes that."

"Did he say that?"

"His food is getting cold. Go."

"All right." Mother got up, rubbing at a place under her chin — a recent physical tick, Ruth noticed.

The floorboards creaked under her mother's footsteps in the hall. Ruth took up her spoon.

Nick asked, "Root, how is John?"

The kids were watching.

"Fine and dandy." She dipped into her stew.

Over the clink of spoons against bowls and quiet slurping, she felt a gaze upon her. Little Jeanne was watching her.

"What?"

Jeanne shook her head.

"I told you to stop worrying."

Jeanne's little girl's voice broke. "Oh, Mommy."

"Eat!" The boulder expanded in Ruth's chest. "Everyone just eat!"

Margaret ducked under the table then came up with a writhing kitten. "Here." She held it out to Jeanne, its clear claws bristling from splayed pink paws.

What would Betty Crocker and her doctor husband say about a table like this, with Ruth's Italian boyfriend chatting and her kids near tears and cats in the soup? They'd get a load of her household in its full glory the day after tomorrow, and would know her to be the wreck that she was.

"Excuse me." Modeling manners — wasn't she fine?

She left the table, rushed through the kitchen, and pushed her way out the flimsy screen door, letting it bang. Outside, crickets cheeped in the dusk; the weary air smelled of heat and dry earth. She kept going until she got to the pasture, where she opened the wooden gate, then strode for Mother's horse. She laid her forehead against the animal's thick neck, the cows shifting politely to make room for the pair of them. JoJo turned her head as if wondering if there were something in it for her, but if not, okay.

Animals didn't know a jerk from a saint.

She started to weep.

# DOROTHY

Open up, John. There's a boy.

Now where were we? Oh, yes: Edward and I were at the art museum. I love that part! Well, the day after, he took me to the zoo.

I'll never forget riding side by side with him in his horse-drawn trap, up the leafy hills of Cincinnati and down, with the wind blowing so hard that it lifted my straw hat from its pins. Edward owned a brand-new Cadillac Runabout, too, red, with chrome lamps sticking out to the sides like great big bug eyes, but he said he didn't want me to be frightened by its terrific speed. I wouldn't have been scared, but that's all right. I felt special enough, riding along with him in his old surrey.

We hadn't gotten far when he turned his head, as large and stately as a lion's. "I remember that you like animals," he told me in his new English accent.

"I do," I said.

"You see, I remember a lot about you."

Did he remember how I smelled, the sound of my laugh, the tapered shape of my fingers? I remembered these things about him.

By the time we reached the zoo, my head was light. I had to pinch myself to keep my feet on the ground as we waited in the shadows for the regular folk to get off the Vine Street streetcar. He would only let us enter after they'd all gone in. He was awfully big on privacy. He was a Lamb, you see, of the Lamb Beer fortune.

Once inside, I had a notion to go to the Monkey House, to see all those simians capering around on their little leathery hands. But Edward thought the crowds rushing into it would "spoil our pleasure." He said, "Let's go somewhere intimate."

I followed him to the Aviary, where he turned around and took my elbow, then guided me into the warm and stuffy dim. It smelled strongly of droppings in there, and was so quiet and empty that you could almost hear the birds breathe.

At the passenger pigeon exhibit, a little sign said, HOME OF THE LAST PASSENGER PIGEONS ON EARTH.

I stopped. Inside their cage, the two boy birds, one named George and the other named I don't remember what, didn't appear to know the gravity of their situation. Heads bobbing like windup toys, they waddled around the girl. They showed off like boys will do, trying to get on her back, though she wouldn't allow it.

After a while, the girl, Martha, had had enough. She fluttered up on whistling wings to the dead branch of her perch, where she sat, staring through the bars of her cage. Only the blink of her white lids gave away that she was alive.

Edward leaned toward my face. "Dode, are you crying?"

I tried to swallow away the lump salting my throat.

"You are crying! Whyever for?" he asked in that accent.

I swallowed enough to say, "She doesn't want her babies to be sad like her."

He smiled. "You're giving her a lot of credit, aren't you, love? Birds don't think."

I was so upset by what I read that I could hardly savor that he called me "love." "It says here that she hasn't laid eggs since the zoo got her. Why else won't she lay, unless she doesn't want her young to be sad? How terrible to be the last female of her kind."

"Cheer up, Dode. She doesn't have to be the last. If she would simply get over her hysteria and lay some eggs, she could solve her own problem. A boy and girl chick could start their own dynasty, like those brother-and-sister kings and queens of ancient Egypt, and fill the skies with their offspring."

The door opened. I followed his glance to two older women, carrying expensive silk parasols. They nodded at him, then looked at me.

We left the zoo soon after. There was a park that he said he liked on the other side of Cincinnati.

After that, as July heated up the summer, he took me to parks nearly every day. "I simply cannot get enough of the fresh air!" he would exclaim from behind the windshield of his open Cadillac. He drove his automobile now, better to get to the distant grounds which he said were so much more interesting than those nearby.

I was all right with that.

We appointed ourselves to be experts on the parks of the region, making a big show of evaluating which had the best band shells, the best ornamental bridges, the best rose arbors. It was when judging one of those rose arbors, beneath some sweet-smelling last blooms under which he had playfully positioned me, that he pressed his lips to mine.

We didn't talk much on the ride back. The smell of roses, and the feel of his lips against my own, lingered in my mind as the car roared toward the sinking sun.

He stopped a few blocks from home.

*Get out,* he said. *Meet me in the stables.*

My heart pounded. I knew my life was changing.

I crunched down the cinder-paved alley, past fires smoldering in ash-cans, past rats slithering over garbage heaps, past horses pawing in their stables. At the biggest and grandest stable, a miniature of the many-gabled house behind it down to the stained-glass circular window of a little white lamb, I stopped. Home. Without being told, I knew to hide. I did so behind my favorite sycamore, my shoulder to bark peeling away to expose the smooth white trunk. After what seemed like hours, the stableman blew out his lamp and left.

I rolled open the door. The stable was as familiar to me as the scar on my thumb from picking up Father's razor as a child. Edward and I had played in the manure-tinged gloom when young. But it looked different to me that steamy July night, foreign, and not just because much of it had been given over to autos those days. Pale blue moonlight poured inside, drenching a painted stall, the flutes of a horse's ears, a muscular rump. I closed the door and went over and laid my head on the warm neck of JoJo, the Lambs' young gray-and-white cart horse, a forgotten gift for Mrs. Lamb's little niece when she'd visited last fall from Connecticut.

The stable door rumbled open.

"Dode. You there?"

I raised my head. I could hardly hear my own whisper over the pulsing of my blood. "Yes."

"Where is my good girl?"

I ran to him. He kissed me so tenderly that I cried out when he pulled back. I needed more.

He drew his finger over my cheekbone. "A tear, love?"

He didn't wait for a response. "I brought you something."

From behind his back, he held out a little metal box. The moonlight caught the bumps and curves of the cherubs carved on top.

"Open it."

My blood surged. Was it a ring box? Was there a ring?

I couldn't find the latch.

He put my finger on a frail little knob on the bottom. "Here."

When I pressed, the lid snapped back. Out popped a feathered bird. It trilled as it jerked back and forth and lifted its wings.

I laughed, as much as out of disappointment as in surprise.

"It came all the way from Germany." He kissed me. "For you, to remember our day."

"How does it work?"

"Does it matter?" He kissed me harder. "You are such a funny girl."

"I don't know about that."

His hands roamed my body. Each part unfurled under his touch, straining like a naked hatchling to its parent.

All of a sudden, nothing must be between us. We swam through the layers of clothes separating us. When flesh reached flesh, we stopped. I gasped at the warmth of his arm sliding under my bare thighs, and at the thrill of him lifting me.

I was reeling from the pain and pleasure of being loved when Father spoke. It took a beat for his voice to register.

"Dorothy."

Edward flinched as if stung. We froze together like two lewd statues.

My voice seemed to come from someone else. "It's all right, Father!"

Father's reply seared the silence.

"It is NOT *all right.*"

# PART TWO

# NINE

*En route*

June was running home from high school with an armful of books, out of breath. She recklessly crossed State Street, drawing a clang of the streetcar man's bell. The State School kids were pumping away on their creaky swings as she ran up the path to the porch, threw open the front door, swirled into the living room, and dumped her schoolbooks next to Ruth on the davenport. Hands triumphantly on hips, she waited for her sister to look up from a book the size of a dictionary.

"Guess what?"

Ruth saved her place in the book with her finger. "What?"

"Of all the seniors at school, I was one of six chosen to model in the window of Wolf and Dessauer's!"

June let the salient points of her announcement resonate. One of six! Chosen to model! W & D's, the biggest department store in town! Such a feat would be the crowning achievement of June's — anyone's! — almost eighteen years.

"Congratulations. There is no higher honor than being picked to shill for a store by standing around in their clothes like a dummy." Ruth returned to her reading.

June gave her sister a pitying look. Thus spoke one who would never be chosen.

June began her preparations immediately. Trips back and forth across the living room with a book on her head ensued, causing the cut-glass pendants on dead Aunt Edna's clock to jingle on the bureau. She practiced clenching in her stomach beyond the point of concavity. Assorted smiles were auditioned before the flecked glass of the bedroom mirror.

She embarked on the more serious operations the night before the show. To make her already shiny hair gleam, she followed the advice of Mary Pickford in *Photoplay* and doused it in olive oil and wrapped it in a hot towel, after which it reeked like a salad. With increasing panic, she'd repeatedly scrubbed all three feet of it with Watkins Mulsified Cocoanut Oil Shampoo, which, though it promised not to injure her hair, left her with a frazzled mane that still smelled strongly of olives. She slathered her already dewy young face with Pond's cold cream, as recommended in *Woman's Day* by Lady Diana Manners, the Most Beautiful Woman of the English Aristocracy. Then she shocked her greased skin with Listerine as an astringent, just as the ads suggested.

Ruth watched the entire performance over her library copy of *War and Peace.*

After breakfasting on a grapefruit half in the morning (as recommended by starlet Gloria Swanson), June nervously bid Ruth farewell and had Ned drive her downtown in the store delivery truck so as not to mess her hair with a walk. She had told her mother that she didn't have to come to see her. The show was nothing. Really. Don't come.

She arrived before any of the other girls and presented herself to the director, a Miss Gerding, a clipboard-clutching blonde whose chic beauty was somehow enhanced by the shiny mole above her lip. She looked June up and down.

"Hm. Nice eyes. Cat-like. Here." She lovingly pulled a midnight-blue gown from a rack and held it out. "Get dressed over there. When you're in the window, no talking, no gum-chewing, no laughing, no smiling. You're a mannequin, remember? We'll do something about that hair when you get out. Do you know how to put it in a psyche knot?"

June gawked at her dress. She dared not believe her good luck: with its yards of deep blue draped georgette crepe, sheer straps and back, and loose satin sash, it was a movie star's gown, a New York socialite's dress. She had never dreamed of wearing something so extraordinary. A quick glance at the rack proved it to be the showstopping garment of the event.

The other girls clattered in on strapped shoes, trailed by proud mothers and sisters, and were assessed by Miss Gerding before receiving their assignments. Soon the dressing room was abuzz with female relatives giving advice amid the rustle of clothing.

June swished out of her booth.

One of the mothers was fanning herself in an overstuffed flowered chair. "Why, dear, that dress looks lovely on you!"

"Thank you." June threw a bashful glance in the full-length mirror. Who was that sophisticated woman in the Hollywood gown? The dark blue set off her golden skin and brought out the honey in her hair, waving down her back.

A dressing curtain parted for a stylish mother in low-waisted silk. One glance at

June, and she tapped the arm in which Miss Gerding carried her clipboard.

"Excuse me, Miss. I apologize for telling you your business, but in all honesty, that dress would look better on my daughter Elizabeth."

Miss Gerding's chic mole rode up and down as she examined June. "I think it looks swell where it is."

The mother smiled regretfully. "Elizabeth. Elizabeth! Come here."

A girl came out of her dressing room, her lower lip drooping like the black tights of her knit bathing costume. June knew her from school — Elizabeth Adams, the only girl who had her own automobile.

"I'm sorry," Elizabeth's mother said to Miss Gerding, "but Dr. Adams would never approve of this."

Elizabeth plucked at the heavy knit tunic. "Daddy would *hate* it."

One of the other mothers laid a hand on Miss Gerding's arm. "You do know who Dr. Adams is?" She didn't allow Miss Gerding to answer. "Sweetie, you cannot put Elizabeth Adams in a bathing suit. It just won't do. Who is this other girl?"

The mothers looked at June, then traded glances. One of them gave her head a tiny shake.

Minutes later, June was tugging up droopy black stockings in her dressing room.

Her whole life, June had quietly taken whatever knocks had come her way. Discomforts, embarrassments, injustices — she took all with the same stony resolve. According to Mother, as a toddler she wouldn't cry in her crib when ill but would patiently lie in her own vomit. In kindergarten, she'd stared blankly when a pigtailed classmate screamed at her for using the girl's handkerchief to wipe a doll's bottom. She let her eighth-grade teacher wrongly accuse her of cheating when she'd scored perfectly on a difficult test. In high school, when she heard people whispering about Mother, she stood by, her heart blazing, with a smile on her face. She had said nothing in defense when people spread cruel rumors about Ruth and a boy. Why protest so bothered her, even traumatized her, she couldn't say. But it did. She preferred abuse to conflict, even if she were seething.

Not today. As she filed out in her scratchy suit with her fellow dummies, she shook with thoughts of revenge. How to punish her tormentors? How to make them pay?

She took her place in the window. And then she knew: she would marry a doctor someday. No, better than that. *She* would be *somebody.* Somebody big. Somebody everyone admired, even Mrs. Doctor Adams. Everyone would wish they were her. And then she would snub them.

But for now, all she could do as she itched and smoldered at the end of the dummy line was to not look at the crowd gathered below. She would not give them the satisfaction of seeing their smirks at her and her lumpy suit. She stared through the plate glass at the brick storefronts with their flapping awnings across the street, as if by some trick of nature, not seeing the crowd meant that they couldn't see her.

She felt a small irritation as she trained her sights above the sea of hats and heads. Something was niggling at her with the mild pressure of a collar turned wrong-side in against your neck. Someone, she realized, was staring at her. She commanded herself not to look.

She looked.

In the front row, next to a farmer-come-to-town in bib dungarees, was Ruth. Her plain teenage face was tight with pride and admiration.

June's heart filled and softened like a sponge in warm water. *Dear baby sister. My truest friend. How I adore you.*

It hit her like a punch to the arm. She

135

wasn't the only one who needed her to be somebody. Odd Dorothy had two daughters.

She squared her shoulders and caught Ruth's gaze. *I'll carry you, little sister. I'm not leaving you behind.*


"You look comfortable."

June opened her eyes to her husband, his thick butternut hair combed back in an expensive cut.

He leaned across the aisle to raise his voice over the roar of the propellers. "Sorry, darling. I didn't realize you were sleeping. I asked you if you were excited to see your hometown and then you got quiet." He laughed. "I wondered why it was taking you so long to answer."

June gripped the armrests of her cushioned seat to brace herself against the vibrations buzzing up through her feet and legs to her internal organs. At least, so far, this leg of the journey had not been as treacherous as the one last night. During that nightmare jaunt, the plane had alternated bucking and shuddering like a Conestoga on a rutted trail with sudden plunges in altitude. A cry would go up from the eleven other mortals trapped in the tin tube whenever they suddenly plummeted — hats, bags, blankets flying. She'd been so terrorized that she'd hardly gotten in a wink once they had arrived in Chicago, in spite of the plush bedding and linens at the Drake. She must have fallen asleep just now from exhaustion.

"Aren't you glad that I insisted on flying?"

She was astonished to find that he wasn't joking. They'd almost died last night.

"Yes, darling."

Terror aside, it seemed like a tremendous extravagance. June had seen what he'd paid at the ticket office in Chicago — $17.40 a person just for the leg to Fort Wayne. The entire round-trip from Minneapolis for the two of them came to $106, more than Dad had cleared over several months in his store. Dad, with his love for science and invention, would have loved an airplane trip — he *deserved* an airplane trip for all of the good he did for people — but since when did being deserving count?

"Go back to sleep, darling. We'll be in Fort Wayne soon enough." Richard shook open his newspaper.

She peered out the curtained porthole, past the riveted aluminum wing and through the shreds of clouds, to the fields sleeping far below. Cows dotted green pastures; windmills and silos marked the homesteads of honest farmers. At this distance the earth seemed such an innocent place, a peaceable kingdom where nothing could ever hurt you.

The stewardess, a young woman with a side cap jauntily perched on her springy auburn curls, balanced herself between them with a tray clattering with dinnerware. "Breakfast!"

Richard looked up. "Hello, sweetheart."

She bent down to place the tray in front of him.

"Oh, no, honey." He crooked a finger at the stewardess. She stooped closer to hear his pretend-whisper, those curls near to his lips. "Give it to my wife. We want to be nice to her. She's Betty Crocker."

June forced herself to smile as the stewardess did a double take.

"Oh, my goodness, you are Betty Crocker! You look just like your picture in the advertisements."

Richard laughed. June flashed him a frown before refixing her smile.

The stewardess laid the tray on June's portable table then stood back, her hand to her Peter Pan collar. "Oh, my goodness, I love your radio show, Miss — ?"

"She's actually married." He turned to June. "Don't you tell people that?" Before she could answer, he said, "I guess she keeps me a secret."

"I love your show, Mrs. — Crocker?"

Richard winked. "Bingo."

"I'm sorry, I didn't know who you were. I was told you were Dr. and Mrs. White-leather."

He lowered his voice. "She has to travel incognito. You understand."

Her curls bounced in a nod. "Oh. Yes. Certainly. You must be the most popular woman in America!" She bunched her shoulders with giddiness. "All those stars that you know! Tell me, what is Fred Astaire like?"

June maintained her smile. "Very nice."

"I'll say! Not like that bachelor you had on last week, talking about what he was looking for in a wife. I'm sorry, but he made my blood boil. Imagine — wanting a girl to cook on a wood-burning stove just like his mother! *His* wife would not "cheat" by using modern conveniences. The nerve! I'd like to take away his modern conveniences — see how he does without a car!"

Richard winced. "Ouch!"

"The only bachelor more insufferable," the stewardess said, warmed up now, "was that mechanic you had on. Can you believe that his requirement for a wife was that she smile, no matter what? In these times!"

"That's what I require." Richard grinned

up at the girl.

The stewardess's smile wavered as she looked to June for confirmation.

Anger flared up. When Richard made fun of Betty Crocker, he was demeaning June's work. He was demeaning *her.* "A smile goes a mile," she said lightly.

"That's just what my mother says!" The stewardess nudged her cap. "I've served a lot of stars on this plane — Carole Lombard, Bette Davis, Joan Crawford — but you're my very favorite. You're the only one *who understands.*"

"She does pretty much know everything," Richard said.

"She does!" the stewardess agreed. "This might sound silly, but when I get in a pinch, I try to ask myself, 'What would Betty do?' "

June glanced away. Heaven help us, Kitty Hunter was right.

"I ask myself that, too," said Richard. "All the time."

When the stewardess wove her way back to the rear of the airplane, June said, "Please don't tease about Betty."

"You or the girl?"

"Both. You insult us."

He cocked his head at her. "I do believe you're serious."

"I am."

"I'm sorry."

The stewardess returned with Richard's meal. After setting it before him, she turned to June. "May I ask you something?"

June prepared herself. So many of the women who wrote to Betty asked personal things in their letters, as if Betty's knowledge of flour and women extended to matters of the heart. The truth was, in most situations, June hadn't the slightest idea what to do. She needed her own Betty to solve her problems.

"Of course."

"My cakes are always overdone. I follow the recipe perfectly — I don't even tap down the flour in the measuring cup, like you say not to do in your little booklets. Still, they're tough."

June inwardly sighed with relief. Cake diagnosing she could do.

"I wonder if it has to do with the pan. Are you using modern, standardized-sized ones? Measure them and see. If they are bigger than the standard eight or nine inch for layer cakes — some of the older pans are — it can make all the difference. You could be overbaking."

"Thank you! I'll check my pans."

Another passenger beckoned. The stewardess turned then stopped. "What a life you must lead, Mrs. Crocker. Do you have any funny stories about the stars?"

Richard sugared his grapefruit. "Tell her how Joan Crawford travels with a gun in her purse."

The stewardess gasped. "She does!"

June shook her head.

"Oh, my goodness, I hope not! She was on this very plane!"

"Did you check her purse?" Richard looked up innocently.

"He's teasing," said June.

The stewardess, reluctantly, left.

"Richard," June scolded when she was gone.

"You have to see the humor —"

"I don't."

He picked up his spoon. "Where's the girl who used to laugh at all my jokes? You're turning into your sister. Why is everyone in your family so grim?"

"My father wasn't grim."

"Old Bud? He was a good chap, I'll grant you that. But let's face it, darling, he had a terrible sense of business. He literally gave away the store."

"He was trying to help people!"

"Well, he hurt his own loved ones while he was at it, didn't he? Making all of you scrimp and scramble and live like paupers.

He died young from worrying about it, too."

Pain welled up in her chest. She couldn't bear a word said against her father. Dad was the one who had her ride her bike to the store to meet him for lunch. He was the one who took her to the library so that she could gather precious armfuls of books in a quiet room that smelled of binding glue and dust. It was he who enrolled her in swimming lessons at the YWCA downtown, where he rented her a musty red wool bathing suit and a dingy white rubber cap so that she could jump into the echoing depths of the indoor pool; he who got her dressed when she was small, once forgetting to put on her underwear when readying her for church when she was a toddler, a mistake only discovered when she could . . . not . . . *budge* . . . down the metal slide in her Sunday School room; he who brought baby squirrels or birds in his pocket for her and Ruth from his walk home from the store; who helped her with her math homework; who lent a patient ear when she needed advice about her friends. It was he who, after she'd told him, sheepishly, that she'd first bled, silently brought her some of Mother's flannel pads and her sanitary belt. June had to figure out on her own how to wear them. She never thought of asking her

143

distant mother.

Of course it was him to whom she'd gone in a panic the week before her wedding to Richard. She'd wanted to call it off. She told Dad that she'd never fit into Richard's world, that she would never know their manners, their customs, just how to be, and worse, much worse, that she wasn't sure she loved him. Dad had told her that she was just having cold feet. Everyone did. She'd get over it.

"Did you have cold feet with Mother?" she'd asked.

He'd smiled. "No. Never."

An odd hot feeling had overcome her. She would have almost said it was jealousy.

Richard reached across the aisle. "I'm sorry, darling. That was thoughtless of me. Are you angry?"

She shook her head.

"Well, I have something that might put me in your good graces again." He nudged the medical bag at his feet. Squat, brass-clasped, and clad in pimply black-dyed ostrich flesh, the bag went with him every-where by day, then crouched like a fat black toad by their bed at night.

"In your bag? What, Richard?"

"Now, darling, you must be patient. But it's a very good surprise, I promise."

"You truly do enjoy torturing me, don't you?"

"Not as much as you enjoy torturing me." He dug into his grapefruit.

He was kidding her. She watched him eat. *Was* he kidding her? Maybe he did feel tortured. She didn't know why he loved her. With a stab of surprise, she wondered, *did* he actually love her anymore? How was it possible to share a table, a bed, a life with a person for eleven years and be so completely ignorant of his mind? Maybe the failing was with her. Maybe other wives understood their husbands better than she knew hers. Maybe even Ruth, even prickly old Ruth, knew hers, before he had taken ill. Maybe Ruth knew John better than June ever had.

She glanced at Richard. He raised his eyebrows.

"What?" he said.

Richard gave her a home, a reputation, status, everything that she thought she had always wanted. He kept her safe. In exchange, he depended on her to at least be a decent wife.

"Thank you," she said.

"For what?"

"For being good to me. You are, you know. I don't deserve it."

"Where'd that come from?" He sat back

145

in his seat with a grimace.

She gazed out her porthole. He was right. Her thank-you was not enough, not when there were nurses, patients, friends at the club, who would be glad to give him more than thanks. Then what would she do?

She thought of him turning away from her at night.

The skin tingled on her arms. Maybe the time had come already. And she had brought it on herself.

# TEN

*Indiana-Michigan Line, 1934*

Six-thirty in the morning, and the sky was the color of blood. Already Ruth was hot. Baking-inside-your-own-skin hot. All night long, Ruth had twitched around her little bed next to John's with her nightie hiked up around her belly to snatch any stray breeze that might come limping through the screen, to no avail. She had not been able to get six winks, although John slept like the dead, as usual. When she'd come out for breakfast, Mother was waiting in her bedcap and robe for the stove to heat. "This weather's going to come to tears," Mother'd said. Ruth thought that she might be right.

Now, outside in the field, Ruth listened to the tweedle of waking robins and kicked the parched ground, setting off tiny tempests of dirt. Nick was pouring a sack of seed corn into the hopper of the planter. He wanted to do the planting himself, but she wouldn't let him. He'd thought with her sister coming that afternoon that Ruth would be busy with preparations. Ruth had argued that no, she was not doing anything special to get ready for her sister. No red carpet needed rolling out. June was not some sort of star, no matter what others might think.

Chickens rushed over the toes of Ruth's heavy shoes to snatch the few kernels that bounced from the metal hopper as Nick poured and Ruth watched Nick's broad shoulders. When he squatted down to re-check the fittings connecting the planter to the tractor hitch, she let her gaze fall to his hands. She imagined them cradling her to him, his slim hips touching hers —

"Ready." He stood up.

JoJo nickered from behind the fence separating the pasture from the field. John used to joke that JoJo followed Ruth around like Mary's Little Lamb. He used to say that animals knew a kind heart when they saw it. "Animals do not lie," he'd say when she protested.

She still didn't know how to take a compliment.

"Root, look," Nick said. "JoJo thinks that she should work."

Ruth shook off her thoughts. "She used to plow, you know, when we first took over the farm, old as she was. She insisted." She didn't say that was because JoJo would do anything to please her. The horse had adored Ruth since she was a little girl. "We were the ones who had to call a stop to it, although she did trample the rows less than a tractor. Wherever Mother got her, she sure got her money's worth."

"Are you sure you do not want me to do the planting?"

"Nope."

They were gambling that the building heat meant that rain was on the way. The bloody sky might just bear this out; a sky as red as this pointed to a severe gully-washer. Regardless, it was getting late in the season to put planting off any longer. Heat like this had to break, and when it did, it would pour.

Well, let it. She clapped on John's beat-up hat.

Nick stood back. "I do not feel good about letting you do the planting."

Letting her?

He added, "With your sister coming earlier than you thought."

Oh. He was being nice. She had to quit being so crabby. Oversexed and crabby was a nasty combination. She'd been off since Ed Squibb had driven over last night to tell them that June had telephoned. She was

149

going to be arriving a day early because they were taking an airplane. Show-offs.

"Doesn't matter. June can come whenever she wants." It truly didn't matter to Ruth. Not in the least.

"They are flying in an aeroplane!"

Ruth shrugged.

He whistled. "They must be important."

"I bet they think so."

She walked around to the back of the tractor. He lifted her by the waist up onto the metal seat. "Am I going to like this sister?"

"Probably. Everyone else does. She's relentlessly likable." Her waist was still glowing from where his hands had been.

"Just like Betty Crocker."

"Don't get me started." Ruth grabbed the lever of the shift. "Anyhow, June was like that long before she was a barker for flour. I was always in her shadow, growing up."

"I cannot see you in anyone's shadow, Root."

"Well, it's true." She squirmed in the slotted metal cradle of the seat, which felt something like sitting on a warm street grate. "My parents were so busy worshipping at the feet of June, they sort of forgot about me."

"I don't believe it." He stepped aside. "Well, I love you best."

She hit the gas to hide her pleasure, then jerked back as the tractor started off, the hoppers tottering down the rows behind it. "You don't even know her!"

"Does not matter!" he called after her.

Poor JoJo, trailing from behind the fence, raised her dusty neck as if to oversee the operation.

Ruth jostled along on the tractor. It was true, she thought, looking behind her to make sure the seed was coming out properly. When she was young, her parents actually did seem to pretty much forget about her at times. She blamed her mother especially. At least Dad was working at the store and was busy. But what was Mother's excuse when she'd sent Ruth to her first day of half-day kindergarten with June, without any provision for Ruth to get home?

Ruth could remember that afternoon like it just happened. The morning had been a revelation, filled with finger paints and painting smocks, sleeping mats and recess. Still vibrating with the excitement of it all, Ruth stood in front of the school by a brick planter bristling with scratchy shrubs. She watched her classmates march off two by two with their mothers, having been released hours before the older grades. Where was her own mother?

They hadn't discussed what she should do after school. She thought Mother would just appear — the other mothers had. She knew that she shouldn't go home alone. The walk there with June that morning had been an arduous journey through unknown territory occupied by interesting new kids and untold marvels. Ruth had to resist pausing for even the most fascinating discoveries — grapevines and pear trees dripping with fruit, an apparently haunted house, the filling station rich with the dizzying smell of gasoline. She had only dropped June's hand once, just long enough to run over to pet a peach-colored spaniel that was chained to its doghouse.

The last of the kindergarteners had gone and Ruth, still waiting for Mother, was picking the little round leaves from the pricker bushes when a man with a broom came out and took a pack of cigarettes from his shirt.

He struck a match on the planter.

"What are you doing here?"

She rolled her gaze up to him. June had warned her about strangers.

He stepped toward her. "Here, I'll take you to —"

She gasped and ran in the direction she thought she'd come. She didn't stop running until she came to a busy street.

A Model T rattled by, then a horse-drawn wagon loaded with crates of apples. She recognized this corner. It was at the street where the nice dog lived. But which way to turn? She made a choice.

She walked along, scared, thirsty. Her new shoes rubbed sore spots on her feet. Where was the peach-colored dog? When was she getting to him and his doghouse?

A car *ah-ooh-gah*ed at her, jolting her from her skin. She ran now, blurry with tears, until she came to a rusty bridge.

Terror descended. She had not gone over a bridge that morning.

She stood on tiptoes to peer over the flaking rails and into the river. Sticks rode the brown muddy water. Something plunked.

The river was dangerous, Mother said. People drowned in it. Ruth was never, ever, to go near it. Now as she gazed woozily into the thick brown water, it seemed like it might leap up and snatch her from the bridge.

She pulled back with a yelp. She was lost. Maybe forever.

She was walking blind with tears when it occurred to her: the river passed near to her home. They crossed over it whenever they went downtown. It was just a short walk away from where she lived. She could follow it until she saw her street.

Cicadas were wailing, late in the after-noon, when she dragged up her porch steps. "I'm home!" she yelled.

No one answered.

The house was empty. The world seemed inside-out, a bleak nightmare in which she was the last one alive.

She was in front of the mirror, looking at her belly, scratched and muddy from where she had clawed her desperate way up a steep place on the riverbank — now she knew why she'd been forbidden to go there alone — when June came in.

"Ruthie! Where have you been?"

"Mother didn't get me."

"Someone said they saw you by the river. We thought you were dead!"

They clung to each other and bawled. She drank in the comfort of June's skinny arms and her dirty, sweet, musky scent. Ruth's favorite smell in the world. It smelled like home.


Toasted from the sun above and pummeled from the tractor below, Ruth steered the big iron wheels around the end of the row. She'd been on the tractor for most of the morning and she was ready to be done. She was getting depressed up here.

A car mounted the nearby rise in their road. Ruth's gut seized.

*June.*

She ducked her head.

No, couldn't be June already. Anyway, Ruth had nothing to hide. What she'd done, she'd done. June wasn't any worse for the wear from it; in fact, she'd come out way ahead. Ruth held her head up, battered hat and all, and turned her chin belligerently toward the road.

A fancy car roared by, a big touring automobile with a chrome grill that stuck out like a cowcatcher on a train. She watched it as it slunk down the road, on past the ruins of the log cabin built by John's ancestors, and out of sight.

What was that showboat doing out here in no-man's-land? She entertained herself with the possibilities as she bobbled along on the John Deere: some bankers took a wrong turn in Chicago. It was the Squibbs — their rich uncle croaked and left them a bundle and they were joyriding in their new limousine. A bank robber was making an escape in a getaway vehicle — actually, that was not a joke. Dillinger was striking all over the area. Just a couple months ago, he hit as close as Auburn. He was said to have hidden out in a farmhouse just up the road.

When she came to the end of the row, she stopped, tractor motor running, and looked out over the naked furrows of neighboring fields spreading out in all directions. In the distance, the sun glinted on the dome of the Squibbs' silo and on the tin of their house's rooftop, and further off, on the horizon, from the outbuildings on the Martin place. Acres of fields and pastureland lay between her house and the Squibbs'. If she screamed, there was no one to hear her.

Her skin prickled even as the sun beat down.

She frowned at JoJo, quivering her haunches to shoo off flies. Calm down, Ruth. More likely it was some city folks with a summer place on one of the nearby lakes, James, Snow, and the like, taking a tour of the "scenic" countryside.

She gave the tractor gas.

On she swayed, the hot sun cooking her back. A lake sounded pretty nice right now. The image of a speedboat cutting across cool gray water flashed through her memory. In her mind, she was back in her brother-in-law's gleaming mahogany speedboat during her first visit to Minnesota, back when Margaret was a baby and she was pregnant with Jeanne. Back when John was whole.

■ ■ ■ ■

The sleek mahogany boat idled in the middle of the lake. Marinating in the smell of gasoline and mildew, Ruth rocked on the cushioned second-row seat with John, as roly-poly in oversized white cloth life jackets as Tweedledee and Tweedledum. Richard, perched on the wooden divider between seating compartments, was looking down on them with a grin.

"What do you think of the boat, John?"

"Nice," John said.

" 'Nice'?" Richard's navy blazer sleeve trembled in the wind as he knocked back a drink. He handed the glass to June, sitting down in the passenger seat. " 'Nice'? They only make ten of these crafts a year."

June cradled the glass, a small smile fixed upon her face. She often looked upset around Richard, Ruth noticed, though Ruth doubted anyone else could tell. Usually when a person smiled, it meant they were happy, but with June, not necessarily. A smile could mean she was panicking. Or furious. Anything that a smile didn't usually mean. Ruth wondered if anyone else knew that about her.

"Want to drive it?" Richard asked.

John tightened his arm around Ruth. "No, thanks."

"You should. You can do it, my man. It's just like driving a tractor." Richard winked at Ruth. "Only a tad more suave."

John patted Ruth's shoulder. "No, thanks."

Ruth found herself speaking up over the rumble of the idling engine. "I'll drive."

"You will?" Richard's tone was amused as he beamed down on her. "June doesn't even drive my baby."

Ruth didn't care about driving that tub. It was just that John was acting like a hick. "I can drive your 'baby.' I drive the truck all the time."

John palmed the top of her head. "You might as well say yes, Richard. She won't stop until you do."

Ruth leaned out of his grip, more to get away from John, who was suddenly infuriating her with his inferiority to Richard, than to make her way out of their compartment. Richard, thinking that she was insisting on driving, reached down to pull her up to him.

"See what I mean?" said John.

June hugged the empty glass. "I admire Ruth. She doesn't give up until she gets what she wants, let the chips fall where they may."

Ruth paused, midway across the divider. The hair rose on her scalp. Was June actually going to make trouble? Here? Out in the middle of the lake? For the first time in her life? Ruth felt her mouth crook. What bee had gotten in June's bonnet?

Richard made a show of helping Ruth into the front though her pregnant belly wasn't all that big yet. "She can drive my boat any day."

"Problem is," said June, "Ruth wants to drive everyone's boat."

Ruth slid between her and Richard. "Three's a crowd," she said cheerfully.

June smiled at her, then, abruptly, pushed up out of her seat. She swung her legs elegantly over the divider and dropped down next to John. Ruth saw them glance at each other, and then, very pointedly, away.

Ruth should have thought out this stupid move. She should have watched her smart mouth. Putting them together was the last thing she had wanted to do.

She made herself listen as Richard showed her the controls. She frowned at the switches and gauges, her inner self scrutinizing John and June from the back of her head. Even without seeing them, she could sense them studiously looking out either side of the boat.

Ruth knew that she would never completely have John. Oh, she might have won the legal right to sleep with him, might have borne a child for him, might have had the honor of enduring the nausea and sprung varicose veins of carrying another. She might have been the chosen one who got to get up before dawn to milk the cows with him and to salve infected udders, the lucky winner who got to wash his clothes, cook his meals, and raise his kids. But even having all this, she didn't really have him. She could never control his heart. She could never make him not love June.

Ruth had not dimmed his love for her sister in the slightest by marrying him — she might well have increased it. She could feel them now, perched behind her in the boat, nobly resisting their beautiful love. Their yearning was so palpable she could reach back and wave her hand through it.

The realization poured through her like molten lead: John didn't have to have a physical affair to betray her. Even if he never acted on his love for June, Ruth would hurt just as much as if he had. For while a stolen act of the flesh was over in a flash, the craving for what-might-have-been knew no end.

Ruth goosed the boat, sending it shooting across the water.

The mahogany boat scudded from her memory, leaving Ruth atop the tractor, glaring at nothing and everything. She was still there, Ruth the human rubber strap, binding together farm and family, though stretched to the point of snapping. Her dismal mood had settled in like a heavy cold when the big car returned.

JoJo swiveled pricked ears toward the dust-covered showboat taking up the entire width of the dirt road as it barreled their way. Now the gray clouds billowing up from its whitewall tires seemed to lessen. The car was slowing down, slowing down, until it crept up . . . and stopped.

A solitary fellow stared through his rolled-up window. Huh — big-city man must think her quaint, a lowly farm woman working the land.

"Take a picture," she yelled. "It'll last longer!"

He sat there, engine running.

Her pulse picked up. Maybe she shouldn't have yelled.

Should she run?

The big car rolled forward, then took on speed. When a cloud of dust was boiling behind it, she aimed the tractor back down the row.

People!

# DOROTHY

Back to sleep already? But you haven't touched your Ovaltine. Sure you don't want some? I saw in a magazine that it "solves the food problem in cases of diphtheria, typhoid, and pneumonia."

Well, we won't worry about that. Time for a little sponge bath before June gets here! Ivory Soap — "so pure it floats." Don't you love how clean it smells?

Lift your arm, dearie.

So, as I was saying, soon as they found out I was late, my parents sent me away. They cast me out on JoJo, who the Lambs got rid of for her place in the stable — Mrs. Lamb's car needed her spot.

I can still see us, plodding our way down country roads. We ate from gardens — muskmelons and carrots with the dirt still clinging to them, pole beans and tomatoes from the vine. I slept under bushes, hayricks, or under JoJo herself, where I'd gaze up at the pink flesh of her belly, now contracting, now expanding, now contracting with her breath, reminding me that we were alive.

On the eighth day, a Sunday, we reached Fort Wayne, where I sought the address I'd committed to memory: 602 Tennessee. At sunset, I knocked on the door of a tar-paper cottage close enough to the river that the air smelled like turtles.

No answer.

Knocked again.

No answer.

I was turning around to go when I was jerked inside. Mother's cousin Mildred sat me down, told me to shut up, and stated her terms.

Monday I was to do the laundry.

Tuesday was ironing: Clothes. Sheets. Towels. Undies. Hankies. Pillowcases.

Wednesday the floors got scrubbed. The rugs got beat.

Thursday, it was pies. And cookies. And cakes. Enough dessert for every night of the week.

Friday it was wood. Chop it.

Saturday, draw water for the bath. This was on top of the water I had to carry for daily use, not to mention the three squares a day that needed cooking.

No church on Sunday. No visitors ever.

She watched me from her high-backed peachy-beige chair, the cords of her neck taking turns at swishing her square jaw. Her hair and eyes were the dirt-brown of the knitting that foamed from her busy needles.

"Well?"

I said yes.

But I was young. When I wasn't chopping wood, crimping crusts, or heating irons, and Mildred was at her factory job at the electric works, I found time to explore in spite of my growing belly. I developed a taste for the chocolate-covered doughnuts at G. C. Murphy's. I took JoJo out to Robinson Park, where I rode on the merry-go-round by myself, though my heart did burn at the sight of all the couples. I took walks to the iron bridge in Lawton Park, where I dropped shiny buckeyes, pried fresh from prickly shells, into the thick brown water of Spy Run Creek. When my belly got too big, I stayed home and watched snow pile up to the windowsills.

Each night, as Cousin Mildred knitted, bubbles rising in the glass of beer next to her elbow, I waited in my room until an excess of drink and wool had slumped her in her throne. Then I would retrieve my secret prize.

Caressing the bumpy cherubs on the lid, I

wound the key then pressed the fragile knob.

Every time it popped open, I laughed. How my darling trilled and warbled, switching to and fro as it jerked its feathered wings, every bit as lively as a living, breathing bird. I was touched to think how much Edward loved me to give me such an expensive gift.

He was coming for me, I knew it. I looked for him to be plunging through the fresh white snow. When he didn't come then, I waited to see him picking through the soot-blackened crust. When not then, I watched as the robins returned; while it rained; when the violets raised bright faces in the grass. It came as a shock to me, then, when my water broke and still Edward hadn't arrived.

I was in the outhouse when it happened, after lunch. The gushing confused me for a moment — I couldn't feel the water pouring out of me, yet there was a puddle at my shoes.

Mildred was knitting an oblong as brown as a beard when I waddled in.

"The baby is coming."

Mud-brown eyes looked over glasses, but her needles kept twitching.

Maybe she didn't hear me. "The baby's coming. We need to send for the doctor."

I gauged my belly for pain. None yet.

Maybe having a baby wasn't so hard.

Mildred twitched her beak, put her instruments in a basket, then threw a brown shawl of her own making over her shoulders and left. Not knowing what to do with myself, I pumped the washtub full of water and got out the washboard.

What must have been hours later, I was scrubbing beer stains from Cousin Mildred's slip when she came into the kitchen with a man. His blue eyes, patrician nose, and red lips would have been handsome had they not been fighting for the center of his face. Vacant stretches of flesh spread out to his forehead, ears, and chin. I couldn't help but stare at him, trying to pull his features apart in my mind.

He said, "Get undressed."

I blushed and asked him where.

He turned to Mildred. "Where do you want her to go?"

Mildred nodded to the kitchen table. "On there. She can scrub it afterward."

I stared into the cloudy water licking the sides of the galvanized washtub. A pain was cranking down on my belly like a vise into a strip of balsa wood.

Mildred came over and jerked my hands from the water and with them, the dripping slip. She peered at it, then stuck her finger through the hole where the beer stain had been. "What have you done, you stupid girl?"

Before long, I was on the kitchen table, another contraction cinching my abdomen, tightening, hardening, lifting it like a rock.

I heard myself scream. "Mother! Help me!"

On a hard-backed chair across the little kitchen, Mildred looped yarn around her needle tips. "*She* doesn't want to help you."

The contraction held, gripping so hard I felt torn in two. And then, it uncoiled, slowly. I fell back, my hair plastered to my cheek. I would bring out this baby safely for Edward.

Another contraction began to crank down on me.

The doctor, drinking coffee at the sink, put down his cup and came over and trained those double-barrel eyes between my legs.

"Hmm. Breech."

"Breech?"

"All I see is your baby's butt. Damn thing is trying to back its way into the world."

I was surprised a doctor would talk so crudely. I thought they were more educated than that. But all I could do was grind out a groan. Every fiber in my body was straining to push that baby out.

The doctor lightly slapped my naked thigh, like he would a balky pony. "You can't push, kiddo. If you let it get sucked back in between pains, you'll cut off its oxygen and it'll have brain damage. Do you want your kid in the State School?"

Mildred said, "Let her push."

# ELEVEN

*Indiana-Michigan Line, 1934*

Having fed John and tidied him, Dorothy went out on the back step to escape the heat already building up in the house. The wind sent whorls of hot dust skipping across the barnyard and ruffling the gritty feathers of the chickens. Dorothy was sure she could hear the hiss of the soil drying, or maybe it was the grass dying in the yard. The life was leaking out of *something.*

She picked up Venus, who'd been rubbing her ankles with her head like she was peeling a potato. She held the vibrating cat to her face, the better to not see Ruth, who had finished cleaning up after planting and was now fast-walking around the side of the house to the machinery shed into which Nick had recently gone.

She let the cat spring from her arms. She was acquainted with yearning for a man that you couldn't have. She knew the craving that ate into you when you woke up in the morning, and kept on gnawing while your husband fixed breakfast for the family, while you watched the kids run down the road for school, while you tinted pictures for Mr. Cryder, while you paid the life insurance man, picked weeds, opened cans for dinner, did the dishes, cleaned up the kids, read them stories, made them sleep, and then came out to your husband, who was sitting at the dining table in the lamplight, with bills spread before him as he figured out how to rob Peter to pay Paul. The yearning consumed you every waking moment, and many sleeping ones, too, just boring into you, chewing and chewing, like a moth larva into your best wool sweater.

Had William known of her obsession? You would not think so, not as kindly as he had treated her. Who would scheme and plot his way toward making his wife's whims come true, scrimping and sacrificing, yet knowing all the while that she didn't love him?

*Florida.* The word conjured up palm trees and coconuts, trained parrots and bathing caps, shuffleboard games and dark glasses, with June's doctor-husband waving from the porch of their resort hotel. The year before William's death, June had sent for her in Minnesota. While June went to work at her new job helping Betty Crocker, Dorothy'd sat in June's mansion with that nice Adela and watched June's home movies. She had studied the Florida reel keenly, with Richard's fancy new projector ticking in the dark, filing away the details like William did with his ham radio books. She had long dreamed of picking up a seashell on the beach like June in the movie, to listen if you really could hear the ocean roar.

She'd had the itch to go to Florida for years, making the mistake of telling William so, back before the girls were in high school. Once he'd heard, he was a man possessed. They were going there! Nightly, he scrutinized his books, searching for the money, even though he was always falling short with the bills.

Her arms crossed over her nightie, she would come out to him, still up working. "Oh, don't worry about it, William. We'll get there someday. We're not dead yet."

He would put down his pencil, his brown eyes pinched behind his wire glasses, his long chin even longer with sorrow. He absentmindedly patted Ginny, the raggedy dog who had followed him home and now never left his side. "We'll find the money somehow, Dorothy."

Sometimes she feared that he had shortened his life by worrying about money for the Florida trip. You don't do what he did for a wife who's in love with another man. But now, as she stood on the back steps, a queasy bubble of guilt slithered through her stomach.

*Do you?*

She bustled down the treads.

"Ruth!" she yelled from the middle of the farmyard. The chickens tottered over, thinking she might have something for them. "Ruth!" *Oh, Ruth, don't do something that you will hate yourself for.*

Ruth's kids, all bobbed haircuts and knobby knees, tumbled out of the house.

"Is Aunt June here?" Jeanne cried.

Margaret elbowed her way past her. "Where's Aunt June?"

"Wait!" The twins shouted, in a second tier of elbowing. "Wait for us! No fair!"

Ruth stepped out of the machine shed, twitching at her dress. "What, Mother? Why is everyone yelling?"

Dorothy felt as foolish as Henny Penny. But the sky really was falling for Ruth, she just didn't know it.

"I — I thought I saw something."

Nick strolled from the machine shed, rubbing a tractor part with an oily rag. He stopped next to Ruth.

Just then, one of the twins pointed a grubby finger. "Look!"

Against the heat-bleached sky, a distant car, yellow as a rain slicker, unfurled a dust cloud into the far-off fields. The vehicle rambled past the Squibbs' farmstead, dipped in a hollow, then reappeared to roll past pastures in which black and white Holsteins lifted heavy heads to watch. It chugged into woods that contained the tumbledown plank cabin of John's ancestors, then popped back out alongside the trampled field that Ruth had just planted, past the dried-up watering pond, past wire fencing spun between knotty log posts, behind which JoJo nosed at weeds.

A hot breeze flicked the bedspread on the side-yard clothesline when at last the car turned down Ruth's dirt drive. The kids jumped and cheered as it lumbered past tree trunks painted white halfway up, past the house with its scraggly skirt of privets and into the yard, where it rumbled to a stop.

Dorothy's heart surged as June stepped out of the cab and removed her dark glasses. With her blond waves and her yellow traveling suit with its crisp lapels, she looked like a movie star. But Dorothy didn't tell her that. She wouldn't be doing June any favors by giving her a big head.

"Stand up straight, Junie."

June laughed in that way that had so tickled — so *relieved* — Dorothy since June was a baby. "Hello, Mother."

# TWELVE

*Indiana-Michigan Line, 1934*

Silk-stockinged legs swung out of the taxi. Ruth's sister, June, planted brown and white spectator pumps in the dirt of the farmyard, unfolded her willowy figure, stood, then brushed off her lemon-yellow suit with the hand not carrying her train case. Ruth swiveled her gaze to her daughters, gaping at their aunt as if she were a goddess descending to earth, then back to that ridiculous suit. It was yellower than the cab. On a farm. With dirt, barn cats, and eighteen chickens. Good luck with that jacket in this heat. And those pearls! Who was she trying to impress, the cows?

"Margaret! Jeanne!" June held out her arms, Lady Bountiful. They ran to her. They never ran to Ruth that way.

June's husband, Richard, got out, gave a regal stretch, then looked around as if he were Old King Cole about to call for his fiddlers three. June hugged the big girls then beckoned to the little ones.

"Irene," she said in a teasing tone. "Ilene. Come on."

The pair hung back, holding hands. Nearly eight years old and they were acting like babies. Ruth was almost annoyed at them. She *was* annoyed at Nick, next to her, shifting uncomfortably as sweat darkened the chambray under his arms.

"It's just Aunt June," she called to them. "Don't be afraid of her."

June gave Ruth that smile that made Ruth so furious. Just frown if you want to frown!

June waved the girls in. "Come on, pumpkins."

They ran to her with a squeal. Little traitors.

The driver dropped their suitcases — stitched leather, not cardboard like hers — by the porch. Richard handed him money, tucked his wallet in his pocket, and approached the twins. "What do we have here? Puppies?"

The bigger girls shied closer to June. The twins, now having regressed into infants, burrowed their faces into her side. Ruth wondered idly if they might stain that sunshine suit.

"Say hi to Uncle Richard," she ordered.

They clung to her sister.

A fancy touring car zoomed by — not the one she'd seen earlier, she didn't think — making the taxi wait at the end of the drive before it could leave. Wouldn't you know, June comes and they have a regular traffic jam of luxury liners out here. It wasn't yet eleven in the morning.

June gently extracted the twins from her suit. "Girls, put out your hand like this." She extended her own white gloved hand. "And then say, 'So nice to see you, Uncle Richard.'"

They looked up at Aunt June, big-eyed as owls. Margaret inched toward Richard, then crept out her hand.

Enough of this nonsense. They knew better. They weren't born in a barn. Hand out, Ruth thrust herself at her sister's husband, sweat soaking the thin cotton of her dress.

"So nice to see you, Uncle Richard."

She regretted the mockery in her voice the minute she felt his soft hand in hers. He must think she was a beast. She had not yet recovered when, in one polished move, he bent forward and brushed her cheek with a peck.

"How are you, Ruth?"

She froze, flabbergasted. Was she supposed to kiss him back? It was like all those other unwritten rules made by society people to trip you up. If you'd been brought up by a recluse, how were you supposed to know that classy folks *never* mentioned the price of a possession, no matter how great a deal you got? Or that it was gauche to heap your plate at a potluck? Or if you were supposed to kiss back your brother-in-law when kissed? She had purposely made sure she was seated the other times she'd greeted him, to avoid this kind of nonsense.

In a snap decision, she darted forward, catching his ear with her open mouth. She saw the wetness upon his lobe as she pulled back. She steamed with humiliation.

"Good to see you," he said. His excellent breeding didn't allow him to flinch.

Suffering, she turned to June, who surprised her with a hug. Adults in her family didn't hug. She raised her hands awkwardly toward June's arms. Her hands were still in midair, lifted as in worship, when June released her.

"Ruth, you look marvelous!"

Self-cut hair, homemade dress, dusty brogans. Real marvelous. "You, too."

"I mean you really do. You look — happy."

Ruth recrossed her arms. She had never known what to do with a compliment.

Evidently undaunted by Ruth's plastering, Richard grabbed Mother. "Dorothy!"

Mother demonstrated the familial rigor mortis when he nailed her with a kiss. At least she had the sense not to tag him with a sloppy one.

He pulled back to behold Mother. "How are you feeling, Dorothy?" He cocked his head, smiling as he waited for an answer, as if he really wanted to know.

Mother looked confused. "Fine." She let June hug her.

"Well, here we are, Mother," June exclaimed, "at your command!"

She could lay off the Betty Crocker act anytime now. Everyone knew why she suddenly made the trip — she felt sorry for Ruth. Mother must have told June how badly the farm was doing. What was Ruth supposed to do? Fall to her knees and beg for more help?

Ruth caught sight of Nick standing behind her, smiling uncomfortably. She gave him a fierce wave forward.

Was she to introduce him to June and Richard, or introduce them to him? More of those hateful rules!

"June and Richard, this is —"

For crying out loud! She forgot his name!

Everything froze for a long painful moment.

Nick broke the spell. "I'm Nick. I help out Ruth here."

June shook his hand and glanced at Ruth.

Ruth pursed her lips. *I'm dying. You happy?*

"Nice to meet you, Nick," June said.

Nick murmured something in Italian then ducked his head before returning to Ruth's side. She felt a hand on the small of her back. He was rubbing her damp dress, much as her children used to finger their baby blankets.

Ruth flinched and stepped away, leaving his hand rubbing the air.

June's gaze lingered on his hand before she raised it to Ruth's face.

She saw.

# THIRTEEN

*Indiana-Michigan Line, 1934*

June couldn't remember her sister ever being happy. If Ruth was given a baby doll for her birthday, she asked why it didn't have eyes that closed like June's doll did. When Dad burned trash in the rusty barrel in the backyard, she was sure June got the privilege of stirring the ashes more often than she had. At swim lessons at the YWCA, Ruth was certain that the skinny lady at the front desk rented June the less mildewed bathing cap. If Mother pinned satin bows in their hair, Ruth thought June's must be bigger or silkier or prettier. She was always sure she was being cheated.

June would agree — Ruth did seem to get shortchanged when it came to luck. It was Ruth's bicycle tire that would go flat when June and she were out riding as girls. It was Ruth, when she and June were walking their bikes along the State School fence, to whom the dull-eyed grown boys would offer their private parts through the iron bars, sending both she and June screaming. It had been Ruth's kitten that had taken ill with distemper and died; Ruth who'd fallen while ice-skating and fractured her tailbone; Ruth's effort as a toddler to sit close to Mother that would break Mother's finger.

Throughout all of this, June took no pleasure in her sister's misery, no joy in her misfortunes. She wanted the best for her sister, to this day, even after what she'd done. This afternoon, therefore, as she studied her sister, looking unexpectedly youthful and refreshed as she kissed Richard hello — an astonishingly sociable move for Ruth — June felt nothing but relief. She didn't know how her sister carried on from day to day. Just the thought of John, lying mute on his bed in the bowels of that dark house, made June nauseous. The fact is, she had avoided seeing him since he'd become ill, always thinking she'd come as soon as he awoke. She never dreamed that his illness could drag on for so many years.

Ruth's hired man removed his hat. "I'm Nick. I help out Ruth here."

June shook hands with him. Goodness, he had striking eyes. Such a brilliant blue. How was Ruth able to work with those looking at her?

She glanced at Ruth to share her amusement but Ruth just gave her a crabby look.

She touched her pearls. *Oh, dear, I am not the one who's done wrong here, sister.*

Well, she'd be the better person. "Nice to meet you," she told Nick.

He ducked his head. "The pleasure is mine."

He's actually very sweet, she thought as he rejoined Ruth.

She was still smiling at him when his hand slid to the base of Ruth's back. Was he . . . rubbing her?

Ruth wrenched away from him but still June saw that hand. She couldn't look away from it.

*Oh, no. No. Oh, John.*

Ruth shouted, "Girls, stop that!"

June rolled her sickened gaze to where two of Ruth's daughters were gripping her suitcase in a fight to the death over who could carry it into the house. Richard, dabbing his handkerchief at his neck, stepped over and took it from them.

"Sorry, ladies, but you'd better let me have that. Betty Crocker, I mean, your aunt June, is a clotheshorse and doesn't pack lightly. Try to lug this and you'll pull your rhomboid major and twist your latissimus dorsi."

Nearly-eight-year-old Ilene, her too-large top front teeth half-grown-in and as ridged as a rake, screwed up her face at him. "What?"

He slipped the suitcase handle from her then whispered, "You'll hurt your back."

Nick strode over to where Richard's suitcase stood in the grass, snatched it up, leaped up the chipping green-painted concrete steps, then held the door open. Once everybody had passed beneath the bull's-eye of sweat under the arm of his chambray shirt, he entered the stuffy crowded kitchen himself, as if Ruth's lover were just another member of the family. Did no one else find this objectionable?

June looked to the other side of the room to her mother, who was clasping her hands as in a prayer of joy. Of course Mother had no idea of what was going on between Ruth and the hired hand. Mother had always lived inside her own little shell, disconnected from her family and everyone else. Not only could she not stop bad behavior, she wouldn't be able to recognize it if she saw it.

Closer at hand, Richard was talking at Ruth; Ruth was watching her lover; the lover was trying to tell June something. June could see his aquamarine eyes sparkling and his smooth lips moving, but she could not get her mind to focus. In her peripheral vision, she saw Mother hustle from the room.

Seconds ticked away like the timer on a bomb, her heartbeat ratcheting up with each tick, until, at last, June burst out — "Excuse me!"

A blush infiltrated the lover's face as his mouth eased closed. Other than taking advantage of an invalid, he seemed like a nice enough man and June was almost sorry she was rude. She sighed deeply as he slunk over to help Richard with the bags, then gathered her voice to raise it above Ruth's children, who were shouting over one another in their excitement, and over the general din of too many people in one sweltering kitchen.

"I'd like to see John!"

Her words reverberated through the room. Ruth stopped directing Richard and Nick toward the rickety stairs with the bags. "All right."

"I'd like to see him, too," said Richard.

June looked at her husband in surprise. Richard had patronized John when he was well and hadn't troubled himself with John when he was ill. And, was it so terrible to admit — she wanted to see John alone.

"Don't you think that too many of us at one time will alarm him?" she asked.

The biggest girl, Margaret, tightened her grip on her prize — June's train case. "If he's sleeping, he won't notice."

"Actually," said Richard, "he could. It has been found that many *encephalitis lethargica* patients can attend to everything going on around them, even when seemingly asleep. Although they can't respond, make no mistake about it — they are fully awake."

Ruth ran her finger along the cast-iron top of the range. "He's aware of things when he's sleeping?"

"If he's like other *encephalitis lethargica* victims, he can be quite alert while somnolent."

"I know that he can understand what's going on when he's awake, sometimes even if his eyes are closed, but I thought that when he was asleep . . ." Ruth twitched grease off her fingers. "He just doesn't seem very conscious, that's all."

"I'm afraid that he is." Richard tousled a twin's hair. "The poor souls, trapped inside their bodies but watching everything. They're buried alive, like in an Edgar Allan Poe tale."

Margaret swung June's train case like a

187

bell. "In 'The Black Cat' and 'The Tell-Tale Heart,' the buried break out in the end and get their revenge."

Her mother turned on her. "What kind of trash is that?"

Margaret shrank back. "We read it in school."

"Mommy, no." Jeanne, long-chinned and skinny, tried to take her mother's hand.

Ruth tucked her hand under her armpit. "Well, those are horrid stories. I can't believe that they teach them to kids."

June had not yet unpacked her bags and already she was desperate to leave. She would leave, right now, if it weren't for John and the children.

She turned to her sister. "Where is he?"

Ruth pointed down the hall off the kitchen. "Good luck."

■ ■ ■ ■

# PART THREE

■ ■ ■ ■

# FOURTEEN

*Fort Wayne, Indiana, 1921*

Ruth, hunched on the davenport, rewrapped herself in the old olive-green army blanket then tucked back into shoveling cereal from her chipped bowl. About a body's length away, next to the front door through which she had just let him in, along with a blast of biting cold, stood her sister's caller, hat in hand.

Huh, he was good-looking. Well, so what? Ruth had nearly been engaged to her own handsome fellow, when she was sixteen. And hers had been rich, as rich as any of the swells June had dragged home before she'd gone to art school.

Robin was her guy's name. Ruth and he had been sweethearts when he was a senior in high school and she was wandering through her sophomore year. While Robin wasn't one of the doctor's or lawyer's sons so prized by Sister June, his father did own

191

a bottling company that produced a bright blue soda pop called I Dazzle U, of which Robin was grotesquely proud.

The pop business afforded the scion of the family a Stutz Bearcat, the only one in town, in which Robin, all cocked straw Panama hat and nonchalance, loved to prowl, his arm slung over Ruth's shoulder in the same possessive manner in which he draped his hand on the steering wheel. With girlfriend in tow, Robin loved nothing more than to tool around town in search of someone drinking the azure family brand, and if he did, he'd strangulate the ball of his horn: *Ah-OO-gah!*

From the start, Ruth had found his behavior repulsive, but at first she enjoyed the excitement of seeing people — be they men raking leaves, boys crouching over marbles, or women leading little children — stop to stand in awe of the bright yellow sporting car growling down the street with her, Odd Dorothy Dowdy's daughter, in it. She wore, with defiant pride, Robin's class ring, wrapped with pink yarn to size it down for her, and was flattered by his assumption that they would be married.

But Bearcat rides come at a price. Ruth had not yet given her virginity to him (something about him — his skinny worm that he'd made her touch? — made her resist that final frontier), so Robin had her make up for it by requiring her constant attention. He needed her every minute after school, every weekend, every holiday. Even her best friend, Barbara, had been banished as too demanding of her time.

Woe to Ruth, should she be talking to a boy when Robin picked her up from school! Robin would yell, he would snub, he would sulk. His pop sightings produced but a tiny, petulant *oog.* Ruth, sixteen and dumb, went along with him.

The end came when she was working one Saturday afternoon in her father's quiet store, restocking the jars lined up on the counter of candy root beer barrels, gumdrops, and wax lips. She'd been chatting with her father's sole employee, Ned, dear to her for his prizewinning pair of ears and his ability to laugh at even her weakest jokes. He was giving her a pincushion shaped like a bag of Gold Medal Flour — he'd won it by mailing in a completed puzzle to a woman named Betty Crocker at the flour company in Minneapolis — when Robin stalked in and demanded that she leave.

Robin was furious, not so much because Ruth was talking to a male, although that was forbidden (no matter that Ned was seventeen years Ruth's senior and lived with his mother), but because Lord Robin had been kept waiting in his Bearcat for five minutes. No one kept *him* waiting, especially not his girl. Especially not his girl who was supposed to be loose but hadn't been loose enough. And, most especially, not a girl whose father was broke. He'd flung down the Gold Medal pincushion — he didn't care if some witch named Betty Crocker sent it — grabbed Ruth by the arm, and steered her outside.

Once they were in his car, he roared around the block and down the cinder-paved alley behind Dad's store, where JoJo was grazing outside her stable. Sweet, clunky JoJo, who would follow Ruth for a pat and then thank her with a nudge of pink velvet muzzle, was switching her tail with contentment as Robin idled the car. She was cropping weeds around a fencepost when, with a cruel grin, he leaned into his horn.

JoJo reared up. Eyes flashing white, she bolted across the yard and into the wire fence. Her flesh was rippling with terror when Ruth reached her. Blood arose from the track of wounds in the pink skin of her belly.

Minutes later, Robin blasted off, rusty pocked cinders flying behind the Bearcat like burnt-out meteorites, his class ring reunited with his pinky. Ruth had decided that if this was what catching a big shot got you, she'd rather be an old maid.

Now she gave June's latest dupe a thorough going-over, while June, home from art school for Christmas, was back in their bedroom getting ready for a "romantic" walk with him in the snow.

Ruth didn't get it. Was her gold-digging sister slipping? This one didn't look rich. If he was, he sure had a lousy tailor. His wrists stuck out of the cuffs of his red plaid jacket by a couple inches. He had buckled up his rubber boots like a farmer when, from the magazines that Ruth had memorized, she knew that all hep city cats wore them hanging wide open. He was tall, Abraham Lincoln tall, with old Abe's cheekbones and shock of black hair.

There was something calm about him that really bugged her. He didn't seem the least bit daunted by the ratty davenport, the bare carpet, the beat-up piano, or even Ruth as he waited. He didn't try to smile at her in spite of her studied boorishness, like June's other hopefuls did. He just watched her, like she was watching him.

After a while, he said, "That cereal must be good."

"Yep."

"What kind is it?"

She wiped her chin. "Pep."

"Pep. Isn't that the brand that you're supposed to eat when having 'The Hollywood Breakfast'?"

"This isn't a Hollywood Breakfast. If it were, I'd be having orange juice and toast. Anyhow, I don't let movie stars tell me what kind of breakfast to eat. I don't pay attention to silly advertisements."

"Yet you knew what a Hollywood Breakfast is." He shrugged when she did a double take.

His upper lip was just enough puffier than his lower one to hint of an overbite, so that she couldn't hate him for being too handsome. She could smell his scent from where she sat — Ivory Soap and male. He smelled good. Darn it.

He stayed by the door. "You're Ruth, right?"

June hadn't brought a boy home since she'd gone to college. Ruth looked at him more closely. Why this one?

He looked right back. "What do you like to do when you're not eating the Pep portion of the Hollywood Breakfast?"

"She reads." June trotted in from the little hall, effortlessly charming in a camel-hair tam-o'-shanter, baggy coat, and fashionably open galoshes. She dressed like the merry coeds in *Time* magazine although Dad could hardly pay the mortgage. She claimed that her clothes were from a secondhand store, which was probably true. She could make anything look good. She could probably spin gold from straw, too.

"What do you like to read?" he asked.

June answered for her. "She's a fan of Sinclair Lewis and other hotheads."

"Hot head, hot heart," John said, but he wasn't smiling. He looked at Ruth calmly, as if curious about the creature inside. "What are you going to do when you grow up?"

She squinted at him. Was he making fun of her?

He seemed to hear her thoughts. "Are you going to do something with all that reading?"

She looked dumbly at her book. She'd never thought about what she'd *do.* Girls from her class got married, had babies, became grandmas. If they were lucky, they didn't marry jerks. Precious few went to college. She herself didn't want to go — it was just another place for people to look down on her.

June took his hand. "Let's go."

Ruth stared after them as they left, her teenage heart withering. June's Abe Lincoln had pulled back the curtain on her soul and she did not like what she saw. She saw a chicken. One who squawked a lot but was actually just afraid to stick her neck out. A big fat chicken, scared of failing.

Her gaze drifted down into her bowl, where a few flakes of cereal floated in milk, the remains of her not-quite Hollywood Breakfast. She had not thought that girls like her were even allowed to dream.

She hardly knew how to start.

# FIFTEEN

*Fort Wayne, Indiana, 1921*

June hadn't made it all the way out to the living room before realizing that the wool tam-o'-shanter was a bad idea. Her forehead itched from contact with it. She was just about to go back and take it off when she heard John ask Ruth what she liked to read.

She couldn't help herself — she was proud of her quirky little sister. Ruth was the smarter and the braver of the two of them. She read at least a book a week. And she had once whacked Mr. Horn with a broom! Her hero! But Ruth had become reclusive and surly since June had gone to art school. For no apparent reason, her already sharp tongue was growing barbs. It hurt June to think of her bold little sister becoming a sour old spinster.

"She's a fan of Sinclair Lewis," she called out. When Ruth scowled, the nut, June added affectionately, "And other hotheads."

"Hot head, hot heart."

She was surprised to see John watching her sister. She stepped forward and put her hand on his arm.

"What are you going to do when you grow up?" he asked Ruth. "Are you going to do something with all that reading?"

June took his hand and squeezed it. "Let's go."

There was a delay before he glanced at her and squeezed back.

He held her door for her. She savored his warmth as she passed under his arm. She shouldn't be falling for him. She had worked too hard to get where she was — Odd Dorothy's daughter, going to the School of the Art Institute of Chicago and living in the fashionably bohemian artists' colony north of the Loop called Tower Town. All right, she was living in a charitable women's club just outside of Tower Town, but she had flown from her dreary childhood home and had had *plans.* She couldn't be slowed down. Meeting John when he was visiting Chicago from his farm on the Indiana-Michigan line, and liking him, too much, had not been part of the plan.

They trampled across the tiny covered porch and down three wooden steps, the buckles of her galoshes jingling, and then landed on the shoveled walkway to the street. The metallic creaking of swings filled the frigid December air.

Until the age of five or six, June thought nothing of having a brick fortress across the street from their house. Hers was set among knobby pines that bled milky sap and was guarded by an eight-foot-tall iron fence to which the residents of the castle clung in all weathers — when they weren't standing in the middle of the play yard or pumping away on one of the eight vulcanized-rubber swings. Behind the swinging residents loomed the palace power plant, with its shining mounds of coal and a cylindrical brick chimney as tall as a princess's tower. But Rapunzel's golden tresses did not cascade down from the tower-top, as much as June imagined in her daydreams for it to be so. Most unregally, the smokestack belched sticky soot, which settled over the neighborhood in a fine black web, including on her bedroom windowsill.

On occasion, an older resident would escape, his or her identity tipped off by the hospital gown or, in the case of one memorable fellow, an ensemble consisting solely of brown work shoes. When word got out that an inmate was on the loose, neighbors went inside and locked their doors, as if retardation was catching. Only her mother, contrary in all things, went outside as if to talk to the escapees, although she could never get one to stop for her.

When June was seven, she had been stripping the privet bushes in her yard of their tiny pretend-grapes when two women on bicycles came puffing down her street. She lowered her chipped cup, suspending her game of "little lost child" long enough to stare. Look at the pretty ladies in their white shirtwaists with black neckties! Look at their big balloon sleeves — why, they're bigger than their heads. And look at the size of their straw hats. You could keep a litter of kittens in them.

"Isn't she cute?" one of the ladies said to the other as if June were not right in front of her and couldn't hear.

"Poor thing, how does she stand living across from this place?" said the other.

"Poor baby!"

"I wish I had a penny to give her."

June's cup hung from her fingertips, its contents forgotten, as they pedaled away. Until that moment, she'd taken the fortress across the street, the spewing smokestack, and the moaning residents as much for granted as the grass in her yard. It was just there.

But now she knew. The Fort Wayne School for Feeble-Minded Children was not nice. Living within view of it was not nice. She herself was not nice. She'd had an inkling that her mother was not nice — no one outside of the family would ever talk to her — and she knew from their Sunday drives down Forest Park Boulevard that her family was not rich, or even special, but she understood now that she was as pitied as her mother.

She had no school chums over after that — maybe a boy or two, later, in high school, to challenge how much he liked her. And then she would break up with him because he knew too much.

Now a cloud crept over her spirits as she picked along the ruts in the soot-capped snow with John. Behind the spiked iron palings, residents milled aimlessly, some stopping as abruptly as windup toys. A lone student determinedly cranked a swing.

John waved. The student, a thick young woman in a gray coat buttoned all the way down to her work shoes, clung to rusty chains and stared.

He saw June's expression. "What?"

"No one ever does that."

"Does what?"

"Waves."

"Waves to the kids in there? Why not?" He waved again as if to make a point. The young woman's thick features slowly animated as she lifted her fingers.

He saluted her before turning back to June. "Poor kid. If we ever have a child like that, we're keeping her at home. We are not going to institutionalize her. Agreed?"

A swift pang jabbed her. He assumed she would be part of his future, his wife, the mother of his children. But she couldn't be. As much as she adored him. As much as she felt secure and happy and like her true self around him. She was going to be somebody. No matter what. And he was just a farmer.

She waved at the girl, who grinned as if she could not believe her good fortune. "I would never put a child in there," June told him.

She did not say "our" child. She glanced at him, loping through the snow next to her. Did he notice?

She hadn't told him why she couldn't marry him. He hadn't even asked her yet. But he would. They both knew he would. She had never both wanted and not wanted something so badly in her life.

A pounding came from the direction of the schoolyard, and kept up long enough for them to locate it. On a third-story window of the institution, a girl was beating on the glass, her face mashed against the pane. She slid down, making a snail's trail with her lips, and then was snatched from sight.

"Good Lord!" John cried. "Shouldn't we do something?"

"You think that there's something you can do?"

He frowned at June then back up at the window. "So we're just supposed to give up? We see things we don't like, and we're just supposed to forget them?"

June started walking.

"June, wait." He caught up with her. "Are you all right?"

She wasn't all right. There was something terribly wrong with her. He wouldn't want her if he knew. She was damaged, empty, unlovable, and unloving. Her mother was incapable of love and now she was incapable of it, too.

He put his arm around her. She tipped her head against him.

*Please. Don't give up on me.*

# Sixteen

*Fort Wayne, Indiana, 1921*

At the head of the dining room table that evening, William swallowed another spoonful of canned stew. "So what does your family raise on their farm, John?"

Dorothy lifted her sights from a peeling spot on the oilcloth and found Ruth watching June's beau, John, from across the table. She pushed her glasses up the bridge of her nose. Ruth had worn the same look when June received a doll for Christmas and Ruth had gotten a set of jacks. It had been on Ruth's face when June won the Little Miss Sunbeam contest and all Ruth got was a loaf of bread.

*Oh, Ruthie. You can't have him. Why do you always want what's June's?*

John finished his own bite of dinner. "Corn," he told William. "Alfalfa. Oats. We have fifteen milk cows."

"Must keep you busy," William said mildly.

"Busy enough that my dad wants me to stay on the farm."

If her girls weren't right in the head, it was Dorothy's fault. She had done them damage. She had not meant to. Not having much of a background in mothering, she had tried to raise them as recommended by Dr. L. Emmett Holt in his expert book, *The Care and Feeding of Children.*

She had worn the green and yellow covers of the book ragged. Dr. Holt, the "world-renowned authority on infants and children" (as it said in his book), strictly advised against playing with a baby at all before he or she was six months of age, and after that, the less playing with it, the better. He said stimulating babies made them nervous and irritable and to "suffer in many respects," the very thought of which sent lightning bolts of terror through her.

Dorothy had not received Dr. Holt's book nor benefited from his knowledge until after June was a year of age. And Dorothy had played with Junie constantly when she was tiny, something Dorothy was sick about to this day. How was she to know that she wasn't to cradle her darling, when every bone in her body had yearned to do just that?

She did not make the same mistake with Baby Ruth. It was strictly business with Ruthie for her first six months of life, just as Dr. Holt prescribed. But by the time Dorothy felt that she could play with little Ruthie and not ruin her, Ruthie no longer wanted to play. She just stared at Dorothy as if she knew what a bad mother she was. Ruth had always been such a smart little thing.

Now Dorothy burst out, "Better a farm than in the city!"

Her family looked at her in surprise. She shrank a little under their gaze. "Better a farm than a city full of murderers and gangsters. They shoot people at Death Corner every day, right in front of witnesses. June's rooms are less than a mile from there."

She had spent most of her adult life worrying about June. She didn't know how to stop.

"How do you know about Death Corner?" June asked.

"Ruth told me."

"Ruth!" June exclaimed.

Ruth was still staring at John. "What would you do if you didn't farm?"

He lit up. "I'd write."

"Write what?" Ruth asked.

"I don't know. That's the hard part. A book? Magazine stories? There seems to be a big call for advertising copy, or scripts for the radio — that's the newest thing. I'd love to be one of those fellows. But I have no connections. I don't know how to get started."

William dipped a slice of store bread in his stew. "Farming's an honest living." He sunk his teeth into the resulting mush.

"It is." John shoved back his hair. "Don't get me wrong, Mr. Dowdy. I love working with the land — our piece has been in the family for generations. But I've been putting words together since I was a boy — I can't help myself. What I'd like to write most is a novel, if I could."

"He's really talented," June said with authority. "All of his letters —" She paused to look at Ruth, as if making sure that she understood that he wrote to her often. "— all of his letters are so clever."

John scowled, a midwesterner's thank-you.

"I don't see why you don't just write books," said Ruth, "*and* run the farm."

John turned to look at her, as did June. As did Dorothy. Was that rouge on Ruth's cheeks? For crying out loud — was that June's good sweater she had on?

"How did you two meet?" William asked.

"At the Art Institute." June laid her hand on his arm. "It was his first visit to Chicago, and seeing art was at the top of his list. My kind of man! We met in front of one of Monet's *Haystacks*. This attractive stranger said he had thought that *he* was the only person in the world who'd ever thought that a pile of hay could look melancholy, but now here was Monet." She looked up at him. "I told him that made three of us."

But he and Ruth were still staring at each other. "You're right," he said after a moment. "You're absolutely right. I am just making excuses for myself. I could do both if I really wanted to." He smiled at her. "Thanks. I needed to hear that."

Ruth sat back with a creak of her dining room chair, lips pursed with not-quite-squelched pride. "You're welcome."

Later, when June and her beau had gone out for another walk in the dark, and Ruth had holed up in the girls' room with a book, Dorothy had come back out to the dining room after washing the dishes, where William had his bills spread out over the oilcloth and was engrossed in his nightly torture.

"June seems to like this boy," Dorothy said.

William took a card from under his pile.

Dorothy said, "Ruth does, too."

William held out the card.

"What's this? A postcard? Who's it from?" Dorothy's heart jumped. Had they found her after all these years?

In the dim light, she could make out a scene in which Model Ts and army tents were jammed together under a canopy of tall pines bearded with moss. The caption read, *A "Tin Can Tourist" Camp in Florida.* The back was blank.

"I'm thinking I could get a tent, rope, stakes, and everything else we need to go camping at the Army Surplus store and then load up the truck and go." William rubbed his hands. "Who'd make better tin-can tourists than us, right, Dorothy? I can get all the cans — maybe a little dented — that anyone could ever want."

Dorothy drooped, her heart still banging.

"They call them tin-can tourists because they live on canned goods. Or because they take big cans of water with them wherever they go — that's the other theory. I've put aside some of those, too. Either way, that's us."

Dorothy didn't care where the term "tin-can tourist" came from. Her dream of going to Florida did not include camping. It did feature staying in a hotel, swimming in a sparkling pool, and playing shuffleboard while wearing smoked glasses and a white cabled tennis sweater trimmed in navy blue. It featured Edward.

"We can camp our way down to Florida," William was saying. "Plenty of farmers will let you set up in their pasture for a dime. Some of the bigger towns have municipal campgrounds. I'll send for a Conoco Touraide Guide and map out the trip. I'm thinking May would be a good month. How does May sound, Dorothy?"

She still thought of Edward every day. Was he looking for her? She had not been able to keep in touch with him. He knew why.

"I don't want to camp," she said.

"We won't be roughing it. There are showers at some of the municipal campgrounds. And you don't have to sleep in a sleeping bag if you don't want. I'll give you the front seat of the truck."

He came over and held her. "Don't worry, I'm going to get you to Florida, Dorothy. You are going to hear the ocean in a seashell, just like you want." His voice rumbled in his chest as he cradled her against him. "We're not dead yet."

# SEVENTEEN

*Fort Wayne, Indiana, 1921*

Ruth believed that one thing June hadn't had to learn, having her prettiness to fall back on, was what boys liked best. It wasn't what you thought. What they craved, more than looking at a pretty girl, maybe even more than necking with one, was for girls to find them interesting.

Ruth, a middling scorer in the looks game, had to figure this out early. It was how she'd gotten Robin. Oh, sure, she'd had to vamp a little to get Robin to look her way — you know, stare at him without flinching when he stared back, and keep her mouth slightly open like a dope. She'd learned that from the movies. It wasn't a bad idea to make boys feel like they had a chance at what was under your sweater, either, not that they'd find much there besides Kleenex, in her case, when they looked.

But if you *really* wanted to hook them,

Ruth figured out when she was just sixteen, you had to listen to them. Act like you gave a rat's rear about their stupid Bearcat. It helped if they actually had something interesting to say. Like this John who June had brought home did.

She closed her book and stalked into the front room, to the door out which he and her sister had gone after dinner, talking and laughing. She opened it and searched the frozen night.

Fact was, he appealed to Ruth. He was modest, he wasn't a dummy, and he smelled good. He wanted to be a writer. He really cared about things, too, like she did. He asked her what she wanted to be when she grew up. Well, what if she wanted to be his wife?

Oh, she knew she was being preposterous. Even discounting the fact that he would never look at a girl like her if he was sweet on someone like June, just having feelings for him made her the worst kind of traitor. June was her best friend in the world — a little soft in the head, maybe, but the very best friend, for as long as Ruth could remember. Literally. One of Ruth's earliest memories starred June.

What had Ruth been, two? Three? Yet Ruth could still see snatches of it in her head. There was Mother, weeding the moss roses next to the porch step. There was her hand, resting on a flagstone while she was pulling dandelions with the other.

Up toddles Ruth. The sight of her slim, golden-skinned mother, her beautiful hand plucking through the tissuey bright blossoms, fills her with such yearning that she has to get close. She bustles up, wedges herself under her mother's arm, and plops down.

*Crr-ack!* It sounds like a stick snapping. Mother jumps up, clutching her finger.

*Ow ow ow ow ow!*

Ruth totters off. She falls down, totters off again. Bad girl! She hides herself where no one can find her — under the desk in the living room — Mother's tinting desk — where she listens to herself cry until she falls asleep.

She wakes to the sight of skinny legs, and then golden braids hanging down.

June lowers her head sideways to the opening under the desk. "What are you doing?"

Ruth can't talk.

"Aren't you coming out?"

Ruth wedges tighter against the desk.

"Can I come in?"

Ruth makes room.

215

They crouch together under the desk. Ruth can hear the barking of the neighbor dog and the *squawk* pause *squawk* pause of the swings across the street.

Mother's buttoned shoes appear outside the desk. "What are you girls doing?"

"Nothing," they say together.

"Touch red," June whispers to Ruth.

When Mother walks away, June says, "You're supposed to say 'touch red' whenever you say something at the same time, or else you will have a fight. Mrs. Demetroff said so."

In a home that only serves canned goods, Mrs. Demetroff, the next-door neighbor lady known for giving them just-baked treats from her kitchen, is right up there with Jesus.

"Say it — 'touch red.' "

Ruth's heart hurts with love as she gazes up at her sister. "Touch red."


"Ruthie," Dad called from the table, "could you shut the door, please? It's cold."

She slammed it shut. He glanced up from working on his account books as she stomped by. "Where are you going, kitten?"

"Nowhere." She almost laughed. It was the truth. Unless she did something about it. Nobody was doing something about it for her.

She skulked to the landing of the basement, where her pet rabbit, Jack, huddled in the corner of his cage. Dad had rescued Jack when he was just a blind and hairless kit, after a neighbor had mowed over his nest, and Ruth had raised him. Now he hopped to her hopefully, on the chance that Ruth would have a piece of lettuce. Poor fellow depended on Ruth to take care of him. All he knew was his cage. He wouldn't make it out of their own backyard without a neighbor cat pouncing on him.

She put her finger through the wire mesh. "What am I going to do about you?"

But she wasn't talking about Jack.

# EIGHTEEN

*Chicago, Illinois, 1922*

Christmas vacation had ended and June was back in school. She was lounging on the ratty silk tapestry on her roommate's bed, studying color theory, but her eyes were not on her book. Over on the worn tapestry covering her own bed — June and her roommate had gone on a shopping spree in Chinatown last semester, further evidenced by the opened red and turquoise paper umbrellas hanging from the ceiling — John was sluicing through the heavy glossy pages of her textbook on art history. Men were forbidden in the rooms of the Three Arts Club, a brick fortress built by social reformer Jane Addams and her circle a few years earlier.

The reformers' idea was to provide an inexpensive safehouse for the girls from small towns and farms across the Midwest who were drawn to the Bohemian section of

Chicago called Tower Town. A squeaky-clean, chaperoned artists' colony just outside the sprawling, louche, infamous one, the Three Arts Club offered not just large rooms at a YWCA price, but plush sitting rooms, a library, a tea room, a dining room, performance stages, and bathrooms in every hall. Men weren't allowed — definitely no men. That was the point of this cloister.

June risked losing her fancy digs by having John in there. But there was something about this man, lying on her bed in his farmer's go-to-town plain white shirt, black vest, and black trousers, that made her break the rules, including her own. He confused her and thrilled her and frightened her at once. She didn't know what to do about him.

He shut the book with a clap.

"Oh!" She patted her throat. "You scared me!"

He got up on his elbow. "You're supposed to be studying."

She laughed. "I am. You."

It's easy to bring color to a farmer's face — just say something complimentary.

He rested his head on his palm and pretended that he hadn't heard. "I've noticed something."

She wished he would come over and kiss

her. Her lips actually burned for it. "What?"

"Why are there no famous women painters? I looked through this entire book —" He tapped the volume lying in front of him. "— and didn't find a one."

"That's just how it was, pretty much until Mary Cassatt and a couple other female Impressionists came along near the end of the last century." Why didn't he come over and kiss her?

"Women started painting recently, then. Is that it?"

The flesh of his upper lip was a little puffier than the lower, giving him the slightest, sweetest overbite. She couldn't take her gaze from it. "Not really. Women were painting back in the Renaissance — Sofonisba Anguissola in Italy, Judith Leyster in the Netherlands, Clara Peeters in Antwerp, several others. But they didn't have much of an output. At least I don't know of it. It's possible that they painted a lot but people assumed that men had done it. Either way, over time their reputations faded away, until now they are pretty much overlooked."

"You." He shook his finger at her. "Don't let yourself be overlooked."

Did he not know that by marrying him, and by being isolated on a farm, she would greatly compound the odds of that very thing? After talking with Dad, he had asked her to marry him before he had left her parents' house over Christmas. She had not given him an answer.

He reached for her over the space between the beds. She made no move to connect with him, as much as she craved him.

"You should keep studying," he said. "Become such a master that no one can overlook you, wherever you are. Even on a farm."

Her face heated. He'd heard her thoughts, as he often seemed to. Well, it was not that simple. Even as young and inexperienced as she was, she suspected that being good at something wasn't the only necessary ingredient of success.

"I suppose that having families might have gotten in their way," she said. "Having children to care for would cut into their work time. Men don't have that problem."

They looked at each other, her frustration and desire, his determination to have her for good, flying between them.

"There was also the issue," she said, "of women not getting adequate training back then. They couldn't tackle the classical themes so popular in the Renaissance because they weren't allowed to paint from the nude."

He smiled crookedly. "They weren't allowed to paint while they were naked?"

Relief washed over her — confrontation avoided, for now.

"No, you nut," she said affectionately. "The painters kept their clothes on. Women couldn't paint nude models. It was considered to be unseemly for them to see bare bodies."

"Men could see — and paint — naked models but women couldn't?"

"They're called 'nude models' in the art world. 'Naked' sounds more sexual. And, no, women couldn't see or paint them. You'll notice that all of their subjects have clothes on. They weren't allowed to study what was underneath."

"That's not fair." He was frowning when he said, "I think I should make up for it."

"Oh, really?"

He started unbuttoning his vest. "Don't say I won't do anything for your art."

June had taken many life classes in her studies. She was no stranger to a nude. A year had passed since that first time at the Institute when a handsome young man had come padding down the polished marble steps of the Grand Staircase, the patter of his bare feet echoing from the balconies, and, in front of the men and women of her class with their sketchbooks poised, had let his robe slide from his muscled body. How she blushed at his exposure, then at herself for blushing, even as the image of his body parts embossed themselves on her brain.

For months afterward, she couldn't talk to a man without picturing what lurked beneath his trousers, be it her teacher while discussing shading, a fellow student telling a joke, or a policeman patrolling the Michigan Avenue bridge, twirling his billy club. She had quickly come to appreciate the necessity, no, the *mercy,* of clothing.

"Where's your drawing paper?" He dropped his vest and started undoing his shirt. "Quit smiling. I'm serious about this. I want to be the fellow known as the man behind the great woman."

A blade twisted in her chest. The hard truth was, she wanted *him* to be a great man. She wanted her husband to be a great man. For a woman, being a somebody meant marrying a somebody, no matter what she might achieve on her own, and with his father's health recently failing, John was more embroiled in the farm than ever. He was always going to be a farmer. Yes, the notion that a woman had to marry a somebody to be somebody was unfair and ugly and maddening. It made her furious and sick to just think it. But that did not make it less true.

A knock came on the door.

She scowled. Besides pooling their money for an ancient phonograph, the paper umbrellas, and the ratty tapestries, she and her roommate, Norma, a licorice-haired actress from French Lick, Indiana, had bought a small silk pillow embroidered with the word JAZZ in scarlet letters. They'd worked out a system of hanging the pillow from the bedroom doorknob in the event of illegal male stowaways. June, who took classes by day and worked demonstrating potato peelers at Carson Pirie Scott by night, and whose beau lived on a farm over two hundred miles away, seldom had call for it, unlike Norma with her loud actor fellows from Tower Town. June was sure she'd hung it out today. It was not like Norma not to honor it.

The knock sounded again. "June?" came a familiar voice.

*Is that your sister?* John mouthed.

June was shaking her head with incredulousness when the bedroom door swung open, the little JAZZ pillow bouncing against it.

Ruth's flushed face swelled into view. She

looked between them, backed up, then burst out laughing.

# NINETEEN

*Chicago, Illinois, 1922*

Ruth had a nose for when someone was hiding something. Personal experience. So when she arrived in June's place in Chicago and June's little dark-bobbed Betty Boop of a roommate tried too hard to entertain her with loud chitchat, Ruth had made a beeline for the elephant in the room: the closed bedroom door. She'd thrown it open. But she had not expected to see John, stripped to his waist, standing by June's bed.

She groaned and backed straight onto the toes of Betty Boop, who was literally hard on her heels. For crying out loud, she'd caught them in the act! Even as she was groaning, she wondered how many times a couple could do it in a day. She laughed out loud at her own depravity.

"What are you doing here?" June demanded.

Ruth was taken aback for a moment.

June's golden skin and those goldy-green cat eyes could be unnerving if your guard wasn't up. People aren't supposed to be so pretty.

"Hi to you, too."

June shut the door, behind which John was scrambling for his clothes. Trailing perfume, she took Ruth's arm to lead her away. "Sorry — hi. But I wasn't exactly expecting my little sister who lives another state away."

"Surprise." Ruth shrugged her off. She wasn't a baby who could be led. Actually, she'd never been much of a baby even when she was a baby. She'd never had the luxury of being doted on and dandled, at least not that she ever knew of. But who was counting?

"How did you get here?"

Ruth shrugged. "There are these miraculous machines called trains."

John came out with his vest open. "Ruth!" June cried. "You took a train by yourself?"

"Why not?"

June and John swapped glances, Mama and Papa Katzenjammer worried about their Kid. They were almost cute.

"Why would you take such a risk?" June demanded.

It wasn't like she hopped trains for the joy

of it. There was a method to her madness. She had been boning up on all things flapper since she had seen June in her hep cat glory at Christmas, reverently consulting *Photoplay* and *Time* and the newspapers for tips on how she might achieve that look, too. She hadn't even let up on the train ride there, where she'd swayed on her seat across from a mother and three little boys in red felt cowboy hats, her gaze glued to a clipping that was limp from use. She could recite from it now, all thirteen items that were the hallmark of a flapper:

1. Hat of soft silk or felt
2. Bobbed hair
3. Flapper curl on forehead
4. Flapper collar
5. Flapper earrings
6. Slipover sweater
7. Flapper beads
8. Metallic belt
9. Bracelet of strung jet
10. Knee-length fringed skirt
11. Exposed, bare knees
12. Rolled hose with fancy garter
13. Flat-heeled little girl sandals

Ruth had made the trip to Chicago to acquire some of these items, as Fort Wayne was not exactly a hotbed of hepness. If her sister could be a flapper, so could she.

"Does Dad know?" June asked.

"Not yet." Was that a flapper curl on her sister's forehead? Was that a round flapper collar on her blouse? That getup would look swanker with a hep metallic belt.

June's voice rose. "Does Mother?"

"What do you think?"

"Ruth! I don't know what's worse — Mother knowing and panicking about disease and murder on the railroads, or her not knowing and panicking about your being abducted."

Ruth folded her arms. "You mistake me for you. You, she'd miss. Me, she won't even notice that I'm gone."

"That's not true. Why would you say that?"

"Maybe because it's true? She did forget me my first day of kindergarten."

"Stop it. How'd you find my apartment?"

"I told the policeman at the station you were in the Three Arts Club. He knew exactly where that was even before I gave him your address. And then I walked it."

"That's over two miles! In a city you don't know! Through a wild part of town!"

Ruth followed John's hand as he cupped it around June's shoulder, loosening an itchy splinter in her own chest. "That's how far you walk to the Art Institute. I passed it on the way here."

"I take the streetcar. And that's not the point. You could have gotten lost and stumbled into a truly dangerous area."

"Death Corner? Hurray!"

"Quit kidding around. It's not safe for a woman to go wandering around here."

"You do it." Back home, Ruth bragged to all the snobs at her school that her sister lived in Chicago. June hadn't finished packing to leave for it before Ruth had aspired to live there herself. The fact of the matter was that for Ruth's whole life, her greatest wish had been to *be* June, no matter that she hadn't the beauty, the sweet temperament, the artistic talent, or any of the other admirable qualities that June had by the bushelful. Any effort for her to be June was sure to fail, but that had never stopped Ruth before. She didn't know who else to be. Unless it was John's wife.

Betty Boop bellowed, "You ought to go down to the office and call your parents."

Ruth winced. Dear Lord, where'd that little girl get the foghorn voice?

"I'll take her down." John let go of her sister and dipped back in the bedroom.

Boop laughed. "You're not supposed to

be past the lobby," she said when he came out shrugging on his coat, "let alone using the telephone."

"We'll go find a phone booth down the street. You —" He pointed at June. "Study, Famous Artist. I'll be back."

Ruth was glad for the noise their footsteps made in the stairwell as she and John trampled down the stairs. She didn't know what to say to him. She hadn't expected to have him to herself so soon.

She wondered if he would be so friendly if he knew what had been written about her on the door of the girls' bathroom at school.

# TWENTY

*Chicago, 1922*

Downstairs, Ruth scanned the situation: A girl was torturing the keys of the piano on the stage. Across the hall, the dining room rang with the clink of china as the Three Arts staff set tables for dinner. A matron with a shiny bun like Olive Oyl sat near the entrance hall door, writing at a desk.

Acutely aware of the frustratingly attractive man inside the red and black checkered wool coat sleeve she was tugging, Ruth plucked her sister's boyfriend across the hall and into an empty sitting room, where a fire was dying in the green-tiled fireplace.

She mustered a tough front to cover her fluttering insides. "Let me talk to that dragon at the drawbridge. I'll distract her and you can sneak out."

He threw an amused glance at her hand on his arm and let himself be led, as would a benign St. Bernard being bullied by a child. "You're as crafty as your sister."

She drew back. Her angelic sister was crafty? "June?"

"How do you think I got up there?" He stepped back into the shadows and shooed her on. "Go."

She stared at him a moment. He was treating her like a friend. Like she wasn't a little sister, or a loser, or a whore.

"Go!" he whispered.

The matron — a different one than who had checked in Ruth, luckily — fell for Ruth's line about being a needy art student interested in renting a room there. Maybe it was the patch that Mother had carefully sewn on the sleeve of her long maroon coat, not so invisible after all. The old bat at the desk looked at it then got out a clipboard with an application. Didn't matter. It was worth the temporary wave of shame to see a six-foot-four man in a lumberjack coat go tiptoeing by.

Minutes later, she fell in step next to him in front of the apartment buildings out on Dearborn Street. Gusts of wind pierced her coat as automobiles stuttered past. Between crusty black banks of long-ago shoveled snow, a man in a baggy coat strode by, then a pair of women, their cloche hats pulled down low and their bare knees pinched and red above their rolled-down hose. Grand iron-railed stairways led up into sumptuous houses with lamps turned on against the early evening gloom. Ruth peered through windows, wondering about the sophisticates inside, as foreign to her as Martians. How happy they must be, living their exotic lives.

"There might be a phone booth on Clark, down near all those cheap hotels," John said.

Although he'd worn what apparently was his Sunday best — the same that he'd worn to visit June at home over Christmas — Ruth could see now that he didn't fit in here in Chicago. His opened red and black coat was too short; he wore no tie; his white shirt was buttoned up to his chin; his flat cap with ear flaps was no debonair fedora. He was perfectly dressed . . . to deliver wood in the city.

Good-looking as he was, for a moment she was embarrassed to be seen with him, before fury at herself torched up in her chest. Who was she but a small-town flat tire? Unlike all the ducky dolls sashaying by, her knees were buried beneath her pinched-waist long coat, a full skirt, and white cotton stockings. She might as well have worn a sign that read OLD MAID IN TRAINING. She saw her future and was frightened.

"Hey," he said, "what's your hurry?"

"I'm going to Death Corner," she snapped.

"You mean where the police look the other way as gangsters shoot each other up and innocent bystanders get killed every other day?"

"I believe that would be the 'Death' part."

"Not under my watch, you're not."

She kept walking. That's how she got anything done — she just kept doing it even though people told her otherwise. She'd surveyed the map of Chicago before coming. She needed to stay on Clark to the Newbery Library, turn right on Oak Street, and then forge down several blocks to arrive at Death Corner and all the tenements there. But when they got to the stone pile of the library, he grabbed her hand and placed it on his arm.

"Telephone is this way." He kept them going straight.

She suspected they looked ridiculous, a giant farmer and an adolescent old maid, promenading down the street, although having her hand on his arm did please her. She let him guide her on, regardless of the fact that her nose ached with the cold, a blister screamed from her heel, and the way to Death Corner was receding in the other direction.

On the other side of the library, under some bare young trees in a little park, an older woman stood on a wooden crate and shouted into a megaphone, her baggy flapper garb billowing around her. Ruth's heart quickened: they were in Bughouse Square! Dear Lord, let it be as wild as the guidebooks said.

"Women!" the old flapper cried into her megaphone. "Are you letting your destiny be controlled by the fear of unwanted pregnancy? Let me tell you what your doctor, your husband — maybe your own mother — will never tell you. There are ways to protect yourself!"

A crowd formed around Ruth to hear the woman speak. Ruth planted her feet on the wet sidewalk when John tried to move her on. "I want to listen."

A sightseeing bus stuffed with tourists under its canvas lid turned the corner and slowly rattled down the street between the library and the park. Several passengers had Brownie box cameras raised, in wait for the bus to come to a stop.

Next to Ruth, a laborer in bulky coveralls yelled at the tourists. "Hey, what are you gawking at?"

"You all are going straight to Hell!" a

camera-toter shouted back.

"Well, that's good news." A stocky man in shirtsleeves and suspenders spoke around his cigar as he handed out flyers near Ruth. "Heaven's fine for climate but give me Hell for the society." He shoved a bill into Ruth's hands. "Can't take credit; that's Mark Twain's quote."

She had just enough time to read the paper between her wool-encased fingers.

TONITE!

"IS
FREE
LOVE
POSSIBLE?"

DEBATE

"Prof." Jack Dunham,
University of Chicago Campus
Vs.
Fred Hardy, Bookman

Dil Pickle Club
Thru Hole in Wall at 10 Tooker Place
Down Tooker Alley to the Green Lite
Over the Orange Door

Members of the Dil Pickle Club furnish
the "swell" music at our Friday Nite
Dancing Classes

John took it from her. "She's just a kid," he told the man, handing it back.

He looked John up and down. "Say, a big man like you — are you a nut about anything? Farm debt? Decreasing prices for crops? Corruption in Washington? Want to come talk to the Picklers?"

"No."

John positioned himself between Ruth and the man. She asked around him, "Who are the Picklers?"

"Oh, you know." The man gave his cigar a chomp. "Just authors. Hoboes. Professors. Every kind of nonconformist or rabble-rouser passing through Chicago. Rich slummers. Me. Sinclair is supposed to grace our party tonight. We've got good jazz. You like jazz?"

Ruth maneuvered past John. "*Upton* Sinclair?"

"None other." The Pickler poked a handbill into the next person's ribs.

"Forget about the telephone," said John. "I'm taking you back to June."

The Pickler kept a keen gaze on John as he delivered another flyer. "Who are you, big guy, to boss this woman around?"

"Oh, he's all right," said Ruth.

"You sure? I don't tolerate bullies."

"He's fine."

The man scowled and moved on.

"Your sister was right about you," John said.

"Upton Sinclair!" Ruth breathed. She hardly felt John aiming her over the trampled snow of the park lawn back toward Dearborn Street. "How brave Upton Sinclair was to go to the stockyards and expose the conditions there. And not just for the people, but for the animals. The poor lambs! It's the lambs that upset me the most. Trusting those Judas goats."

John searched over the heads of the crowd closing in to hear the speaker. "Goats?"

"Haven't you ever heard of the stockyard Judas goats?"

"No."

"They're actually rams, though they call them goats. They've been trained to lead the lambs to slaughter."

"This way." He put pressure on the small of her back to get her moving again.

His touch weakened her. She let herself be guided toward the lower edge of the park, across the street from the townhouses of Gilded Age millionaires. "The little lambs come crying in from the trains, and these Judas goats calm them down, nudging them with their heads until they get quiet. When they have the lambs' trust, off they trot, gay as a boy at a fair. The little lambs follow them down the chute, kicking up their heels, happy — until the men meet them with sledgehammers."

"Excuse us." John pushed his way through stragglers.

"What kind of person would think that was okay to do to a little creature? Yet that person, some meatpacking baron, is living over there on Lake Shore Drive right now, drinking whiskey with the mayor and having his shoes buffed."

He looked down at her. "Why are you so angry?"

Her heart took a jolt, as if he'd flung a tub of cold water on her.

"I'm not angry."

"Yes, you are. And so is your sister. Only she hides her anger, and you wear yours like a badge of honor. Is that the only way you know how to get attention?"

Words were her shield between people and herself, flashed to make her look smart and dangerous. They were supposed to ward people off, people like Robin's old steady, who wrote *Ruth Dowdy goes all the way* on the back of the girls' bathroom door.

But the words weren't supposed to keep you away. Not you.

She wheeled onto the street and into the path of a car. Its *ah-OOH-gah* blasted her back to her days with Robin and his Bearcat, in which she did *not* go all the way, although close, because she was so stupid, so desperate, that she had wanted him to like her.

John grabbed her. "You trying to get yourself killed?"

She marched diagonally across the street, causing a car to screech to a stop, then darted down the first alleyway, into a crowd of ladies and gentlemen in stylish dress shuffling toward what looked to be a bricked-up stable. A single green bulb shone down on the entrance, its weird light illuminating the word DANGER daubed on the crumbling bricks. More words were splashed on the orange-painted door, but Ruth couldn't make them out through the furs, veiled hats, and fedoras blocking the way.

"What is that place?" she asked a woman nested within a high silver fox collar. An ostrich feather wafted from a band around her head.

She crooked bright red lips. "The Dil Pickle Club."

Ruth shrugged away from John to get in the line behind her.

He sighed wearily. "What are you doing?"

"Seeing Upton Sinclair."

"You *know* you shouldn't go in. Why do you have to give me such trouble?"

She turned away from him. *Was* causing trouble the only way she knew to get what she wanted? What was it exactly that she did want?

The furs and fedoras parted, revealing the splintered orange door. Ruth read out loud: " 'Step High, Stoop Low, and Leave Your Dignity Outside.' "

"Great," John muttered.

She pushed the door open.

# TWENTY-ONE

*Chicago, Illinois, 1922*

Inside the vestibule of the Dil Pickle Club, Ruth let her eyes adjust to the smoke and the dark. John pushed back his cap until the ear flaps were even with his eyes as he strained to read. " 'Elevate Your Mind to a Lower Level of Thinking.' That does it." He took her arm.

She shook him off. "Let me go. I'd like to see."

He spread his hands as if stuck up by a bank robber. "All right. All right. Have it your way. Your sister's going to kill me anyhow."

"Admit it, you want to see this place, too."

He scowled at her. "Just be quick about it, would you?"

Puffed with this small victory, she waded into the main room, a hot, smoky cave seething with hundreds of club-goers. Couples milled around brightly painted tables and chairs. Knots of men argued at a counter being wiped by a waiter. Jazz oozed from the band of Negro musicians playing in the corner. There were more Negroes in the crowd, more than Ruth had ever seen in her life, dressed like movie stars, and workers in coveralls, and women in sleeveless frocks. There were rich people, plenty of rich people, with their Hollywood suits and beaded gowns, and professor-types in tweed. Had she died and gone to heaven?

Her admiring gaze trailed up one woman's slinky gold lamé dress, then slowed on the woman's jutting Adam's apple, before halting altogether on the stubble peppering the woman's jaw. Once Ruth had absorbed that truth, she scanned the room again, wondering which boys were girls, and which girls were boys, and then wondering, in a sobering flash, if it actually really mattered.

Chuckling at the sensations that this colorful new universe rat-a-tat-tatted at her from all directions, she wormed her way to the counter, where a man was ordering a drink. His order placed, he waited, his brow pointed at the shellacked wood as if his head were top-heavy with brains. There was something familiar about the twin white haystacks heaped to either side of the pink line of his part, and about his long and horsey upper lip.

Behind the counter, the server poured something from a fountain tap, then handed the owner of the haystacks the glass. "What're you working on now, Mr. Sandburg?"

Ruth winged John with her elbow. *Carl Sandburg!* she mouthed. *The poet!*

Mr. Sandburg raised a bristly brow. "Lincoln's early years."

"Poems about Lincoln?"

"No. A biography this time. Well, maybe a few poems on the side. I can't help myself."

"I know what you mean. Poetry will have its way." The counterman wiped his hands on his apron then came down to Ruth. "What'll you have, sweetheart?"

"Whatever he's having."

"That would be soda pop. Thank you, Prohibition. Say, are you old enough to be in here?"

John bellied up next to her. "Whatever she ordered, it's for me, okay? We don't want any trouble."

Mr. Sandburg sipped his drink. "You her dad?"

The counterman slid a drink at John. "Here you go."

Starry-headed, Ruth pushed away from the counter as John dredged some coins from his pants pocket. A man in a pinstripe suit slid a flask from inside his lapel and tipped it over the drink. When he saw Ruth watching, he winked. "On the house."

She wandered over to the band, where John caught up with her.

"Do you realize who that was?" Ruth shouted in his ear.

"What?"

"At the counter — do you know who that was?"

He turned back around and looked as he took a sip. Carl Sandburg raised his glass.

"This is so exciting!" She tipped John's glass her way.

He held it away from her. "No, ma'am."

"Why? What is it?"

He smacked his lips. "Some kind of strange hooch."

The horns blared.

"Is it good? I think that man meant it for me but I'll share."

"What? I can't hear you!"

She plunged two fingers into the drink, then formed a damp flapper curl in the middle of her forehead. She took the newspaper clipping of the flapper from her purse and held it up next to her face. "Did I get it right?"

John snatched the clipping from her then

stuffed it into his pocket. "Why aren't you happy just being who you are?"

She couldn't hear him over the galloping music. "What?"

"WHY DO YOU LIKE TO CAUSE TROUBLE?"

She yelled back, "BECAUSE THAT'S WHAT I'M SUPPOSED TO DO."

Next to her a couple bounced forward, kicked, and bounced back to the music. The Charleston!

"Dance with me!"

"No." He took another drink. "Why?"

"Why what?"

"Why do you believe that you're supposed to cause trouble?"

Ruth stored away the dancers' moves for practice at home. "To make June look good!"

He shook his head. "June's going to look good no matter what you do."

"Thanks a lot." She turned away.

He grabbed her. His serious expression surprised her. "It's the truth. She's going to shine no matter how you act, so why make yourself look bad? What are you getting out of it?"

She wilted. "Do I really look bad?"

He hesitated. "Oh, kid."

In that moment, she saw that he understood her. Her. Not her latest creation, Bad Ruth. Ruth Who Yelled Before She Got Yelled At. But the real her — Hurt, Desperate, Sad Ruth. Lonely Ruth.

She grabbed his face and kissed him.

He pulled back, blushing so hard that his skin nearly lit the dimness. "What are you doing? Are you crazy?"

"Yes! I love you!"

"Oh, kid, you do not love me. You don't even know me." He took a drink, then when he saw her still watching him, took another.

Her chest ached with earnestness. "I know that you're good. I know that you're decent and kind."

"You don't know that."

"I do know!" She swallowed. "I do know that you are a wonderful human being."

He stared at her through the throb of the clarinets. "You're seventeen."

"Almost eighteen. I graduate this spring. That doesn't mean I don't know things."

"Don't, Ruth."

She grabbed his face and kissed him again. "Stop that! I'm serious."

She did it again.

He was red-faced and flustered. "Look, you flatter me. But really — don't."

"Why not?"

He stared at her. "Because I like it too much."

She waited for him to say more. When he didn't, she kissed him again.

He was glaring this time as he pulled away from her. "Now you're starting to make me mad."

"You like me."

He reared back, stumbling a little. She wouldn't let him go.

"I can't, Ruth."

She peered into his eyes. "Don't you understand? I see you, and you see me, I mean really, truly see me. I may not be experienced but I know enough to realize that doesn't happen much." She reached up and touched his face. "You know it's true."

He shut his eyes. When he opened them and spoke, his words were fuzzy around the edges. "I love your sister. Don't you get that?"

She raised on her tiptoes and, carefully, touched her lips to his.

"This is all I 'get.' "

She kissed him, softly at first, then, feeling his mouth yielding, harder. She felt his forearms against her back, his hands pressing her shoulder blades through her coat. She leaned into the solidity of his body as music, commotion, blared around them.

She was melting into him, the charge from his flesh dizzying her, when she heard a sharp "Ruth!"

She opened her eyes. It was moments before her mind could assemble the pieces. Past pink-faced Carl Sandburg with his twin white haystacks of hair, past the dungareed laborer talking up the flapper in a gold lamé dress, past the beautiful Negroes, past the girls who were boys and the boys who were girls, past the hat-check girl reading *The Age of Innocence,* running toward the door was her sister, June.

■ ■ ■ ■

# PART FOUR

■ ■ ■ ■

# DOROTHY

Junie's here. They'll be coming back to see you, dearie. Anything I can get you before they do?

— What? Keep telling my story? Now? Well, all right. If that's what you want.

After the baby was born, I stayed on with my cousin Mildred. Though I had an infant waking to feed three times a night, I still had to do the wash, keep the house, and cook three meals a day, complete with dessert, always with dessert, even if it were just some kind of crisp made from whatever fruit was in season. How I came to loathe cooking for that woman! I was so worn out that I fell asleep sitting up while doing the mending at night. But where else was an unwed mother going to go? Edward had not come for us, yet.

One afternoon, when the baby was six months old, she was napping in her basket while I was browning some chicken backs for dinner, when a knock sounded on the front door.

My heart did a flip. Edward?

Mildred wasn't home from work yet, so I took the pan off the stove, wiped my hands on my apron, checked the baby, and answered.

Papa was standing on the doorstep.

"Father?"

With a crush of fallen leaves, he came in and took off his bowler hat. He still had a full head of black hair, his best feature. I don't know why I expected him to look different. It had not quite been a year, although my own hair had gotten shot through with gray. I wanted to tell him that I missed him, and Mother, and that I had worked hard and been good. Could he forgive me? But before I could find the words, he wiped his feet as if he were still on the doormat, then cleared his throat.

"Can I see the baby?"

Not a letter had come from Mother or him since they had sent me away. I thought they had washed their hands of me. But he wanted to see the baby! Did this mean that they forgave me? Did this mean that I could go home?

I ran to get the baby.

When I brought her in, one of her cheeks

flushed from sleeping, he touched her head. "She looks just like you."

I kissed her to hide my delight. Bragging about your child was like bragging about yourself, so I said the worst things about her that I could.

"She's a little spoiled. She won't let me put her down once I pick her up. And she has to eat the minute she gets hungry. You're a little crybaby, aren't you?" I kissed her again.

He withdrew his hand and tucked it under his arm. "Dorothy, the Lambs want her."

I could not quite understand what my father had asked. His words seemed like a foreign language. "What?"

"The Lambs want her."

"My baby? They want my baby?"

"I'm supposed to get her." He glared past my shoulder. "And take her back."

My heart stumbled. I must have stumbled with it.

He grimaced. "It won't be so bad."

Then it dawned on me. Wait a minute! Edward wanted us! *Oh, Edward, I knew it!*

"When should we go?"

My thoughts raced ahead — *what should I wear? What would the baby wear? Oh, Edward, wait until you see our beautiful child!*

The baby, seeing my excitement, chuckled.

Father said, "Not you, Dorothy."

I shook my head. I didn't know what he meant.

"I can stand living with them, if that's what everyone wants."

"No, Dorothy. They just want her."

"But — we go together. We go together, don't we, Father?"

"She can't stay here. Mildred doesn't want a baby crying in her house." He glanced around the shack. "Anyhow, it will be a better life for her."

I still didn't understand. "They want to keep her?"

He kept his gaze on Mildred's chair. "That's what they say."

"Will we live with you and Mother in the house?"

"I told you, it's just her."

"She will live with them," I stated.

He still wouldn't look at me. "Don't make this harder than it already is."

A bubble of hope rose. "Will Edward be there?"

"That I do not know."

*Calm yourself. Edward must want this. Picture our daughter as heir to the Lambs' beautiful home, with its silver wallpaper and stained-glass windows, the staircase that sails up three flights. Her inheritance. She will want this.*

"He will call for me."

"I didn't say that."

I clung to my thinning hope. Surely once things were right, Edward would call for me. Surely he would be sorry he'd made me wait and worry and wonder, but he'd had to smooth things over with his parents. He'd had to make things right. That must be hard for them. It wouldn't be easy to accept the housekeeper's grandchild as your own.

I understood now. It was temporary. Not for keeps.

Father put aside Mildred's knitting and sat in her ugly peach chair. He fingered the wooden armrest as I laid the baby on the floor and then flew around the cottage, gathering her necessities. The baby was still nursing but could be weaned, though my breasts throbbed — or was it my heart, cushioned behind them — just thinking about it.

At last I picked up the baby and faced my father. He held out his arms. The baby gazed up at him with those kittenish eyes.

My voice caught. "She can't be without her blanket."

"No."

I leaned down and inhaled the smell of the baby's corn-floss hair, her scalp, her breath — medicine to hold me until we were together again.

She cried when Father took her. She only knew one word, though that was smart for a baby her age. She called it as he took her out the door.

"Maa!"

# Twenty-Two

*Indiana-Michigan Line, 1934*

Ruth fanned herself in the late morning heat. Too many people were packed in her kitchen. Every single living relative was crammed in this oven — well, except Mother, always the odd man out. Heaven knows where she wandered off to. Even without her, a person could suffocate to death in here, as buried alive by chattering family as Mr. Poe's black cat, bricked up inside a wall. Why did Margaret have to mention that story? Now Ruth kept picturing bricks being plunked down, the mortar oozing between them while she watched, bound like a mummy behind them.

*For crying out loud. What is wrong with you?*

She scowled up at Nick, loaded down like a pack mule with June's luggage as he plodded up the stairs. Then she swung her frown back down at Richard, yammering at her with that big head of hair. He was saying *something* but all she could hear was what he'd said earlier. Encephalitis lethargica *patients can attend to everything going on around them, even when seemingly asleep. They are fully awake.*

She refocused in time to see that June and her ridiculous yellow suit were halfway down the hall to John's bedroom.

"Hey!"

June stopped.

"Let me make sure that everything's all right first." Ruth could smell her sister's expensive perfume when she squeezed past her.

Over the years, Ruth had gotten used to John sleeping in the background as she lived her life. Sure, Nick and she had talked outside John's window, plenty of times. They had laughed. There was that time he'd picked her up and ran her kicking and squealing around the yard, after she had teased him.

And the time he'd lifted his shirt for her to scratch his back and he ended up taking it off.

And the time they had kissed under the clothesline, sheets billowing around them like angel wings.

And all those times that she had followed Nick to the barn.

Her tell-tale heart sunk like an anvil dumped into a lake.

She slowed her steps but it was a short hall. The posse arrived at the closed bedroom door before she was ready to deal with it.

She blocked the way in. "A big crowd might be too much for him."

"I'm going in." June shifted forward in her sunshine suit as if she might actually ram past her.

"Not without me you aren't."

"I won't hurt him, Ruth."

Anyone else would have thought that June's sweet smile meant she was joking. Ruth knew better.

Maybe Ruth had hurt John. Maybe she had meant to. Maybe she was so furious at him for leaving her that she was punishing him. And maybe by punishing him, she was punishing her own guilty self. Because she loved him. Loved him more than she could bear. She had from the moment she'd first seen him.

She flung the door open.

# TWENTY-THREE

*Chicago, 1922*

June pushed her way through the crowd of the Dil Pickle Club, the slashes of people's mouths and eyes blurring in her vision. John was kissing her sister. Her John. Her sister.

She stumbled into a dark-skinned man, who then held her wrist to steady her. "Are you all right, Miss?"

The kindness in his voice swelled the salt lump in her throat.

She nodded, plunged on, then ricocheted from a staggering woman in fox furs and into the arms of a man fuming of alcohol.

"Hey, what's a pretty girl like you doing crying?" He clung to her as he blinked to clear his eyes. "Wow. You are pretty. Anyone ever tell you that you have kitty-cat eyes? Here, kitty, kitty, kitty."

She tried to break free.

"Hey! Hey! Where you going, kitty? I'm trying to help you."

"Let go!"

A man shaggy with raccoon fur stepped up. As June shrank back from him, it registered that he was handsome and young. He wore his mass of light brown hair combed back in a pompadour.

"Now let her go, Bob. That's a good boy." He pried the drunk's fingers from her sleeve. "Let — her — go."

He escorted her toward the hat-check counter. "Are you okay?"

She rubbed her arms and looked over her shoulder.

"Sorry about my friend. Would you believe it, he's a physician here in town. I'm afraid we were slipped some rather wicked booze. He's not a bad fellow — most of the time. He's actually saved a few lives in his day."

June looked over her shoulder again. John wasn't even trying to find her.

Her rescuer raised his voice above the scream of a trumpet. "Are you here with someone?"

The wooden floor seemed to have developed a magnetic force that was dragging her downward. How luxurious it would be to give in and sink down into it. She forced her mouth to move. "I'm all right."

"Well, Miss All Right, I'm Mister Okay. Pleased to make your acquaintance." He

263

stuck out a neat hand.

She moved her own hundred-pound hand toward his. Had she imagined what she'd seen? Hope fluttered in the iron cage of her ribs. Could that be it? She'd only imagined that she'd seen John kissing her sister?

Through the crowd, she saw John staggering past a white-thatched man in a bow-tie. When he caught her glance, he raised a floppy hand then plowed her way.

"Say, Miss All Right, you're looking a little green. Did you get some of that coffin varnish, too?"

John stopped heavily behind her. "Hey."

"Do you know him?" asked her rescuer.

Oh, for the release of tears. Healing, cleansing tears. If only she knew how! She stood there, erect and quiet, as her heart clawed through her chest.

"June," John slurred.

She turned around. "Where's Ruth?"

John rotated woodenly to look behind himself then stumbled back. "I don't know."

"You're disgusting."

"I know! It's hitting me hard. I don't know what I had."

June's rescuer smirked. "Liquor, by the looks of it."

"I'm not much of a drinker," John slurred.

"No lie."

"I'll take Ruth home," June said coldly. "If I can find her."

Her rescuer put out his hand to John. "I'm Richard Whiteleather. I was helping your friend —"

"Girlfriend," John said thickly. "Fiancée, if she'll let me."

Richard looked between them, raising his brows. "You two?"

"I don't know him," June said. This, she realized, was the truth.

John reached out for her.

She shied away from him. "Stay away from me. I mean it."

"Okay!"

"And stay away from my sister. She's just a kid."

"Okay!"

He was so beautiful, and dejected, that she wanted to relent. Maybe she had imagined it after all. Maybe they could just forget it.

But at that moment, Ruth pushed her way through a circle of Picklers crisscrossing hands over knees in the Charleston. She shouted over the riot of trumpets, laughter, and shuffling feet. "June!"

She trotted up, breathless. "June! I'm sorry. It shouldn't have happened that way."

*That way?*

Richard put out his hand. "Hi there. Can I help you?"

"Who are you?" Ruth snapped. He withdrew his hand as she turned to June. "Junie, we need to talk."

"It didn't mean anything to us," John slurred. "I swear, it didn't mean a thing."

Ruth looked up at him, stricken. It obviously meant something, very much, to her.

June felt all emotion bleed from her, all sorrow, all pain, all disappointment, gone. Nothing could hurt her if she did not feel.

"Take care of him," she told her sister. She walked away.

# TWENTY-FOUR

*Indiana-Michigan Line, 1926*

The sky had been as crisp and clean as a freshly ironed handkerchief that September day in '26. Even with her pregnant belly grinding on her pubic bone (she should have known she was carrying twins), three burnt black coffins of bread smoldering on the stove, and her two kids crying in the house, Ruth's heart had soared at the perfect bluebird-blueness of it as she strolled in the barnyard (well, as much of a stroll as she could muster, being more of a charger). She could actually *feel* her youthfulness pulsing in her twenty-two-year-old cells. She broke into the song that had been playing on the radio.

" 'When the red, red robin comes bob, bob, bobbin' along. Along!' "

She stopped when she came to John, then shifted the basket she was carrying against her protruding stomach. "Hey, you."

He was sitting on a bale of hay just inside the barn, his knees jutting out like a grasshopper, his dusty hat pulled low on his head. He rarely sat still — never, when he was working.

"Gorgeous out, isn't it? Who wants cream?" Their private joke.

He kept his face pointed at his work boots.

He didn't have to be so serious. He was twenty-seven years old and all sinews and muscle. Just looking at him made her blood rise.

"Oh, come on, old man!"

He looked up. Under the brim of his hat, his Abe Lincoln face, with those high cheekbones, was blank.

She raised her voice over the chickens who had spied her basket of scraps and were squabbling at her feet in a flurry of down feathers. "You okay?"

A long moment passed. "Throat hurts."

Strange. John never admitted when he was ill.

"Why don't you go in the house and lie down then?" She knew that he wouldn't. "At least go gargle with some salt water. Go on in and I'll be there in a minute."

When she returned from gathering eggs in the henhouse, he was still sitting in the entrance to the barn.

"John, aren't you going to get up?"

It took him a while to lift his face. "Yes."

The rest of him didn't move.

Unease slid through her guts, but she had to go in the house. Margaret and Jeanne were only three and two years old then and she'd left them in the playpen. Later, after she'd baked a cake, put some clothes in bleach to soak, frosted the cake, and given the girls lunch before laying them down for a nap — with the ridiculous "Red, Red Robin" stuck in her mind all the while — she went back outside with a sandwich for John since he had not come in to eat. The hair on her arms prickled. He was perched on the same bale, in the same position.

"John!"

He kept his gaze on his boots.

Her pulse thumping in her ears, she stepped closer. She thought the question bizarre even as she blurted it.

"What are the names of your daughters?"

In the distance, cowbells clunked sedately. She was aware of the acrid smell of animal drifting from the barn.

When he raised his head, his pupils were blank with fear, as if he knew what not knowing their names meant.

Terror blazed through her. "John!"

He yanked free when she tried to pull him

to his feet, then he scrambled on all fours into the barn and curled up in a corner.

"John, what are you doing?"

When she touched him, he bunched tighter.

They had no phone. She ran through the yard, chickens flying up shrieking, then she snatched the girls from their bed and ran with them, still clinging to their blankets, to the Model T. They cried from the front seat as she pulled the choke by the radiator, hopped in the car to jam in the key and adjust the throttle, hopped back out to crank the car, then threw herself back inside. Cats galloped for cover as she sped from the yard and toward neighboring farms for help.

John was balled up asleep in the barn when the neighbor men came. They approached him slowly.

"Now, John." George Squibb reached out his hand. "Let me help you." He touched John's shoulder.

John's eyes flew open. He screamed like an animal that would bite if cornered.

They surrounded him warily, menfolk around a rabid dog, when Dr. Akin roared up in his Buick. He jumped out and ordered the men to lash John down to keep him from hurting himself. Upon a signal, they leaped on John and dragged him to the back bedroom, where they bound his wrists and ankles as Ruth watched, her two-year-old straddling her hip and her three-year-old burrowing into her leg.

They hadn't needed to tie him up. He was asleep before they were done, and could not be awakened.

Five days later, Ruth had pressed Jeanne to her hard gob of pregnant belly as Dr. Akin positioned then repositioned the cupped end of his stethoscope against John's chest. Ruth stroked her daughter's satiny hair and grasped for any distraction: organ music, wheezing from the parlor, the wedding march that signaled the start of Betty Crocker's radio program; Margaret in the kitchen talking to Mother, who'd come to help; Aunt Edna's cuckoo clock yodeling from the dining room. *HOO-hoo. HOO-hoo. HOO-hoo.* Ruth fought the sudden impulse to jump up, snatch that little birdy, and smash it.

Dr. Akin straightened his wiry body with a sigh, then slowly unclipped his instrument from behind his ears. "I'm sorry to tell you this, Ruth, but I believe that John has *encephalitis lethargica.* That's —"

Ruth had held up her hand to stop him.

271

The newspapers had been talking about the mysterious disease that turned people into zombies since she was back in high school. When the Spanish flu came a few years later, doctors thought the ailments might be related. But Spanish flu had come and gone in two years, taking a chunk of the world's population with it, while the sleeping sickness kept churning on. Nobody knew what caused it, nor who it would attack nor why. Not even the richest lady in America had escaped it — Mrs. J. Pierpont Morgan, Jr., had died of it last year. But it always attacked other people's wives, other people's husbands. Not Ruth's.

Behind smudged glasses, Dr. Akin blinked lashes the beige of milky Sanka. "The fact is, he might not ever fully recover. Few with this type of *encephalitis lethargica* do. From what I've seen, they can go on like this for years. The issue isn't that the patients can't do things. John's muscle tone and reflexes are normal. Why, he's probably physically capable of running a mile. It's just that they drop off to sleep before they can finish a task. As much as they might want to do something, they can't without falling asleep."

She pulled Jeanne's thumb from her mouth. The baby inside her kicked. "There has to be a cure."

Dr. Akin put his stethoscope in his bag. "At times he might be able to sustain a response. He might be able to talk to you some, perhaps take a few steps. There isn't much rhyme or reason to this. Remember — he *wants* to do things, it's just that he's too sleepy."

From the parlor, Betty Crocker recited a recipe in her fruity voice. What a prissy know-it-all! Why didn't Mother turn that thing off?

"At least we can make him comfortable." Dr. Akin shut his bag. "There are institutions that can take him if it gets to be too much."

Ruth stared at him even as the world changed under her feet, vast stony plates grinding to a halt.

The doctor patted her arm and left.

She would make John comfortable. She would make her children comfortable. She could even make the unborn baby ramming against her tailbone comfortable. But dear God, what about her?

# Twenty-Five

*Indiana-Michigan Line, 1934*

Like a cat whose tail had been stepped on, Mother shot up from where she'd been sitting by John's bed when the posse entered the bedroom. She faced Ruth, eyes bugged behind her glasses. "He's still sleeping."

And yet Mother had been chatting away to him. Ruth led in John's examiners: June, Old King Cole, the kids. Nick didn't come, which was wise of him.

She looked down at her husband. His skin, draping over his sharp cheekbones, had thinned from being mostly bedbound all these years, but his features were much the same. June would still find him attractive. He was, Ruth realized as they gathered around his bed, still attractive.

Truth was, Ruth avoided looking at him whenever possible. For good reason. When she gazed down at his arms, she didn't see motionless lumps under the patchwork quilt. What she saw were veined and muscular powerhouses in the act of hoisting up hay bales, digging postholes, or pulling breech calves from the womb. In her eyes, his legs, useless now, were towers of strength that tramped up and down fields, paced the floor with baby Margaret when she nearly died from scarlet fever, or ran toward Ruth in the rain. His body, still as a log, she saw sliding under the Ford with a wrench, hunching against a blizzard in an open wool coat, or moving against her, filling her with holy delight. This was what she saw when she looked at him. And so, she did not often look.

She glanced away before glaring at the wall. "John, wake up. June's here."

"John, wake up. June's here."

June winced at her sister's tone. Did she have to be so rough?

She tried to keep her gaze on John, sprawled on the bed below her, but it was like clinging to a hot baking dish with bare hands. Dear God, who was this silent ruin of flesh and bones? John looked nothing like himself, nothing like the man for whom she'd yearned all these years. Until this moment, she had not believed that his illness could be this . . . complete. She knew he slept a lot. She knew he hadn't the strength to run the farm. But she had not known that he'd been robbed of any kind of livable life. He was a living dead man. Her John. Ruth should have told her. Didn't she know she would have dropped everything and come?

He opened his eyes. She flinched as if jabbed.

His flesh blossomed with color when he found her. Life surged into his eyes, into his bones. He struggled to move his mouth, as if it had been glued closed and he had to fight to break the seal.

"Hi. Betty."

Stupid words spilled out. "You know about Betty?"

"You're — famous."

Richard pushed next to her. "Hello, John. Remember me? Mr. Crocker?"

"Hi. Doc."

She wasn't giving him over so quickly. "John, how do you feel? What can I get you?"

His chest heaved under his covers. "Just — my legs."

She felt the kids backing away behind her.

"John." Ruth's voice was brittle. "Just let Richard look at you, would you?"

June understood that Ruth's words were

meant for her. She got out of the way, joining the kids at the back of the room, where she recorded Richard's frown as he took John's pulse, the children's wary expressions, and Mother's rabbit gaze as she ran her thumb under her chin. Mother wouldn't have the slightest idea how this kind of despair felt. Dad had always coddled her.

Now Ruth was demanding, "What do you mean? Cure him how?"

Richard turned to see if June was listening before he answered. "A colleague at the hospital has just had success in treating *encephalitis lethargica.*"

"I thought there was no cure," Ruth said bitterly.

"That is the prevailing thought. And true, there has been no hope for the hyperkinetic form of the disease. He doesn't have rapid motor movements, uncontrollable twitching, anxiousness, or general restlessness, does he?"

"No."

"Same for the amyostatic-akinetic form, which presents like Parkinson's disease. The patient has Parkinson's-like tremors and dramatic reduction in muscle strength and difficulty with moving."

"Are you asking if he shakes?"

"Yes."

"No. He doesn't. He just sleeps."

Richard patted John. "Then, as you probably know, our friend here has the somnolent-ophthalmoplegic form, the most prevalent type. It starts with a high fever and the patient falling asleep randomly, even while walking or talking, then moves into psychosis, derangement, or hallucinations before the individual assumes an oft-fatal comatose state. How long was John in a coma, Ruth?"

"Five days."

June reached for one of the twins then let her burrow into her.

"I see. He's lucky he lived through it. And then comes the end stage. Patients go into a state of akinetic mutism, lacking the will to move or express themselves in any fashion. It is thought that they will stay this way for the rest of their lives."

"We know this!" Ruth said. "Tell us something new!"

Down on the bed, John opened his eyes. Everything in June lurched for him, even as she stood with the children.

"As I was going to say," Richard said, "there has been no hope. Until now."

Must he make such a production of it? "What is it, darling?" June asked.

"One of my colleagues has found what

might be a simple therapy — simple but surprisingly efficacious: vitamin B-12."

"Vitamins!" Ruth scoffed.

"My colleague's patient had a complete recovery after receiving injections. I saw the patient myself — talking, walking. She even did a little dance — the polka, I believe. This after being, well, in crude parlance, a zombie, for six years."

"For crying out loud," Ruth muttered.

Silence fell over the room. John stared at Richard as the *cheer-cheer-cheer* of a cardinal sifted through the rusting screened window. June tightened her hold on her niece. "What does this mean for John?"

Richard smiled. "How good are you at dancing, John?"

Mother exclaimed and clasped her hands.

"Enough!" Ruth glared at him. "Say these *vitamins* could work. How long until we would see results? Or do you even know?"

"I'm not certain, I'll admit. If there's no improvement in eight hours, I'll give him another injection. I have enough serum for two weeks, QID — four times a day. If it works, I could get you more and show you how to administer it." He paused, then raised his voice for John, who had drifted off again. "I'll admit, this isn't foolproof. They've only tried it on the one subject, not exactly a rigorously conducted study, although her response was remarkable."

"Then why get our hopes up?" Ruth cried.

He turned to her with his friendliest doctor expression, the one he reserved, June knew, for cancer patients with inoperable tumors. "If there's a chance for recovery, don't you think it's preferable to doing nothing?"

John reopened his eyes and, searching Richard's face, inched his hand across the bed until he grasped him.

"Fix me."

The clank of cowbells drifted into the room, along with the smell of withered grass. Heat was building outside, and it wasn't even noon.

"All right, sir," Richard said, "if you're game, I will see about fixing you up. June, help me prepare, would you, darling?"

He strode to the washstand with its bowl and thick porcelain pitcher, where she poured water over his hands, let him lather up, then rinsed him. When they were done, they went back to the bed, where Ruth was sinking onto the mattress. John slipped his hand into Ruth's, and Ruth squeezed it hard.

June took the blow. What did she expect?

Ruth was his wife, not her. If John were cured, Ruth and he would go back to their happy married life. That was the way it should be.

Mother edged toward the bed.

"Come closer, Dorothy," Richard called. "You ought to be able to watch this, since you're the one who instigated this reunion. June, fetch my bag."

Glass tinkled inside the satchel when she picked it up. Mother instigated the reunion?

"What signs are we to look for that it's working?" Mother asked.

"John fox-trotting on the bed, evidently," Ruth said.

Mother put her hand over her mouth. "Will it be that fast? Shouldn't we have lunch first?"

"You, planning for lunch?" said Ruth. "How long do cans take to open?"

"Unlatch my bag, would you, darling, and get my head mirror?"

Ruth was scared, June thought, opening the bag. She's rudest when she's frightened. She thought of Ruth, her pimpled face fierce, cracking Mr. Horn with the broom. June had never dwelled on it, but Ruth must have been scared out of her mind then.

June fitted the head mirror over Richard's hair. "Can you sit?" he asked John.

When John couldn't manage it, June helped Ruth prop him upright, then she retreated to a corner of the room. Ruth's place was next to the bed, not hers.

Richard flipped the shiny disc over his eye then peered into John's pupil.

"Kids," said Mother. "Can you see this?"

The children stayed glued in the doorway. The very room seemed to hold its breath as Richard examined John, slumped against the headboard. One of the girls coughed.

At last, Richard drew back. "All right, John. We're going to give this treatment a whirl."

He fished in his bag, tore some cotton wool from a roll, wiped John's arm with alcohol from a brown bottle, then opened a small vial. A medicinal smell permeated the air.

A hand on her back — June flinched and turned. It was Mother.

Richard filled a syringe.

# TWENTY-SIX

*Chicago, 1922*
June brushed past the would-be revelers outside the Dil Pickle Club door. She only stopped to catch her breath in the alleyway when she had cleared the line of them.

Richard came to a halt beside her, his raccoon fur wafting in the light of a streetlamp. "I'm sorry that he upset you. What kind of numbskull treats his girl like that?"

Already she regretted blurting out to him that she'd seen John and Ruth kissing. "I don't care. He can do what he wants." She pulled her baggy coat closer. The damp in Chicago's wind pierced straight to the bone. "I should be going."

"I can't let you wander off alone."

"I don't live far." Should she have told him that? She didn't know who this young fellow was. This was Tower Town — an expensively dressed fellow could be a mobster or a con man. She'd seen some in the club.

"No matter if you live across the street: you're not traipsing around this part of town without me. Doctor's orders."

June must have had a suspicious look on her face because he took out his wallet. She peered at the card he produced: the American Medical Association.

He shrugged when she looked back up at him. "I know. I don't look like a sawbones, do I?"

She liked him more for his modesty.

He walked her home that night, then called on her the next day at the Three Arts Club. While he seemed a little less humble perched behind the wheel of his topless roadster, with his fedora tilted across his brow and the fur of his raccoon coat rippling in the wind, he was sweet just the same. He took her driving through Lincoln Park with its naked winter trees and empty bandstand, then, as she held down her bottle-green cloche, they roared past the self-satisfied façade of the Drake Hotel. They conquered Michigan Avenue, rumbling past old churches and new offices, past the mock-medieval Water Tower, beneath the concrete gingerbread dripping from the Wrigley Building, and over the sea-green

Chicago River, to the row of frilly Gilded Age skyscrapers overlooking Grant Park.

Pausing long enough to growl back at the bronze lions in front of the Art Institute, they charged into the park, zinging along the railroad lines and racing a locomotive to the modern-day temple of the Field Museum, beyond which the car came to the end of a dirt road and stopped.

The roadster vibrated in idle. Ahead of them steam shovels, their yellow paint glazed with icy snow, were parked in an earthen pit like dinosaurs frozen in the act of grazing. A broad snowy field separated them from Lake Michigan, which lolled behind blocks of ice tossed haphazardly onto the shore as if by a race of giants.

Richard raised his voice above the wind groaning off the lake. "They're digging a new stadium."

She could see where the big machines had bitten off chunks of the pit in which they were trapped.

"Thank you." Her silk neck scarf snapped in the wind. "I needed this."

"I needed this, too. Thank you." He had taken off his hat and the wind had unstuck his pompadour, whipping his hair in his eyes, making him appear more boyish. "You're different from other girls. Wiser.

Calmer."

"It's all an act." She wasn't kidding.

"Well, don't stop being you. You're special."

She looked into his light brown eyes. This was the part where men kissed her. Maybe she would not mind it so much, especially when she pictured John kissing Ruth. She leaned into him. He gave her arm a squeeze, and then let her go. He started the car.

She smiled to herself. Interesting fellow.

Richard returned to his home in St. Paul the next day, after which time he sent roses daily, and letters, until at last she agreed to come to St. Paul to visit over the summer, during which time she would stay in his mother's house. It was his mother with whom she would fall in love, or at least the idea of being her daughter. She was engaged to Richard before the end of May.

# Twenty-Seven

*Indiana-Michigan line, 1934*

The framed watercolor above the washstand of a curly-haired sleeping child, the work of an obvious amateur — June, in fact, when she'd been in high school — irritated Ruth with its naive serenity. The ticking of one of dead Aunt Edna's clocks on the dresser also bugged her, as did the cardinal who wouldn't shut up outside with its annoying *cheer-cheer-cheer.* Oh, there were plenty of irritants to keep her occupied while she waited to see how her future would be. Would she be a wife? A caregiver? A divorcée? Her fate hung on something so stupid as a vitamin.

Ruth rolled her scowl to her sister and Richard, both sitting next to John on the bed. She toggled between imagining the rickety bed breaking under their weight and wondering how in the world June stood that husband of hers. Ruth would rather be poor than be shackled to such a phony. She almost hoped that John wouldn't awaken just so Richard couldn't claim credit — well, not really, but if Richard did cure him, it would be hard to stomach. Richard would be sure to crow about his medical miracle to his bigwig buddies and then newspapermen would be crawling all over the farm in no time flat, snapping photos of the Hoosier Lazarus and his pitiful, grateful family, who owed it all to their brother-in-law and his beautiful wife, one of the plucky women who was an ambassador for America's Favorite Mother, Betty Crocker. Ruth could just *see* her family in *Time* magazine, beaming at the revived patriarch somberly ladling gruel from the pitted aluminum pot at their grubby table, the most recent poverty cases documented by the famous photographer Margaret Bourke-White.

Now Richard was dipping that head of hair, big as his ego, toward June, who was drooping in her canary suit as if *she* were the grieving wife. When June looked up, he mouthed to her, *Go.*

She glanced at Ruth.

Ruth recrossed her arms, then wedged them under her small breasts. "Go if you want."

Richard patted June's hand. They exchanged a long gaze that made Ruth burn with envy. Easy for them to be lovers. They had no children, no bills, no drought, no failing crops, no hungry herd, no Mother in their hair, no hope-crushing, dream-curdling, life-snuffing sleeping sickness — nothing — to sully their moonbeams and roses.

Down on the bed, John opened his eyes.

June melted into a smile when she saw him. "Hi."

"You're. Here."

*So am I, John. Your wife. Right here.*

He grinned up at June, too happy to mask his affection. Didn't matter, did it? Good, true John would never be unfaithful. Not even if he loved June more. Not even if he were well. Now, as Ruth watched their old familiarity flash between them, for one black second she was glad that he was felled, glad he had suffered, until her breakfast boiled up to her throat with shame and remorse and anguish.

This was how it felt to lose your mind.

"You gather your strength," June told John. "I'll be near."

He receded back into himself, asleep again.

June got up, her eyes bright. Ruth peered closer: no tears. Why didn't she just go ahead and cry? Why did she always have to be such a martyr?

Richard rubbed June's back, then watched her leave.

"Well," he said, "looks like it's just you and me now, Ruth."

She lifted the corners of her mouth then let them drop. She might have to kill somebody.

From the kitchen, Mother was making lunch noises. The kids were running through the house, until they'd latched on to June.

Richard pointed that pompadour at her. "So how has life been?"

"Oh, just peaches and cream."

He nodded and smiled, as if she weren't being completely surly. "Thank you for having us. Your sister couldn't wait to come."

What was he looking for? Thanks? "Thank you for helping out with the rent," she said stiffly.

"That's all June's doing — not that I don't approve. She puts every penny of her check in an account for you and the kids."

Was he *trying* to rub it in? "Thank you," she mumbled. When she looked down, John's eyes were quivering behind his lids as if he were trying, hard, to listen.

How much *did* he hear?

"I admire how you're managing the farm,

Ruth. Even with help, in these times, that's no mean feat. And with four children and a house to run — I tip my hat to you. You're a remarkable woman."

She jumped to her feet. She didn't stop until she reached the base of the stairs, where she clutched the newel post and gritted back a scream. She saw herself pregnant when she was eighteen, all those years ago. She was not quite showing, her skirt straining over her thickened waist.

"We got married," she was telling Dad.

Pencil in hand, Dad looked up at her from the bills arranged over the dining room table, then swung his face to John, and back to her again. Wrinkles of confusion wreathed his gentle face.

She had smiled stupidly. *No, Dad, he's not June's boyfriend anymore. And no, Dad, I'm not exactly a virgin bride. I never disappoint to disappoint.*

# Twenty-Eight

*Fort Wayne, 1922*

Ruth was in the stable behind Dad's store, where the air was so thick with the smell of animal that she could taste it. She ran her hand down JoJo's firm warm neck, then laid her head against it. She concentrated on the feel of the horse's smooth hair against her cheek — she had to, to keep her heart from thrashing from her chest. John would be here in a moment.

They had become unlikely pen pals since they had stumbled around that night in Tower Town last winter, him trying to walk off the effects of the wicked hooch, her trailing behind him, not knowing what else to do. They'd ended up at an all-night automat, staring at a piece of pie. She couldn't face June. He'd put her on the first train home in the morning without having said a dozen words to her.

After school on the Monday she'd returned, she'd mailed him her olive branch: a piece of sheet music. The cover pictured a brilliantined hep cat fox-trotting a real live wire off her high heels. *CRAZY PEOPLE,* it read. Inside, Ruth had scrawled in red crayon over the musical notes, *What do I say after I say I'm sorry?*

A week passed before the envelope came. When Ruth saw "State Line Road" on the flap, she ripped it open and unfolded the piece of sheet music tucked inside.

*GUILTY,* it read. *A Fox-Trot Ballad.* The woman on one half of the cover dipped her marcelled head in shy remorse. The other half was a scene of a sweet girl-next-door-type turning away from a man.

A quick flip of the cover revealed no other message.

She laughed, then plunked down and wrote him right back. She had deposited her letter in the mailbox on State Street when it occurred to her with a jolt: Who was he saying was guilty?

She stewed about it as she sat in her classes by day, and took care of her assorted animals and rearranged Dad's shelves in the store by night. John's reply came with the last freak snow in the beginning of April. She ran with it to the bedroom, where she scanned the contents.

*It's still unseasonably cold here . . .*
*Turned the far field . . .*
*Three new calves . . .*
*I want June back. Could you help me?*

She wadded up the letter and speared it into the wastebasket by her desk. Had he no idea how offensive that was?

Later that night, she dug it out. With it uncrumpled on the table next to her, she wrote back.

*June is seeing that fellow she'd met in Chicago. Remember him, big hair? Wise mouth? Fur coat? It turns out that he is a doctor in Minneapolis. She spends a lot of time with him and his family — they have a lake house and loads of money. From the looks of her letters to Mother and Dad, they are serious.*

Weeks went by. A month. She graduated from high school; relined all the shelves in Dad's store with fresh butcher paper; bled the Tecumseh Branch of the library dry to the point that in early summer, she had to break down and spend her savings on a book. *This Side of Paradise* it was called, by a newcomer named Fitzgerald.

She locked herself in the room that she had once shared with her sister and read, the high-pitched screech of Mother's paint swab on a photograph coming from the other side of her door. Her heart pounded as she turned the pages. She knew this story. She knew another midwestern boy who was knocking his head against the wall while wooing an unattainable beauty. So what if the boy in the story was rich and John was not? F. Scott, whoever he was, had obviously grown up rich, and was disguising his life in fiction. Well, John was every bit as clever as F. Scotty Fitzgerald. Why didn't he just write a love story that was set on a farm? He had all the material he needed — people were forever wanting what they cannot have, no matter where they were. The grass is always greener, be it on a farm, in the city, or in a jungle.

She finished the book in two sittings. Then, although she was furious at John, she wrapped the book in brown paper, tied it with a string, and mailed it.

Under his address she wrote, *You could write this.*

He showed up on the porch a week later. Across the street, State School kids were creaking away on their swings.

Without any prologue, he demanded, "Do you really think so?"

She knew exactly what he meant. "Write that book? I wouldn't have said so if I didn't."

"But he and I have nothing in common."

"Are you kidding? You're from the Midwest. You're clever. You're wise."

"He's rich!"

"You're interesting."

"I'm a farmer."

"Well, make that interesting. It *will* be interesting, because that's what you know. Make us know it, too."

They talked for hours after that, spilling out their real selves as they walked streets lined with tall wooden houses and small green yards staked with a single tree. They passed horses pulling carts, shuddering Model-Ts, women hanging clothes, and children booting cans and running. Ruth saw them and loved them all.

When they found themselves in the Lakeside Rose Garden, they wandered paths dense with floral perfume. Velvety veined blooms drooped from arbors and strained from flower beds as latticed shadows netted John's earnest face. They settled next to a reflecting pond, where John talked and Ruth dunked the rubbery lily pads until molten drops shimmered on top. He shared his dreams of writing, and she thought about hers, until the shadows of the arbors cast dark towers over the grass.

John said, "I guess it's getting late."

It occurred to her with a start: "Where are you going to stay tonight?"

"I'd better get moving. I was going to thumb a ride home."

"It's too late for that." She threw down the rose leaf she'd been shredding. "You should stay at my house."

"I feel a little odd." He frowned at the grass. "I can't do that."

"You can stay in our stable, then. Unless you mind bunking up with a horse. It's just a few blocks from here. Behind Dad's store."

"Thank you, but I shouldn't."

"Do you have a better plan?"

He drew in a breath. "No."

They started walking again but their conversation came now with difficulty, as if they had just met after a very long time, or were strangers.

When they got to Dad's store, its awning had been lowered for the day and a "closed" sign hung on the plate-glass door. They peered through the windows. Not even Ned was there.

"There's a sink out back," she said, "if you need it. Let me fix up a place for you in the stable."

There, with trembling hands, she lit a lantern, spread an old blanket over the straw, then waited. When she couldn't bear it anymore, she buried her face against Jo-Jo's warm neck.

*Do it. This is your only life.*

He entered the stables. She nearly fainted at the sight of him in the lamplight, upright and strong from labor on his farm.

"I put out a blanket for you."

They gazed through the soft yellow light to the coarse blanket lying on the straw.

"Thank you," he said.

She nodded.

"Really." He drew in a breath. "Thank you. I've never had a friend like you."

Her heart sank as she raised her eyes. Friend?

She turned away.

He stepped close. "Hey. What's wrong?"

She shook her head.

He sighed, then put his arm around her with brotherly ease. "What am I going to do about you, little sister?"

She drank in his smell, then squeezing her eyes closed, turned and pressed herself against the length of his body.

He held her away from him. "Hey! This isn't right."

"It's right if I say it is."

"Ruth."

"Don't I get to say what I want? Don't I

get to say how I feel?"

"This isn't right."

"Why is it always so wrong for me to want something?" She stepped up to him. She could feel the warmth radiating from his flesh as she lifted her face.

They kissed, gently at first, and then with such hunger that it frightened her. When she grappled to release him from his clothes, she thought, *This should be June. But it's me. It's me. It's me.*

# TWENTY-NINE

*Indiana-Michigan line, 1934*

In the kitchen, as Mother clanged a pan on the burner, Ruth's twins, June's eager guides, had grabbed June's hands and pulled her up the creaking stairs to what was to be her boudoir. They crowded behind her now as she unpacked her suitcase, the heat of their young bodies adding to the stuffiness of the room. What kind of oven would this be by night?

Ilene, the twin with the bigger gap between her saw-edged new front teeth — the only way June could tell the little girls apart — darted a finger to a dress. "Pretty!"

"Thank you." June let her caress it, the child's hot, grubby-sweet musk catching at her heart. She smelled like Ruth as a kid.

From the start, June's feelings for Ruth had overwhelmed her. Just the smell, the sight, of baby Ruth released a warmth in little June that was so powerful that she had not known what to do with it. When baby Ruth had taken her first steps, her proud grin forming three chins against her neck and her diaper saggy over chunky plodding legs, June had darted forward and gripped her baby sister's arm, squeezing it, hard, until Ruth had squawked and Mother had screamed.

Dad had whisked June off. She was confused, ashamed, and scared of her own self. She had only wanted to love the baby. After that, whenever she squeezed her little sister's arm, teeth and body clenched with the force of it, her insides hot with love, she made sure her mother was not around. But she loved that little baby. She did.

Now she took a dress from the suitcase and shook it out.

"Our mother never wears pretty dresses," the other twin, Irene, said matter-of-factly.

"You shouldn't say that," June said.

Irene hopped on the bed next to the suitcase. "Mother tells us to always tell the truth."

"She does?"

Irene peered into the bag, a cat inspecting a chipmunk hole. "Yes. She says to never lie."

"That's good." June wondered if by not lying her sister meant that as long as no one asked, she could carry on with her blue-eyed farmhand. No wonder Ruth had not seemed thrilled to see her, even after Mother had written and begged her to come because Ruth "missed her so." That was obviously not the case. "Could you get me a hanger, please?"

Irene ran over to the wardrobe and threw open a door carved with a preschooler's all-head-and-rickety-stick-legs scrawling of a person. She unearthed a hanger from the bottom of the wardrobe, and with it, Mother's cat.

The animal shot under the bed as Irene brought back her wooden trophy. "Here you go!"

Not to be outdone in helpfulness, Ilene rooted around the suitcase and pulled out a pair of pumps pilloried on shoe-trees. "Want me to put these away?"

Her twin, Irene, apparently the dominant one, elbowed her sister out of the way. "What else can I get?"

June held up her jewelry case. "You can put this on the dresser, please."

Irene snatched the box and popped it open. Both girls gasped at the contents, as if the mostly costume jewelry were golden treasure.

"No fair!" Ilene cried.

"Girls!" Ruth called, trudging up the stairs. "Leave Aunt June alone."

"We are helping her!" Ilene said when her mother entered the room.

"She said we could!" cried the other.

"They *are* helping," June lied.

Ruth dropped on the other side of the suitcase. "I know what sort of help they are."

June thought that wasn't kind to say about her daughters. She was surprised when Ruth allowed Ilene to come over and root her way onto her lap, then let her coltish legs dangle to the floor. The child put her thumb to her mouth then took it away when she saw her mother watching. June bet Ruth was a tough mother to please.

Irene snapped the jewelry case open and closed. "Aunt June, why do they call you 'Betty Crocker'? Why don't they call you by your real name?"

" 'June Whiteleather' doesn't sound as catchy, does it?" June said lightly.

Ruth wrapped her arms around the daughter in her lap. Up came the thumb again.

"The problem is," Ruth said, "there is no Betty Crocker."

"That's not you on the radio?" Irene's voice went high, as if she didn't want to believe it.

"Nope," said Ruth. "Not her. I told you that, nut. The radio Betty Crocker is one of the bunch of ladies who pretend that they're her."

June felt a prick of annoyance. This must be one of the instances when the truth must be scrupulously told. "My job is to help Betty."

"But if there's not a Betty Crocker," Ilene said around her thumb, "how can you help her?"

"You have a very good point." Ruth tickled her daughter's ribs. "What Aunt June does," she said over Ilene's giggles, "is works for a company that made up a woman to sell their flour."

Irene kept flipping the jewel case open and closed. "Why don't they just use a real woman to sell their flour?"

The twin on Ruth's lap agreed. "Yes, you should sell it, Aunt June."

"Your aunt was pretty good at selling a bathing suit in high school."

June looked up sharply.

"I'm being complimentary, June."

"Thank you," June said, uncertain. Ruth was even more sour than she remembered her. She reminded herself of the hardships her sister had to bear.

Ruth removed her daughter's thumb from

her mouth with a pop. "The company made up Betty Crocker because a make-believe character can say anything they want her to say. She's not beholden to the truth, you see."

"Huh?" Irene wrinkled her nose.

"But I like Betty Crocker," said her twin. "We hear her on the radio."

"Made-up," said Ruth.

Such a stickler when it suits her, thought June. She wondered what Ruth's policy was with her children on Santa Claus.

"Girls, I want you to know that there are real people behind Betty. Like me. There are twenty-one of us 'Bettys.' We try out recipes and write cooking publications and make suggestions for the radio show. One of my favorite parts of the job is to answer letters from people. We get thousands of them every day, can you imagine?"

"You do?" they breathed. "About flour?"

"About everything. No one tells me what to say in my letters. I have to answer from my heart."

"You mean people write to you about more than how to frost a cake?" Ruth held away her daughter on her lap then fanned her own face. "Geez, you're a little hotbox!"

June took a dress to the wardrobe. "The other girls and I have become regular agony

305

aunts. I suppose women — it's mostly women who write, although we do get our share of marriage proposals from men — believe Betty can solve their problems, which is rather astonishing to me."

"Really? Isn't that what you Bettys are working so hard for, to get women to think that they can fix anything with a cake and a smile — just be sure not to stint on the flour."

"We're just trying to help people, Ruth. These are terrible times."

"Ha. I'm not the one you have to convince how hard these times are. But I'm not sure that lying to people helps them."

"I don't know, maybe it does — not lying, I mean by giving them someone who they can turn to. I suppose many women don't have a soul to sound off to, so they unburden themselves on perfect strangers. You wouldn't believe what they tell Betty Crocker! I've had to become an amateur psychoanalyst."

"I'm sure you're perfect at it."

June leveled her brow at her sister. Was it too much for Ruth to acknowledge that June was trying to do something good? All right, Ruth was less fortunate. All right, she was in a terrible situation. June was absolutely sick about it — even more ill now that she had seen John. But did she have to be punished for her own good luck every waking moment she was around Ruth, when she was not the transgressor here?

Around her thumb, Ilene asked, "Mommy, is Daddy awake yet?" She looked up at her mother.

"No."

The child slouched back against Ruth.

Irene closed the jewelry case with a final pop. "Mommy and Daddy used to sleep in this room. Now it's Grandma's. Stinks like her baby powder."

"And her throat lozenges," Ilene added around her thumb.

"And her girdle." The twins tittered.

"Girls," Ruth said.

June felt terribly weary all of a sudden, flattened, as if the oppressive roar of the airplane propellers were battering her ears again.

"Thanks for helping me to unpack. Uncle Richard and I shall be quite comfy in here."

"Not exactly what you're used to," said Ruth.

"It's lovely. It's wonderful to be out in the country."

"We have twenty-one cats!" piped up Ilene. "Out in the barn."

June smiled. "You are in heaven!"

Ruth rolled her eyes.

This was going all wrong. Everyone should be thrilled — John had a chance to be cured. Their family was reunited. The sisters were back together again. She touched Ruth's arm. "I really am glad to see you."

Ruth's eyes flew open. They were brown, like Dad's, and fierce. "Why?"

June had squeezed this woman's arm as a baby, not knowing what to do with the love surging through her. "I just am."

Ruth blew a breath out her nose, then looked away, before resting her chin on her daughter's head. Suddenly, she said, "Why are you a Betty, anyhow?"

"What?"

"Why do you work as a Betty? You don't need the money."

"I don't know. I suppose because I get to use my creative side." She would not admit that she loved how the girls looked up to her. Ruth would have a field day with that.

"Well, don't stop. I need the money."

When June didn't answer quickly enough, Ruth said grimly, "That was a joke, June. Ha — what I would give to be the one supporting you for a change."

"Lunch!" Mother yelled up the stairs.

"The can's on, ready to be served." Ruth stood up, letting her daughter slide from her lap. "Come on, girls."

The twins sidled over to June. The worship on their faces was obvious even to her.

Ruth shrugged, then sauntered out of the room, leaving them behind.

June clasped their warm hands. "Ladies, let's go eat."

She still didn't know what to do about Ruth.

# THIRTY

*Minneapolis, 1922*

Mrs. Whiteleather was having June draw her portrait that golden October afternoon. They were in the Whiteleathers' magnificent Tudor house on Summit Avenue, in the bright sunroom from which one could almost get a glimpse of the Mississippi if one stood in a certain spot. Richard would purchase a house for June and himself just up the block in the following months. It had been Linda Whiteleather's idea for June to do the portrait, a gift for Dr. Whiteleather, she said.

The sturdy German maid brought in gingerbread squares, still wafting faint steam on their plate. Linda nodded to her, then said to June, "Why the rush to get married?"

June lowered her drawing pencil and took a sip of coffee, waiting until the maid padded away on spongy heels. She was uncomfortable with an audience.

"Richard's in a hurry."

It was the truth. He was tired of taking her to the family lake "cottage" alone, only to have their lovemaking on the sofa stop with caresses under clothing. He wanted complete access. And since getting Ruth's latest news, June was ready for it, too.

Mrs. Whiteleather pushed back a swoop of silver blond. "Oh, Richard's always in a hurry."

"I can look into art school and finish my degree here."

"But you won't. Richard is greedy. He'll want all your time."

Yes, Richard was greedy. He exhausted her with his needy affection, as if he thought that though she did not love him as much as he loved her now, with a relentless bombardment of charm, he could tip the balance. At least his over-affection made the lack of hers less glaring. She was grateful for the cover.

"He's been so supportive."

"I suppose it's my fault that he's so greedy. At least that's what Dr. Freud would have you believe. Dick doesn't approve of my reading Freud, although I should be the disapproving one, as poor an opinion as Freud has of mothers. It's always the mother's fault, isn't it? In my case, perhaps it is."

That could not be! What Ruth would have given for Linda Whiteleather to be her mother. "Richard is lucky to have you!"

Mrs. Whiteleather offered June a slice of gingerbread, then picked up her cup.

"I'm just stating the truth, dear. Maybe there's something to be learned from it." She took a sip, then sighed. "I probably should not admit this, but there was a fellow who consumed entirely too much of my thought when I was a young mother and Dr. Whiteleather was busy with starting his practice. The fellow was unsuitable for me, and I knew it, but the heart wants what the heart wants. I wasted a lot of time scheming how we might be together, pining for what I could not have, before I realized that I was throwing away any chance of happiness with what I *did* have." She put her cup to her lips but didn't drink. "Most of Richard's early childhood had slipped through my fingers before I came to my senses. And so we have our Greedy Gus." She sipped thoughtfully.

Radiating guilt, June bit into her gingerbread. Did Mrs. Whiteleather know about her? Did she know about John? June didn't know how that could be possible.

Mrs. Whiteleather put down her cup and

reached for the polished coffeepot. "Just don't rush, dear. You don't need to. You already have him, I promise."

June watched the coffee twirl from the silver spout as Linda poured. But she wanted to get married now, the sooner the better. The contest between her and her sister, if there ever was one, was over. The door that June had always kept open to John — whether she admitted it to herself or not — was now closed. Ruth was expecting a baby, due sometime in March.

# DOROTHY

Everyone's out there eating lunch. Look here, canned peaches for dessert.

Now that got your attention. There are those nice brown eyes! Are you feeling any better yet? Did that shot help? Not yet?

Well, you gather your strength. My story's just about done.

— A "Pocket Venus." That's what they used to call a tiny little beauty like Edward's mother had been. Even with my stomach boiling as I sat in the Lambs' foyer that day, I couldn't help but like that little bride, so tiny and beautiful, smiling down at me from her life-size portrait. Beneath the sheer tent of her veil, she looked shy, even apologetic. I could not tell which. All I knew was that as a child, I admired her and that smile whenever I passed beneath them.

Now the real-life Mrs. Lamb said, "Tell me about yourself, Dorothy."

I brought my sights from the painting

down to the real Emmaline Lamb, her teeny-tiny figure now as padded as the chair upon which I sat. It was as if time had draped the little bride with a thick fleshy coating, turning the sweet girl into a cruel caricature of herself. I swallowed hard, my insides wringing themselves to shreds. When would she bring my baby out? It had been five months since I'd given her up.

"I've taken up coloring photographs." I wanted to show her that I had gumption. "Tinting, it's called. You have to be very particular about staying in the lines."

"You have time for hobbies? Is there a husband on the scene?"

A shockwave rippled through me. How could she think that? Was she testing my fidelity to Edward? Was this why she had gone these months without answering my letters, without responding to the packages of teething biscuits I'd baked or the bibs I'd so carefully quilted? Not even my parents would answer my postcards. They were trying me by fire.

I'd only come to this realization that morning, while Mildred was out wrangling the cheapest price for yarn at the fabric store. I had been peeling potatoes when it dawned on me — Dorothy! What are you waiting for? What if they are wondering if you will fight for your baby, and for Edward, too? If you are waiting for an invitation, it's never going to come. Go and get your baby!

I had dropped my knife, run into Mildred's room, burrowed through her underwear drawer, pulled a fistful of dollars out of a sock, whipped on my Sunday shirtwaist, grabbed my coat, then bounded all the way to the train station downtown on Baker Street, chilly weather be darned. I would prove to Mrs. Lamb that I'd do anything for my baby, that I was true to Edward, no matter what.

"Oh, no, ma'am. No husband."

Mrs. Lamb smiled with tiny possum teeth — one of the few things that stay little on a person. "Have you found employment? I remember you were quite good at laundering. Not afraid not to spare the bleach."

I thought I heard a baby's laughter. I jumped to my feet.

"Sit down, Dorothy."

"Is that June?"

"You must have heard the parrot in the parlor. Remember Socrates? That bird will outlive us all."

"Please, Mrs. Lamb, may I see her?"

"Dorothy. Dear." She fondled the cameo at her neck. "In light of the child's condition —"

Fire bells clanged in my brain. "Her condition?"

Mrs. Lamb stroked the cameo. "You can't say that you didn't notice."

"Notice what?"

"Her retardation."

My vision went red-black. The floor seemed to have opened up beneath me.

"Severely so. Surely you noticed."

No. No. June was bright and bubbly. She had been doing all the things that six-month-olds should: reach for things, laugh, roll over, make cooing noises. She was smart for her age. *Maa.* She even said *Maa.* She was advanced. Wasn't she?

I thought of her difficult birth. I had tried so hard not to push. Had she been hurt and I was too inexperienced to know it? Bile scorched up to my throat.

"It's only to be expected in her kinship situation. Babies born of it can die, if they aren't horribly damaged like your baby was. It's a very good thing that there are laws against it, don't you think?"

I thought I had not pushed. I replayed the birth, every agonizing minute of it, to see where I'd gone wrong. Sparks were shooting behind my eyes. "Against what?"

"I hate to acknowledge it, too. Believe me, I hate it more than anyone."

I was oozing terror. I could hardly hear her right.

"Edward is your half-brother."

My ears slammed open.

"What?"

"All those years, I pretended that I didn't know about my husband and your mother. I had no other choice. To expose them would only humiliate me. But then my own son, *my own son* —" Her voice was calmer when she resumed. "You can understand how much that hurt, can't you, Dorothy?"

It's true: when in shock, your mind does break from your body. It splits free and looks down on the scene that is threatening it. As I perched on one of those foyer chairs that was too uncomfortable for human use, my inner self left my body. It drifted over to the magnificent maroon-carpeted stairway, with its flame-shaped frosted glass lamp upon the newel post, where it looked down idly upon the poor wretch gaping at the former Pocket Venus.

The poor wretch forced out the words. "Does — Father — know? About me?"

Mrs. Lamb pressed the diamond of her ring to her mouth as if to suck it. "Heaven knows." She lowered her hand to her bosom. "He went along with it all those years. Maybe he just didn't want to see. I didn't, at first."

From the staircase, my inner self noted that over on her chair, the wretch was having a difficult time with speech. Drool pooled at the corners of her mouth as she fought to shape the words. "She said *Maa*!"

Mrs. Lamb lifted a brow.

"Let me — see her. Please!"

"Oh, dear. I'm afraid that's not possible."

Over her shoulder, her bridal-self gazed down apologetically as the current Mrs. Lamb made sure I was listening.

"It was best to institutionalize her, dear."

I watched myself jerk.

"There's a wonderful facility just for children of her kind. It's in Indiana, in Fort Wayne, to be exact. Maybe you're familiar with it, having lived in that little burg — the State School for Feeble-Minded Children? I have a good friend on the board there, a very good friend, indeed. He has assured me that your child has a permanent place there, for the rest of her natural life."

As the wretch choked back her vomit, my inner self coolly realized: that wasn't an apology, or shyness, or sweetness, on little Mrs. Lamb's young face. It was spite.

# THIRTY-ONE

*Indiana-Michigan Line, 1934*

Richard was in his element at lunch, regaling the family with his story about the disturbed patient who had eaten an alarm clock and Richard had to remove it. When Richard had opened the man and revealed his stomach cavity, the alarm was going off.

"True story!" Richard exclaimed. "I'm not kidding."

"Oh, darling." June glanced at Nick, who quickly lowered his gaze. He'd been watching her since she'd sat down.

"June, do your ad men at the flour company know other ad men?" Richard asked. "I could sell my testimonial to Westclox: Baby Ben was licked and yet it ticked."

"I don't think anyone would be interested," June said.

Nick leaned toward her. "What work do you do now for Betty Crocker?"

Over the scraping of thin spoons against

thick bowls, the family, minus Mother, who was sitting with John, turned toward June. Richard, so quickly deposed, frowned before he took a bite.

June wasn't sure how friendly to be to a fellow who was taking advantage of John's illness to dally with her sister. She wondered if he should even be there at the table. But she would rather not have a confrontation. Already the atmosphere was uncomfortable enough with everyone waiting for John's response to the medicine and it being so strangely hot outside, tightening the screw on this already-strained meal.

"Tell him what you do," Ruth said.

June smiled at her, peeved. "We're putting together a publication called *Let the Stars Show You How to Take a Trick a Day.* I just completed a photo shoot that illustrates how to set a table for an elegant supper."

Ruth burst out laughing.

The kids half-smiled at their mother, ready to get in on the joke if she'd explain it.

"You do see the irony," she said to June. She lifted her jelly-jar of milk. "To our elegant family!"

June blew out a silent breath. Curb your annoyance. Ruth was under tremendous pressure. "This particular publication mainly focuses on menus. Of course, there are recipes, too." And illustrated table settings, which she was in charge of, but she knew better than to elaborate on that now.

"Menus?" Ruth scoffed. "Just how many ways are there to serve flour?"

"You'd be surprised," said Richard.

June would not get defensive. "We're providing a service. A lot of women are looking for ways to make interesting meals. It gives them a chance to use their creativity."

"By aping —" Ruth made her voice dramatic. "— *'the stars'?*"

The kids turned back to June as if at a tennis match.

"Betty Crocker has helped a lot of women," she said. "She gives them something to think about other than —"

Ruth spread her hand to encompass the threadbare room. "This?"

June stared at her sister. She was spoiling for a fight. She must be terribly frightened — of John recovering, or of John not recovering, which, June didn't know. She found herself yearning to check on him. Was the medicine working?

Irene piped up. "I wish you worked for Betty Crocker like Aunt June, Mommy."

"I can't," snapped Ruth. "I have to run

this farm. Or would you rather move to town and lose all your cats?"

June stared at her sister. Was that necessary?

"Would we have a toilet?" asked Margaret.

"Would we have lights?" said Ilene.

Ruth wouldn't look at June. "We would not have a house like Aunt June's, so get that out of your head."

Richard lowered his fork. "Listen, how would you girls like to come stay at our house this summer?"

June flashed him a look of warning. He was throwing gasoline on the fire.

"You could watch home movies every night and swim in our pool. Did Aunt June tell you that we have a pool now?"

"The answer's no," said Ruth.

"You and John could come, too. Or you might like that time together here alone, once he makes a recovery."

"I said no."

"Mommy, please!"

"You can't have my kids, too," she snapped at June.

Just then Mother came bustling in, waving a spoon.

"He's up! John's up! He's talking a blue streak! Come quick!"

# THIRTY-TWO

*Indiana-Michigan line, 1934*

They had gathered around Dad's coffin just like this, Ruth thought. Mother's pale eyes had been glazed with the same bewilderment. The girls had been similarly shying back like stray cats. Richard had been considering the body with his typical medical detachment, a puffy-haired Dr. Tulp conducting an anatomy lesson for Rembrandt. Only now it was John who was laid out, on his back on his bed but alive, so much so that he was touching his nose at Richard's command.

"You should be up there," Mother told Ruth, standing in the back of the room with June.

Ruth eased forward a few steps. Richard reached back and grabbed her, then handed her next to John. The wife's place. Regardless if she had betrayed him.

"John?"

He turned his face to her. "Hi."

His wide eyes, his flushed cheeks, made her gasp. Was he really back? Miracles like this did not happen to her.

Behind her, June asked, "How long has it been now?"

Ruth heard the silken swish of Richard's shirtsleeve as he consulted his watch. "Seven minutes."

"Oh, he talked to me longer than that," Mother said.

"Why didn't you come get us sooner?" Ruth cringed inside as he gazed up at her. *Do you know about me and Nick?*

Richard stepped next to her, then cleared his throat into his fist. Give the patient's wife some room. "It won't take too much longer to finish examining him."

She moved aside.

Richard flipped down his head mirror and leaned over John. Outside the hot room, the sky had darkened. Mother lit the lamp next to the bed and was turning down the wick when Richard stood up, then patted John on the shoulder. "Hello, friend. Looks like you're back."

"Well." John cleared his throat. "That was some nap."

Everyone laughed, even the kids, who'd been hanging back at the door. The laughter of relief.

"You want to sit up?" Richard asked.

From the foot of the bed, Mother warbled anxiously, "How do you feel?"

"Good." John looked around the room as Richard helped him sit up. Her pounding heart deafening her, Ruth followed his view of the children squeezing hands, of Mother covering her mouth, of June, the yellow shoulders of her suit bunched toward her ears with anxiety. He stayed with June for a long moment before dragging his gaze to Ruth. "Alive. Finally."

Richard thumped his stethoscope over John's chest, then his back, listening. "Swing your legs around." He helped John hang his legs over the bed.

"Just a moment, big fellow, before you take off. I want to test your reflexes." Richard took his rubber hammer to John's knees. Each leg swung out in turn. "Excellent. I believe you're ready for a stroll."

Leaning on Richard, John trudged to the washstand, his bare feet scudding against the wood floor.

Ruth could see her children's open-mouthed astonishment, her sister's growing delight. What if this was just a flash in the pan? People could be getting their hopes up for nothing. How many times had she hoped and wished and prayed over the past eight years, only to be crushed. Counting on good things happening was a setup for pain.

"He's always walked," she snapped. "He just hasn't much. It has been too hard for him." Trips across the floor usually resulted in his sinking into a chair, dozing.

Richard guided John to Ruth, where he stood looking down on her.

"But I've never felt this good."

She looked away first.

Without Richard's help, he crept over to a wooden chair, where he carefully lowered himself and then held out his arms. "Kids. I promise — I don't bite." He glanced at Ruth. "Do I?"

June held her breath as John trudged across the stifling bedroom. Once he made it to a wooden chair, he grabbed the back, then, his lanky body quaking, lowered himself until he could drop. He grinned as if proud of his achievement. "Kids. I promise — I don't bite." He looked to Ruth as he opened his arms to them. "Do I?"

June saw her sister shrink into herself.

Anger flared. *Don't show him how guilty you are, Ruth. You owe him that much.*

June hugged herself as she stepped forward, smiling. "Don't trust him, children. I distinctly remember him taking a bite out of me, once, years ago. He's got terribly sharp teeth."

John showed his teeth to his children. "What do you think?" To June he said, "I'm sorry, Miss Crocker. I thought you were one of your cookies." He winked at one of the twins. "A sugar cookie."

The children giggled. Gap-toothed Ilene sidled toward his knee. "Daddy." She paused, as if shy about using the term. "How'd you know Aunt June is Betty Crocker?"

He shifted her on his knees. "Your grandmother told me. She likes to chat when she brings me lunch."

Mother and he regarded each other. "So you can hear me, after all."

He kissed his daughter on the top of her head. "Every last word."

"Thought so," Mother said.

They exchanged a look that June did not understand.

Richard brandished the arms of his stethoscope. "Five more minutes, John. Then you should rest."

"But I don't feel tired, Doc. I've got a lot to make up for. I've been lying here all these years, listening, watching, seeing everything.

Oh, how I've wanted to be with you all, but I've been as trapped in my own body as Poe's black cat in the wall — just like you said, Margaret."

"You heard me say that?" Margaret's adolescent voice cracked. "We were out in the kitchen."

"A body can hear just about anything in this house, if he listens. And I've been listening."

He dashed a hank of dark hair out of his eyes. "The things I've wanted to say! To you and you and you and you." He nodded to his children, each in turn. "Margaret, you're just like your mother, your nose always in a book. When you were reading the Boxcar Children books, no one could get a word out of you."

She straightened her wire-rim glasses on her freckled nose. "You knew? Those are my favorites."

"And Irene, you like kittens."

"So do I!" her twin exclaimed, not to be left out.

"I know, honey, but you like the chickens just as much. Even that ill-tempered leghorn with the broken wing. What's her name . . . ?"

Ilene chortled with self-recognition. "Flo!"

He paused at Jeanne, hanging her head.

"And you. Honey, I'll take over the worrying for you now, okay? Everything's going to be all right, I promise."

Tears wet the child's lashes.

Ruth started to leave.

"And you."

Ruth stopped. June had not seen her sister look so guilty since she was a toddler and had broken her mother's finger.

Nick put his head inside the door. "Knock, knock. I heard the good news." He extended his hand as he crossed the room. "Welcome back."

"To my own house, yes. Thank you."

A blush swarmed up Ruth's cheeks.

Richard rose from the edge of the bed. "Look here, good fellow, John only has a few more minutes until I insist that he rests. Maybe he should spend them with his family?"

Nick looked at Ruth, who glanced away.

June regarded her husband, facing down Nick with a good-natured smile. He really could be a decent man.

Nick was still retreating down the hall when John said, "Kids, your old man needs to get back in bed. But don't leave. I want you to tell me all about yourselves." He got up, then sagged back into the chair. June ran to support him.

Ruth brushed past them and out of the room.

"Ruth!" Mother scuttled after her. "Ruthie!'

At the bed, Richard received John from June, then waited for John to lower himself on top of the covers. As soon as John pushed his head back onto the feather pillow, Richard listened again to his heart.

He patted John's arm when he was done. "So far, so good. Congratulations, my good man."

John shook his head in wonder. "Thank you, Doc, for saving me."

"Don't thank me. I'm doing it for the boss."

Their gazes found June. She sank under the weight of them.

# THIRTY-THREE

*Minneapolis, Minnesota, 1926*

June had been married for four years when Ruth and John had made their second trip to see her and Richard in Minneapolis. Angling for a visit from the stork had been her full-time job then, although the actual act of mating took precious little of her effort, harried as Richard was at work. The rest of her time she spent feathering the Whiteleather nest, and entertaining friends and colleagues, to raise Richard's and her standing within their set.

She had gotten good at it, so good that as the other young wives had babies, their share of the burden of organizing events had slipped onto her empty shoulders. With the intensity that only an outsider possesses, she observed those whom she admired and then bettered them as if her life depended on it (which it did). She — she! — became the expert on what to serve at a yachting luncheon or how to set the table for a smart bridge buffet. Her friends would run to *her* wanting to know what to serve for an exotic patio supper (Mexican rice enchiladas and fruit) or how to make a standout table arrangement (try the new mirror place mats).

When asked these things, her gut response was always a frightened *How should I know?* before being Mrs. Richard L. Whiteleather, III, kicked in. What would her friends think if they knew that beneath the French twist hairstyle she had adopted from Richard's mother, beneath the pearls, beneath the frock shipped in from New York, beneath the feathered hats, beneath the carefully cultured accent (also lifted from Mrs. Whiteleather, who had in turn lifted it from the previous Mrs. Whiteleather), that she was the daughter of a recluse and a bankrupt? She intended for them to never find out.

That first Monday of Ruth and John's visit, Richard had taken the morning off from his work, unusual for him — he didn't like to unload his cases on his partner. He was also sacrificing his chance to bounce into his patients' hospital rooms after he'd freed them of bad gallbladders, strangulated hernias, and festering appendices, to receive their undying (literally!) praise. He guzzled down their love like a lush quaffed whiskey. But at least he actually deserved it.

Richard and June had gathered in the den with their visitors after breakfast. Richard sat in his oxblood leather wingback, with his feet — and June — propped before him upon the nailhead-studded ottoman. Ruth perched on the edge of her chintz chair. Next to her, long tall John overflowed his flowered chair like Lincoln in his new Memorial. Their two girls, not much more than toddlers then, were playing with Richard's antique pottery Staffordshire dogs on the floor before the empty fireplace from which the smell of ashes festered, no matter how much potpourri June had hid around the room. The little girls were making the cat-sized russet and white figurines, with their golden painted-on chains and human-like eyes, dance and sing like dolls. They were unaware that their uncle Richard had bought the dogs for a sum, were he ever to be gauche enough to divulge it, that was more than John's monthly income on the farm.

"What about the zoo?" Ruth was saying. "Would you girls like to go there?"

The oldest girl, Margaret, then three and a half and the bridge of her stub nose already sprinkled with pale freckles, set her dog down hard on the rug. Its permanently raised anthropomorphic brows seemed to lift in shock. "The zoo? With animals?"

June could feel her husband beaming his gaze on the dog. He recrossed his leather slippers. "I believe that the zoo might have a few of them."

Margaret shrank into her Peter Pan collar; up came the shoulders of her puffy sleeves.

"Do you like elephants, Margaret?" June said gently. "There's an elephant in our zoo."

Two-year-old Jeanne, suffering from a cold, sniffed at the glistening stream between her nose and mouth. "I want el-falents." She galloped her dog, its human's eyes wide, over to her sister's. The girls made whining sounds as their dogs greeted.

"Well, then, it's settled," said Richard. "El-falents it is." He patted June's back. "You should call Wally, see if he could give us a special tour."

Wally was their friend on the park board. Richard wouldn't do anything if he couldn't get special treatment while doing it, even going to a zoo. It was the Whiteleather way. June wondered if she would ever get used to it.

"Bet you could get him to let you feed the bears," Richard told the girls.

"Are there baby monkeys?" Margaret clinked her dog against her sister's.

Richard, watching his possession, cleared his throat. "I bet so."

Ruth put her cup on the coffee table then pushed it away. "How about we go to your country club? Isn't there a swimming pool there? Girls, would you like to swim?"

"Yes! Yes!" They raised their fragile pets in celebration.

June's gaze rested upon her sister's home-sewn dress and cheap orange lipstick. June had told her friends when she'd first joined the club that she was from a small midwestern town. One of them got the idea that her father owned a bank there and the notion stuck. Why had she not set them straight immediately? Why did she not tell them that her mother-in-law had taught her everything, that because she'd been left on her own so often as a child, she had been almost feral, her and Ruth, until Linda Whiteleather educated her.

"The water's cold," she said. "There's not much else to do there."

Ruth sat back in her chair and crossed her arms, the flimsy rayon of her sleeves scraping against the bulge of her midterm pregnancy. "Really? I imagine people playing shuffleboard and couples playing tennis, and once people have had enough mint juleps, everyone jumps into the fountain. Is there a fountain? Please say that there is."

John turned to his wife. "She said there wasn't much to do."

Ruth ignored him. "I want to go! What's it like, Richard?"

June looked over her shoulder. Richard's gaze was on the china dogs. "I don't know — lovely, I suppose."

June was not taking her sister to the club. What a disaster that would be! What glee Ruth would take in recounting their odd childhood in which all they had to eat for dinner so many nights was a bowl of cereal, a far cry from the luncheon buffet presided over by waiters dressed better than Dad had ever been, and that their mother, the opposite of a gracious hostess, had spent her life hiding inside their home. What boogeyman had Mother conjured in her imagination that kept her from going to PTA meetings, a Girl Scout tea, or just shopping at Wolf & Dessauer, like every other mother in town? All June ever wanted was a mother like everyone else's, or, short of that, at least a mother whom she could talk to.

Richard raised his voice. "Adela!"

Adela appeared with her braids crowning her head, the real queen of the manor. Her gauzy apron had been starched and ironed until it stood out from her dress.

"How about taking my nieces into the kitchen? Bake some cookies with them." Richard took his feet from the ottoman, got up with a crunch of leather chair, then squatted down with the girls. "Adela," he said, releasing the pottery dogs from their small hands, "makes magic cookies."

They cocked their heads at Adela, ready to believe. Little Jeanne's red chapped cheeks shone with mucus. "Magic?" When June had a child, she would never let her face get dirty like that.

"Oh, yes," said Ruth. "Magic Princess Cookies. You eat them and you turn into a princess." She shrugged. "If they don't work, you can always marry well."

*"Ruth."*

Ruth turned to her husband abruptly. "What? I'm joking."

John's voice was calm. "Not now."

"If June doesn't want us to go to the club for some reason — if she's ashamed of us —"

"Ruth. *Not now.*"

June slid her gaze to John. He received her coolly, his face stoic above the wrinkled collar of the same white shirt he had worn in Chicago four years ago.

Every cell in her body yearned to go over and tip her head against his chest, to tell him how sorry, how dreadfully sorry, she was. She had made the mistake of a lifetime in not marrying him, in not throwing caution to the wind and trying, somehow, to stake their places in the world together. She loved him, *loved him,* so much that if he did not hold her this moment, she might go irretrievably insane.

Her gaze drifted to the gold-trussed Staffordshire dog.

"I'll call Wally," she said.

At the Como Park Zoo in St. Paul, their friend Wally rechecked his pocket watch as they strolled between exhibits. He clearly had other work to do. June would have to take him a chocolate cake to make up for their intrusion on his time, once her sister and her family went back home.

Wally stopped before a cage reeking of urine where, behind thick bars, a black bear swayed miserably, swinging its great tan muzzle like a pendulum.

"This is Peggy." Wally put away his pocket watch. "We just acquired her. I understand that she likes to eat bread. Would you girls like to be some of the first to feed her?" He opened the small brown paper bag he'd been carrying.

Ruth's children took slices of white bread, hesitated, then heaved them through the bars, but "Peggy" couldn't be coaxed away from her inner torment.

Wally was soon released and the group moved on to a picnic lunch. They settled on a blanket, with John hugging his knees and Ruth plucking grass into a miniature green haystack. June was opening the basket that Adela had packed while Richard spun tales of the Winter Carnival — ice palaces built there in the park, soaring, translucent castles that shimmered with candlelight before they melted into a pool of nothing-ness — when a honeybee landed on little Jeanne's nose. Even though she hadn't been stung, she had a two-year-old's fear of bugs and couldn't be coaxed out of her hysteria, no matter how many times she was told that bees were her friends that brought her honey. If the group was to eat their sand-wiches in peace, they had to leave.

They piled into Richard's shining new Packard. Richard, a proprietary hand on June's knee, did his best imitation of a Swedish tour guide for Ruth and John in the back seat, their children in their laps. They glided past wide clapboard houses and awninged storefronts, past Richard's boyhood friends' comfortable pillared homes on Mississippi River Boulevard, and across the Erector Set trestles of the Marshall Avenue bridge from St. Paul into Minneapolis. Down the road on the other side of the river they breezed, until they came, at last, to the dense oak woods of Minnehaha Park.

There, lunch was demolished and a stroll was achieved, each married couple properly hand in hand, until a former patient accosted Richard and the girls went running off, leaving June watching the waterfalls with John. They had not been alone since she'd lived in Chicago.

June leaned against the bumpy river rock bridge, keen, it would seem, on the raggedy veil of water shredding before her. In truth, she was nearly immune to the earthy smell of moss and wet wood, to the constant gasp of the falling water. Every cell of her body was focused on John's hand, resting on the warm rounded stone next to hers. Energy crackled in the half-inch space between them.

A squeal from one of John's daughters penetrated her awareness. Ruth was running after the girls, who were tottering down the footpath along the stream. June wondered what her children would have looked like if she'd had children with John. She thought about this often.

"These falls are just as famous in winter," she said, "maybe more so, when they freeze into a solid curtain."

He frowned slightly, as if wondering why she would be talking about falls.

She blundered on. "People think it's a lark to pick their way across the icy ledge behind them. It's a Twin Cities tradition, you know. They say you have not lived until you've done so."

"Who's 'they'?"

She laughed. "Richard."

"Have you walked behind them?"

She shook her head. "I guess I haven't lived."

"I'd say you look like you're doing pretty well."

He lifted his head to peer beyond her, at Ruth, prettily swollen like a fertility goddess. She grabbed Jeanne's hand and they chased after Margaret until they came upon Richard in a bend in the trail, talking with the well-dressed couple who'd snagged him on the way to the falls. He greeted Ruth and the kids jovially, then scooped up Jeanne and put her on his shoulders, to her squealing delight. He was always a good sport.

"You look like you're doing well, too," June told John. "The farm sounds wonderful. Tell me about this new bull that you're going to go get in St. Louis." He was planning to go soon after he returned home. "Is it a special kind?"

When he didn't answer, she gave him a questioning smile.

He frowned at her. "June."

"I have to admit, I don't know a Holstein from a — a —"

"June, I've been wanting to say —" He waited until she saw he was serious. "June, I just want to tell you that I'm sorry."

Her chest tightened. "About what?" she said lightly.

"Don't."

She turned to the falls.

"Just let me apologize."

"There's nothing to apologize for."

He pressed the side of his hand to hers. "You know that there is."

She removed her hand. "I think it's best that you don't."

"You just want to leave it this way?"

How she loved looking at his face! "It has never been a matter of what I want."

She immediately regretted it. She shouldn't punish him like this. It had never been entirely his fault.

343

"There shouldn't have been that last time," he said. "You were with Richard."

"But I wanted it."

"Evidently not as much as I did."

She stared at the waterfall. The groan of water beating rock was relentless. "You were with Ruth."

In the near distance, Richard called, "Hallo!"

She flinched. She turned toward her husband, striding up the path toward them, happy as he often was after talking with adoring patients. When he reached her side, he swung his arm over her shoulders. "I see that it hasn't stopped yet."

She skipped a breath.

Richard looked at her, then at the spilling water, then back at her.

Of course. He'd meant the falls. She laughed, but not quickly enough.

# THIRTY-FOUR

*Indiana-Michigan Line, 1934*

It had beeen a long day. Dorothy lay on one of the grandkids' beds, her shoes off, with the crazy quilt folded back over her stockinged legs, hot as it was, like the pastry of the apple turnovers she used to make for Cousin Mildred. The murmur of voices, the loudest of which was that of her doctor son-in-law, wafted up through the floorboards. Downstairs, John and his family were having a reunion after dinner, now that he had been made to rest all afternoon, which was as long as he would tolerate. She couldn't blame him for wanting to make up for lost time. She would stay out of their way up here with Venus, who had settled on her chest like a sandbag.

She had thought that John could hear her all along. Though he'd rarely opened his eyes while she talked to him when she fed him, there was something about the way he held himself when she laid him back down after ladling in the soup that had led her to suspect it. He wasn't limp like a half-full sack of flour but was so rigid that he seemed to vibrate under her hands. Sometimes when she spoke, energy ran through him like a plucked guitar string, making his eyes quake and fingers tremble. He seemed to be fighting to get out of his body, such a horrible thought that it made bile rise to her throat.

But now a vitamin shot had brought him back to life. Well, they could use a miracle around here. She hadn't expected such a tremendous result when she'd told June that Ruth wanted her to come. She had just been trying to get June's help with Ruth, and here their John had come back to them. What good news for all the sleepers around the world! Think of them rising up from their beds, and of all the happy families, so glad to receive them.

Venus put her paw on Dorothy's lips. She lifted her hand to the fine rows of fur between the cat's ears.

The problem was, with John back, if their marriage was going to work, Dorothy needed to clear out. They didn't need some old woman lurking around when they were trying to find their way as husband and wife again. But how was she going to live alone? She'd never done it. William had spared her of it the one time she'd struck out on her own.

William. What greater power had led him to her in her hour of need? After a two-week courtship during which she'd stayed at his sister Edna's house, he had left college to marry her, a year shy of finishing his degree. She had never felt good about that.

She remembered when the two of them had moved into his parents' house in Angola, soon after they had gotten married — before Edna had died and left her house to them. They'd had trouble that day with the car that William had borrowed to move them. By the time they'd reached his parents' door, he was frazzled, fumbling with the doorknob while juggling the baby's wooden high chair and their suitcase.

William wasn't the only one who was awkward. Dorothy'd had trouble getting Junie in her little dress, even though putting clothes on Junie, as pliant and quiet as she was, was like suiting up a china doll. Taking on a baby and a marriage all at once had been tough on William and her. And her trying to forget Edward — that was no mean feat, either. Edward was always on her mind, even when she stood with her new husband on William's parents' doorstep, a ferocious expression on his long-chinned face as he wrestled with the knob.

She chuckled now at the memory of mild William, his hat knocked back on his head and his hair waggling in his eyes as he wielded Junie's high chair like a weapon. All he'd wanted was to make her happy and here he was making a mess of it. That night, even with his parents battened down in the next bedroom in their flannel nightgowns and caps, she'd made love to him with extra zest. Ruthie had come of it.

Venus pushed her paw against Dorothy's lip, this time with a hook of claw. Well, no use crying over spilled milk. William was gone now. Swiping her eyes with her arm, she pictured the object nestled in a browning shoebox below her. It waited for her beneath the mattress ticking and box springs of the kids' bed, tucked between Ruth's boxes of old photos and important papers. It was the one thing of value that Edward had given her.

No, that wasn't true — Edward had given her something of far greater value. He'd given her that which was most precious to her in this life, and yet she had let her be damaged. She kissed the soft leather of Venus's paw, the miniature sickle of cat's claw nearly, but not quite, piercing her flesh. The paw remained there, riding Dorothy's lip, as she murmured the part of her story that she could not, *she would not,* let another mortal bear.

# DOROTHY

The moon was prowling between clouds like a wolf through a herd of sheep, lighting up and then concealing the dour brick fortress of the School for Feeble-Minded Youth. I clung to the spiked iron palings of the fence, wondering how I was getting in.

I hoped that she wasn't on the top floor. The windows there were fitted with metal fire-escape tubes that swooped from the three-story building like giant ear trumpets. Did they just hurl the children down them when there was fire, like laundry down a chute?

Didn't matter. I was getting her.

I slipped through the open gate as a carriage shuddered its way out. Before the guard could see me, I was sneaking across the grounds.

Moisture seeped into my boots from grass spongy with melted snow and rain. A light peppering of sleet had begun zinging. I was picking my way through the slush, my heart whaling at my chest, when my shin rapped something hard. I stuck out my hand and caught a wet chain. A swing?

I kept going, past an abandoned band-stand, along the brick drive empty of carriages and wagons, to the front of the building with its forbidding rows of windows. The dark seemed to hold its breath. Or was that me?

A flight of concrete steps led into the central tower, where a gas lamp hung in the portal, its flame hissing at the night. I would march inside to whoever was in charge and demand to see my baby.

I trudged up the stairs, then heaved open the door, releasing a thrum of distant disembodied voices and the stink of Lysol and despair. The desk by the door was bare save for a greasy white plate piled with chicken bones. The wooden chair behind it was askew.

"Hello?" My voice echoed down the green plaster hall.

No one answered. I not so much walked as floated toward distant voices. Fear had disconnected my mind from my feet. I glanced in rooms along the way, my brain unwilling — unable — to process the horrors it was seeing: Iron rings on the wall.

Howling mouths. Flurries of limbs and hair.

*Keep moving,* I told myself. *Find somebody to help. Find where they keep the babies.*

An attendant burst from a room in a flash of white gown. I flattened myself against the wall as another flapped forth, then another. Their footsteps beat the tiny gray honeycomb tiles as they flocked to a room ringing with shrieks.

I felt invisible. Or dead.

Down more halls I drifted, and up a broad stairwell, going deeper and deeper into the bowels of the place, where the very walls seemed to contract and dilate with suffering. A sweet medicinal tang masked something pungent.

I peered through doorways, revulsion auguring through my gut. In some rooms, children sat on their cots, still as stones. In others, teenagers tore at their mattresses or at themselves. I saw trembling heaps upon the floor. Heaven help these poor lost children. How could people treat their fellow souls this way? But my baby was not among them. Had Mrs. Lamb lied?

There was one last room. Its door yawned open at the end of the hall. One last dip in, one last mortal blow to my heart, and I was done. Mrs. Lamb would have had her cruel joke.

I drew in a breath and plunged in.

It was in the corner. A single white iron crib.

My heart was pounding so hard that I couldn't see straight. Something was hanging down from the bars of the bed: four leather restraining straps, thick and flaccid as dead snakes.

I lifted my gaze to the mattress, where lay a small white-gowned figure. Its legs were splayed in the manner of porcelain limbs sewn onto the soft cloth body of a doll that had been dropped.

I leaned in.

She rolled her gaze up.

Those eyes. A kitten's eyes.

My heart jammed to my throat.

"Shhhh. Don't scream."

But June was as mute as glass.

## THIRTY-FIVE

*Indiana-Michigan line, 1934*

The hallway in her house smelled like rubbing alcohol. The smell of doctors. Ruth tried to remember if June's house in Minnesota'd had that odor when she and John had visited there the year he'd fallen ill, but all she could recall was the scent of rose potpourri and baking cookies and the stink of her own shame as she'd compared her threadbare life to June's elegant one. If she *really* wanted to hurt herself, she could let herself remember the reek of her anxiety as she watched John and June pretend that they weren't in love. But why would she want to do that?

Dinner had long finished. Out in the parlor, Nick was turning on the radio on the bureau. She paused in the hallway to observe him, enjoying his beauty as he stood back to let the device warm up. The tubes cast an orange glow on the flowered wallpaper as he stroked his chin; she could hear the scratchy sound of his beard. She knew exactly what that stubbly chin felt like against her cheek.

He looked up and saw her, his turquoise eyes scrunching with worry. "Are you all right?"

He didn't ask, "Is John all right?" He didn't ask, "Is your sister all right?" He asked, "Are *you* all right?" It was the right question.

"No."

He gestured with both hands for her to come to him. When she didn't, he frowned then went for the dial. He knew when to let her be.

"George Squibb was here," he said over the radio's whining and whooping. "He said we are to get a 'doozy' of a storm. We could get gusts of fifty miles per hour."

They both looked toward the window. Beyond the screen, the evening sky was decaying from gray to a dark olive green. The wind, the birds, even crickets had gone silent. The animal in Ruth cowered.

"We've got to bring in the stock."

He kept searching for a station. "He said it should be in here in a few hours. And something about it carrying a load of dust."

"Dust!" she scoffed. "We don't get dust.

355

Not this far east."

Muted trumpet music oozed from the radio. He dropped his hand from the dial and faced her. "Root, we must talk."

Anxiety shrunk Ruth's guts as she stared back at him. A woman was crooning on the radio.

*Don't know why*
*There's no sun up in the sky.*
*Stormy weather.*

"Are they playing that as a joke?" Ruth exclaimed. "Put on WOWO! Where's the weather report?"

The kids tramped into the room. Ruth glanced at Nick. No need to scare them yet. "Go upstairs." It was way past their bedtime.

Margaret looked up the stairwell. "Grandma's up there talking to herself."

The twins cocked their heads to listen, then giggled. "She is!"

Ruth flipped her hand at them. "Go give her someone to talk to."

They raced one another up the steps, not waiting to be told again. They weren't bad kids.

Nick watched them go then left the radio. "I can leave the farm if you want me to."

Ruth looked away. Eyes should never be that blue.

"Did you hear me, Root? I will leave, if you want. I never meant —"

Ruth glanced back quickly, ready to bristle. He never meant for what? For her to love him?

"I never meant to hurt anyone," he said.

*Life is bare . . .*

Ruth sighed. Why was that woman still bawling on the radio?

Nick waited until Ruth looked at him again. "I want to do what's best for you and for John."

Ruth's breath stopped. "You want to do what's best for John?"

"Don't you?"

She wanted him to say that he cared for her. That he wanted to do what was best for *her.* Then she would tell him to go, if that's what she had to do. She'd do what was best for her family. She always did. She just wanted someone to think she was special, just for a moment, and to fight for her. Then she'd do the right thing. Was that asking so terribly much?

Richard strode into the front room, all puffed out, big doctor man.

"Say!" he said over the music. "Could you be a good fellow," he asked Nick, "and take me to a telephone? John said there was one at a neighbor's."

Nick glanced at Ruth. "A bad storm is coming."

Richard scowled toward the window as the trumpets sobbed around their mutes. "It does look rather threatening out there. I'd better get the call in before the weather breaks, then."

"I will take you," said Nick, "but I must bring in the cows first."

"I'm afraid this can't wait, chap. It's rather important, you see. Ruth's husband's recovery is making medical history."

Ruth spoke up. "I'll take you."

"Would you?" Richard lowered his raised eyebrows. "That's a good sport."

"No, Root, do not go. It is too dangerous."

It did look like tornado weather. The very idea of tornadoes terrified the kids and it didn't do much for her either. "Maybe we should wait until after the storm passes. The Squibbs are probably already in bed now, anyhow."

Richard pushed back his sleeve to check his watch. "It's not even nine."

"Things are different out here in the country."

"Maybe your neighbors will forgive me when they hear what it's about. Who would want to keep the encephalitis sufferers around the world sleeping another minute?"

"Let me go, Root, not you."

It came out even more bitterly than she'd intended: "Don't you want to ask John if he approves?"

Ruth turned on her heel before Nick could answer. She saw how it was. He wasn't going to fight for her. Oh, she'd refuse him if he did, she had to, she knew that, but couldn't he at least make an effort for her? No man ever had. Even her husband had only married her because he had to.

"Don't forget to bring in JoJo," she snapped over her shoulder.

"I do not forget nobody!"

She walked away. *Prove it.*

The pitcher was getting heavy in June's hands. She needn't be holding it. She could have put it on the floor, like she had the washbowl that went with it, but she did not know what else to do with herself. Richard was writing notes at the makeshift desk he'd made out of the washstand; Ruth's kids were at the foot of John's bed, fidgeting with one another, giggling, and shoving. Only little Jeanne stood apart, sucking on her hair as she hugged herself. They didn't know how to act, June realized. How scared and confused they must be of John, now sitting up on his bed and talking with them. He was a stranger to them, a new head of the household who'd been suddenly dropped into their lives. Not even the oldest of them would likely remember life with an active father. All they'd ever had was Ruth.

He sat forward, quiet for a moment. They stole surreptitious glances at him.

"Girls, tell me what your favorite subject is in school."

They stared at him before the oldest one mustered an answer.

"Art."

The others followed.

"Art."

"Art."

"Reading."

He smiled at the reader, Jeanne. "What's your favorite book?"

The others answered for her with their own favorites.

"*Wizard of Oz.*"

"*Wizard of Oz.*"

"*Wizard of Oz.*"

"*Velveteen Rabbit,*" she said.

"That's a baby book," a twin objected.

She hugged herself tighter. "I like it."

"I do, too," said John. "Poor rabbit, wants to be real but can't be until he's loved. I've always had a soft spot for him."

"I like scary stories," Margaret offered.

"Hence the Poe," said her dad.

Margaret nodded, as did the twins, who were unlikely to have read any Poe. "I like Washington Irving, too," she said, perhaps showing off a little. " 'The Legend of Sleepy Hollow' is creepy. That Headless Horseman — brrr!"

The little ones, no more apt to be familiar with Irving than Poe, were still nodding in enthusiastic agreement when Jeanne said, " 'Rip van Winkle' scares me."

John regarded Jeanne a moment. "It does?"

When she didn't answer, June put down the pitcher and cut in brightly. "Now I'm going to have to go back and read it. Was it that frightening? I can't remember how it ended after Rip van Winkle awakened. Happily, I'm sure."

"No, it doesn't," said Jeanne. "He doesn't like his wife. He is sorry that he woke up."

Richard looked up as if alerted by a change in the room.

"Maybe we ought to let your father rest now," June told the girls.

"That's not necessary. I'm fine." John's face, pinched with exhaustion, said otherwise.

"Isn't it your bedtime?" June asked Margaret.

"We usually would have been in bed an hour ago."

"There you go," June told John. "Case closed."

"Betty's a bully." He winked at his daughters. "Goodnight, girls. See you tomorrow."

The group bolted for the door as if slingshotted. They'd only been looking for an excuse.

June could hear them talking in the hall.

"Grandma's up there talking to herself."

"She is!"

They giggled until Ruth said something inaudible, then June could hear them tramping up the stairs.

John faded back on the bed and closed his eyes.

Richard put his notes in his bag and got up. June moved to leave with him.

"No," he told her. "You stay. Someone should be here with him while I go make a call, to make sure he rests. He's going to have to take it easy at first."

"A call? They don't have a phone."

"I'll get that Nick character to take me to a neighbor's."

She glanced at John, eyes still shut.

"Don't go, Richard!"

"I have to. This kind of news can't wait. We may have made a breakthrough which could affect thousands of patients. Imagine how many families this could put back together."

John spoke without opening his eyes. "He's right."

"You." Richard thumped John's arm. "You just lie here and take it easy. Let Betty Crocker take care of you."

"Mmm," John murmured. Within moments, he was breathing softly with sleep.

"See?" said Richard. "Piece of cake, Betty."

*Cake!* She dropped down on the chair, annoyed, only to jump up when the screen door slammed in the kitchen. Out the window, she could see Nick striding off toward JoJo in the pasture, his lantern a blue glow in the falling green light. Ruth, with her own lantern, stalked to the machine shed, a sudden gust whipping her dress around her knees. She threw open the doors as Richard approached, medical bag in hand, his badge of importance.

June sagged onto the chair next to John. Don't be so hard on Richard, she told herself. Everyone needs a badge of importance, some way of being special. Everyone craves respect, whether we realize it or not.

# Thirty-Six

*Chicago, 1922*

It was ninety-one degrees, hot for early summer in Chicago. The sun drew sweat to the faces of the people milling on the beach in bathing suits, street clothes, or coveralls, and radiated from the dirty sand baking June's bare feet. She glanced at John, toeing the sand next to her, and shivered.

He had shown up at her Three Arts Club rooms that afternoon, where she had been packing. She was to stay with the White-leathers for the rest of the summer, an arrangement to which she'd agreed only when Mrs. Whiteleather had offered it. She had taken the train from St. Paul the previous week to get her things. Richard would be collecting her tomorrow.

"Knock, knock," someone had called through the half-open door. "I hear that there's a famous artist up here."

The blood left June's head. John. She

hadn't spoken to him since the night at the Dil Pickle. She didn't think that she ever would again, nor did she think that she ever wanted to, not since Ruth had let drop that she was corresponding with him.

Her traitor body tingled at the sight of him filling her doorway. Levelly, she said, "Why are you here?"

He ducked his head. "Ouch. Well, I guess I should have expected that."

His black hair was raked to perfection; his white shirt ironed and buttoned to his chin in spite of the heat; a new fedora hung from his large, slender hands. An edge of her heart softened to see him trying so hard.

Her roommate, Norma, sashayed over in her kimono. "Want me to get the house mother?"

"No. That's not necessary. I think he'll do the right thing and leave."

"June, could I please just talk to you?" He stopped, his face earnest. "Just as a friend."

Somehow, several howlingly awkward minutes later, she and John were walking down the frying sidewalks of Tower Town. And somehow — June didn't really know how — several minutes later, in the course of which she'd shed her filmy jacket (a present from Mrs. Whiteleather) and he'd unbuttoned his collar and removed his hat in the heat, they had made their cautious amends. Somehow, by the time they passed bony children flinging themselves into the blast of a gushing fire hydrant, they were giddy with relief. By the time they'd reached the Oak Street Beach, they were good old friends, if by good old friends one meant friends who kept touching each other's arms as they reminisced, friends who laughed a lot at nothing, friends of which one was engaged to Richard.

At the beach, it was as if the skyscrapers looming over the neighborhood had been split open and both sand and humans had come tumbling out. Men in trunks and singlets flirted with women in head-wraps and bathing dresses. Old women in flowered frocks knelt over picnic baskets, doling out sandwiches. Little children hopped about like toads.

Directly before the wall that the two good old friends had found at the edge of the beach where they could sit and dig their bare toes in the sand, a drama was unfolding. A policeman had stopped two young women and, his jacket straining over his portly belly, was now on his knee, huffing and puffing as he applied a tape measure to the bare thigh of first one girl then the other.

"What's going on?" John whispered to his

good old pal.

*Do not let yourself be so happy.* "Decency law. Six inches are allowed between the bottom of a woman's bathing suit and her knees."

From the feet up, the women were covered with bathing slippers and sheer knee socks. But above their knees, their bare thighs — one set thin and stringy, the other chunky with muscles — gleamed like beacons in the dark sea of wool and cotton worn by the other women on the beach.

"I think they're in trouble."

*If only I could burrow into his arms.* "Oh, he'll just send them home. I've seen it before. The offenders are given blankets, then they usually run off, giggling."

As if June's words had ordered her up, a police matron in black dress, stockings, and prim pumps struggled across the sand with a holey green army blanket opened to receive the miscreants. The commotion attracted a crowd, whose excitement grew as the girls dodged the blanket like bulls through a matador's cape.

The burly officer laid fingers thick as cow's utters on the skinny girl's arm. She wriggled from his grip as the matron grasped the other girl and fought to cover her.

"You want to dress like a man?" A by-stander tossed a frankfurter into the melee. "Be one." The wiener bounced from the skinny girl's arm, leaving a smear of mustard.

"Hey!" yelled her friend.

The policeman took advantage of his quarry's momentary distraction to lock her in a squeeze hold and hoist her off her feet. To the cheers of the crowd, he carried her kicking from the beach.

John caught up with June as she stalked away. "That was ugly."

When he could see her face, he said, "Hey. Hey, I'm sorry. We should have left sooner. I can see that it really bothered you."

She couldn't keep the words in. "She reminded me of Ruth."

He winced.

What had she been thinking, imagining that they could be friends — or whatever they were. Ruth would always be between them.

"June. I said I was sorry."

"Let's forget it." She started back to her apartment.

"Look, I bunged things up six ways to Sunday. I know that. But we can do something about it. That's why I came to see you. We don't have to just go along with the way things are going. We can be honest with Ruth and Richard right now. Let's tell them. As soon as we get back."

She stopped. "Why do you have to tell Ruth? I thought she was just your pen pal."

He took off his hat, and then fit it back on. "I don't understand. Don't you want to get back together? Isn't that why you came out here with me?"

"The fact is, Ruth kissed you. And you kissed her."

"That was nothing. It was stupid. I told you that."

Ruth had seen something in him that had encouraged her to kiss him that night. Ruth was smart. She wouldn't have imagined that.

"I don't think she thinks it was stupid. I don't think she thinks that at all."

She pushed ahead, past two little girls holding hands and skipping, past a mother steering a rubber-wheeled baby buggy, past a man selling ice cream from a cart.

"June," he said, following, "is this punishment? Are you punishing me because of a meaningless kiss? Because if so, it worked. I've been miserable since then."

"That's not why."

"How many times have you kissed Richard? My having to picture that — now that's punishment. You can really dole it out."

She slowed. There was some truth to that. She was punishing him. He'd not paid enough for having hurt her and she was making him bleed. Deep down, she could be terribly cold. She didn't know why. She hated this about herself.

"June, let's not be like this. If I can get past your getting engaged to a rich guy, then you can get past me talking to your sister."

She stopped again. "The problem is, I admire Ruth. She's the most honest person among us."

"I admire her, too, but — June, I'm in love with you. I love you, June. You know that I do."

She glanced up at the mansion behind him, then at the seagulls lined up on the peak of its roof. She would never live in a place like this with him. But maybe it didn't matter. Maybe that was the least important thing in the world.

"I love you, too. I really do. You're all I think about."

Relief, then gratitude, then joy dawned across John's face, mirroring June's own growing elation. He was stepping toward her, his eyes rich with affection, when a horn blasted.

Richard puttered his open roadster to the

curb. "Junie! Your roommate said I might find you out here. Johnny, what are you doing in town, old man?"

He didn't wait for John's answer — he might not have gotten one in any case. John was staring at the idling car with disbelief.

Richard hopped out and opened the door for June. "I left last night and just drove straight. I about hit a deer in Wisconsin!" He kissed her on the cheek. "I couldn't wait to see you."

Every nerve was screaming as she got in the car.

"How are you, darling?" Richard jumped back into the car. "Here, let me help you put on your jacket. You coming?" he called up to John.

She put one arm into the sleeve of the filmy wrap and then the other. She looked up at John. *Claim me. I'm yours. But you have got to claim me.*

"Not coming?" Richard let out the clutch. "Whatever you say, friend." He applied the gas.

# Thirty-Seven

*Indiana-Michigan line, 1934*
Ruth treadled the floor pedals and wrestled the wheel as the wind pummeled the Model T. She squinted her eyes. Was that a *crate* tumbling through the beams of the headlights? What in the world was she doing out in weather like this — with June's big-shot husband, for crying out loud? Blasts were whistling their way through the seam of the windshield, snatching at the flared fenders, shoving the flivver off course. At least her brother-in-law, jouncing against the fraying gray-and-white-striped upholstery next to her, had the sense to shut up and let her drive.

He straightened his fedora and raised his voice over the ruckus. "Do you normally have weather like this down here?"

The car's lights swept across a field where tiny tornadoes of dirt were rising up from the furrows like gritty spirits. So much for the seed she'd planted! She leaned over the metal dashboard to look up through the windshield. Her headlights caught birds huddled together on the electrical lines, dozens of them. Gusts blew off stragglers, who then beat their way back to safety.

She threw herself back. "Not really!"

The lights illuminated weeds thrashing in the ghostly light along the road, then lit a mass of hips and hooves — a herd of huddled cows. Squibb should be getting them in the barn. Ruth wished she'd grabbed John's old jacket at the door. The temperature must have dropped twenty degrees in the past fifteen minutes. Richard had better get his phone-calling done quick.

He raised his voice over the wind. "I thought you'd be glad about John!"

She raised hers, too. "I am!" She thought about it. "Thank you!"

Headlight beams approached. The Model T lit up an expanse of chrome grill, coming on fast. Another touring car? Out here in this mess? You had to be kidding!

When its long hood slid close, Ruth peered inside the windows. The driver appeared in the shadowy light, hat pulled low. Ruth waved as they passed. He kept his face pointed forward.

"Who'd have a car like that out here in

the dark," she wondered aloud to Richard, "in this weather? He can't be up to any good." She swallowed. "Did you know that Dillinger has been around here? He was in Auburn, not twenty miles away, recently."

She looked at Richard when he didn't answer.

"I didn't know about the hired hand," he said.

Her anxiety dropped like a curtain; heat leaped up in its place. So that's what this was about. Well, he sure picked fine weather to chastise her in.

"I suppose it was natural," he said.

Richard cut into people for a living. She supposed he'd seen it all. Maybe storms didn't scare him, or crooks out on the roads, or adulterous sisters-in-law. All right. Let him ask her what he wanted, if that made him feel better. Get it over with. Just let her get back to her kids.

"He and I haven't done as much as you think."

He clutched at the door as a blast shook their vehicle. "That's not what I was getting at."

She glanced at him. "If you're trying to make me feel bad, forget it. Trust me, you can't make me feel any worse than I already do."

"I'm not trying to make you feel bad." He bumped along on his seat. "I'm not trying to make you feel anything. What I'm trying to tell you is that I understand."

She turned to face him, swerving the car. "Are you cheating on June? Because you'd better not be."

"Say — be careful! No. Although I'm not sure if she would care."

Good grief, she did not want to talk about whatever was eating him. Especially if it was problems with his pecker. Not out in this ridiculous weather — not ever, to tell the truth. "She loves you."

"Loves me? She doesn't even talk to me."

The Squibbs' dog Scraps bounded out to chase the flivver as Ruth muscled their way nearer to the Squibbs' house. "Don't take it personally." Darn dog! It was going to get itself hit. "June has never talked to anyone about her feelings much. Not even me. She's the most bottled-up person I ever saw."

"Most bottled-up, or the most angry?" He rocked with the car as the wind buffeted it. "I am not a psychoanalyst. But I do know that the most suppressed people are some of the angriest. I sometimes worry that she's angry at me." He laughed. "I suppose at times I can be a little irritating."

Ruth gave him a baleful eye.

"But I've come to see that she's not really miffed at me. She keeps to herself with everyone, including our friends and the women at her work." The wind splatted a newspaper against the windshield, then ripped it away. "Now you say that includes you, too? She loves you more than anyone."

She didn't want to hear that. She surely did not believe it. Not anymore. Not after what she'd done with John, and all the years that had passed. "That's just June for you. She's always been that way."

"Why? Why has she always been that way?"

With Scraps in the lead, Ruth turned off the road and onto the wheel ruts in the grass that constituted the Squibbs' drive, then along a tall hedge of privets that noticeably buffered the wind, reducing the racket within the vehicle. She neared the house, a tall white board affair skirted with latticework. A light was on in the kitchen.

With a metallic gnash of levers, she shut down the car. She lowered her voice with the reduction of noise. "It's because of my mother, I guess. She wasn't a talker, either."

"Then why aren't you that way?"

"You mean not angry?" she said. They both laughed, which made her a little mad.

He took a handkerchief from inside his suit coat then offered it to her. When she shook her head, he dabbed his own brow. "I just thought if I cured John —" He tucked back his hanky with a flash of stitched monogram. "— that she'd be happier with me. Silly of me, I know."

She stared at him. He was scared. This man, brazen enough to slice up people for a living, born with a silver spoon in his mouth, dripping with looks and charm and smarts, used to getting his way in everything, was scared. If this man was scared of June, there was no hope for anyone.

She wanted to change the subject but she had never been nimble at polite conversation, so she just scowled at the key in the ignition. Why wasn't he getting out?

"You know that we've wanted children," he said.

"Ha, take all of mine that you want."

He smiled as if he understood why Ruth would say such an outrageous thing that she obviously did not mean, which burnt her up.

"It has been a painful subject," he said. "One of the reasons I leaped when your mother called was that I thought if I could do some good for you and John, it would lighten June's heart. I had been keeping an eye on the work my colleagues were doing with sleeping sickness, so when they had their recent breakthrough, and then Dorothy rang, I took it as a sign. And now John is well. Everything is meshing."

"Mother phoned?" Mother never used a phone due to the expense, whether a collect call or otherwise. She must have been desperate to see her favorite.

"Ruth, I'd do anything for June —"

"Ha, I've been hearing that line all my life."

"— especially since I'm the reason we can't have children."

Wait a minute. They were having two different conversations, and his had just become the more interesting.

"What?"

He wouldn't repeat what he said, just looked at her. What kind of fool would expose his underbelly like that?

"Does she know?"

He put his doctor bag on his lap. "No." He drew in a breath. "I should have told her a long time ago."

"Why didn't you?"

"I don't know. Ashamed. Guilty." He tugged at his hat. "Afraid that she'd leave me." He slid his gaze at her. "I think you know that I was never the one she loved the most. I've always been the second-best."

Behind his head, the Squibbs' porch light came on.

She scowled at the house. "Aren't you going to make your call?"

He looked over his shoulder, then turned back. He drew in a long breath. "She has a right to know, Ruth."

What'd he expect her to do about it?

He exhaled loudly. "I had better go help the sleepers. Think how this cure will change lives."

She grabbed the door handle. "Oh, trust me, I have."


Dorothy opened her eyes. She'd only meant to rest them after the kids had come up. Fear froze her heart — the kids were still awake. For the love of Mike, had she talked in her sleep?

Wrapped in the patchwork quilt like the wiener in Betty Crocker's "Pigs in a Blanket" concoction, she kept her eyes shut and let her ears do her walking. She listened to dice being rattled in small cupped hands before bursting onto the wooden floor, followed by the tapping of tokens against cardboard and her granddaughters' exclamations. Junie had brought them what was called a Monopoly game — brand-new and all the rage in Philadelphia, according to her doctor son-in-law, who had received it from a patient. People were so enthusiastic about things being all the rage these days. They just chucked out the old without a second thought and brought in the new.

Like with horses. Seemed like only last week that the streets in town were full of them, and now, *poof!* they were gone, as if lifted up by angels and borne away, their hooves dangling down from their knobby knees.

Nothing these days was like it was. Radios blared in every home, telling you how to be and which new products you just had to have to achieve it. You worried about not buying the right kind of toothbrush, soap, or flour. Who knew that unless you used deodorant, you drove folks away with your body odor, until the deodorant makers pointed it out? Who knew that you were supposed to douse your nether parts in Lysol according to the ads, in order to ensure your "dainty feminine allure"? So far, Dorothy hadn't tried it, and she strongly hoped her daughters wouldn't.

She ought to get up. Tell the kids to go to bed. It was way past their bedtime, and they were burning through the kerosene. But she felt oddly immobilized, like a bug being wrapped by a spider. Maybe it was the strange cold wind whistling through the screen. Things were banging around outside. Get up! Something bad was coming.

But then her mother's face came to her, harsh beneath her lace cap. *Just lie there and shut up.*

So good little girl Dorothy folded her hands and did just that, as her grandkids played and radio music wafted up through the floorboards. How she yearned to go downstairs and see Junie. Just looking at her would suffice. Dorothy never took that privilege for granted. Yet she had let Ruthie go out in this weather and she could feel it in her bones — something terrible was going to happen tonight.

Dear God, forgive her. For the honest truth was, she had never worried about Ruthie enough.

# THIRTY-EIGHT

*Indiana-Michigan Line, 1934*

June opened her eyes to John lying on the bed, smiling up at her. He pushed himself onto his elbow. "Hi."

She scrambled to rise from the chair next to the bed. How long had she nodded off?

"Am I that frightening?"

"Of course not. It's just that you surprised me." She brushed at the smear on her yellow skirt. "I didn't mean to fall asleep. I was only going to rest."

"Thank you *for* falling asleep. It was nice having the shoe on the other foot, watching someone else sleep for a change." He grinned. "Actually, it was a treat."

She felt a niggle of guilt, as if fraternizing with John was betraying Ruth somehow. "How long was I asleep?"

"I'm not sure. Less than an hour."

"Where are the kids? And Ruth? She'd gone with Richard to make a phone call."

The laughter of children came from the distance.

"Well, there's your answer about the kids." He frowned. "They're up late."

"Maybe I should go put them in bed."

"No. Your mother will do it. She's a pretty good egg."

She glanced at him.

"She has kept me from going crazy," he said.

*"Mother?"*

He smiled at her as if deciding whether to elaborate. "Let the kids be. They must feel discombobulated. They've just had the rug pulled out from under them."

"They are celebrating," she said firmly. "Their father is back."

Cold air blasted through the bedroom window. The temperature had dropped significantly. She went over and pulled down the sash.

"The radio's on. Maybe Ruth's already home." He shook his head as if amazed. "I don't have to wonder about it anymore, do I? I can get up and go see for myself."

"Yes, you can. Shall we?"

She helped him out of bed and down the hall with her hand on his back, conscious of his warmth under his shirt as they walked along. Tension vibrated between them like a clothesline in the wind.

The radio was playing in the empty parlor when they got there. The room, with its balding velveteen rocker, its faded flowered armchair under the floor lamp, and its buffet with peeling veneer, was a still-life painting of failure, of chances and hope lost.

"They aren't home yet." June left him leaning against the armchair and retreated over to the radio. "I shouldn't have let her go."

" 'Let her go'? Have you met Ruth?"

June smiled.

On the radio, three young women harmonized about the joys of eating Pep Cereal.

John braced himself on the back of the chair. "I wonder if it's still part of the Hollywood Breakfast."

"Pardon?"

He shook his head.

The commercial finished with a flourish of clarinet. The program resumed.

"I've got to give Ruth credit," he said suddenly.

June waited.

"How she has held this place together after the hand I've dealt her is nothing short of heroic."

June became aware that she was holding her breath. She exhaled. "Your illness was not your fault, John."

"Doesn't matter. The result is the same. I ruined her."

"You didn't ruin her. She has the kids, the farm. She has you."

"Some bargain I am."

"Some would kill to have you."

They glanced at each other. She should not have said that. But she did not know how to act. He was once everything to her and now he was to be a distant brother.

He gazed around the room. "The place hasn't changed. I can't wait to take a walk around the farm. There's so much to do." He shook his head. "I still can't believe that I'm standing here." He grinned. "I still can't believe that *you're* standing here."

"What was it like, John?"

"When I was ill?"

"I'm sorry. Maybe I shouldn't ask."

"No. I can talk about it." His measured speech failed to hide his anguish. "What it was like, was like being nailed inside a coffin, and banging, banging on the lid day and night but no one ever comes. I wasn't kidding when I told the kids that it was like being bricked up in a wall while still alive — how did Poe know how that felt? He got it just right. He knew how murderous I felt."

He noticed her face. "I'm sorry. I must

sound like a madman. But, frankly, I *was* mad. It drove me insane to hear my little girls, playing and laughing, and be powerless to reach out to them. Do you know how excruciating that was? I was just a lump on the bed to them — I don't think they thought I was fully human. And now I've come back to life." He gave a dry laugh. "I must terrify them."

She came over and squeezed his arm. "They are happy. They'll show you — give them time. You're here, now, finally. How strong you are! How did you ever manage to survive?"

He glanced at her hand, then spoke as she removed it. "The first few months, I made up messages in the Morse code that your dad taught me."

"Dad taught you Morse code?"

"Rowdy Dowdy taught me a lot of things."

"Dad," she sighed.

"I tapped out code with one finger. Even with my eyes closed, I kept it up all day: *dot dot dot dash dash dash dot dot dot dash dash dash —*"

"SOS."

He looked at her pointedly before continuing. "And then I realized — no one understood. They thought I had a tremor! The more I tapped out the distress signal, the more they worried about my palsy. Ruth even called back the doctor."

A clock ticked as if bearing witness.

"I went into a depression after that. I was at the bottom of a deep black narrow well and no longer tried to get out. I kept thinking, June would have noticed. June would have known. June would have saved me. But she'd been banished."

She looked away. All those years, she'd never come. She'd not been there for him in his time of need, not even as just a friend. She hadn't been banished. She'd been a coward.

"Seasons passed. Leaves fell, and then the snow, and then later, much later, I became aware of the girls playing outside, of the calling birds, of the smell of sunshine on the grass. I began to let myself think again, calming myself when I panicked by figuring out what new crops to grow, what I was going to do around the farm when I woke up, or ways to fix the house. Throughout this time, your mother was talking to me. When she fed me, she told me about herself. She told me about you." He studied her a moment before going on.

"I arranged her stories into a longer one, fictionalized it some, until it had shape and meaning and a kind of music. It became the book that I'd always dreamed of writing."

"That's wonderful."

"I've spent the last few years telling it and then retelling it to myself, drilling it into my brain. I was determined not to forget it, so that I could set it all down on paper as soon as I got well. I guess I can do that now."

"Yes. You can."

"But I always come back to the same thing."

She lifted her eyes.

"To you."

*No, John.*

"I'm just telling you the truth. After all this time, can't I just tell you the truth?"

Jazz violin drifted from the radio.

"Maybe you shouldn't."

"You're thinking of Ruth," he said. "Well, I have thought of her, too. I heard everything, June. I could open my eyes at times, you know. I could see things a man shouldn't have to see."

"She didn't know," June said softly.

"That I could hear her? Is that supposed to make it better?" He gave a bitter laugh. "Maybe that makes it worse."

She turned her head.

He stepped closer. "I've made you feel bad. I'm sorry." He squeezed her hand then laughed. "I forgot that I can do this."

She slipped her hand from his. "Hurting my sister is the same as hurting me."

"Am I hurting her? I don't think she cares enough about me for me to hurt her."

"Oh, John, she cares. I promise you. She cares."

A note of hope crept into his voice. "Do you really think so?"

With sudden clarity, she saw that Ruth mattered to him, a great deal. In the years that they'd been together, through all their hardships and joys — admit it, they'd had joys — Ruth had supplanted her. He needed Ruth. As maddening, wrong-headed, and absolutely irritating as Ruth could be, he leaned on her, whether he could admit it to himself or not.

They both looked upward at a sudden thumping on the ceiling. The children were playing in their room. They heard the murmur of her mother talking to them.

They pulled their gazes down to each other.

"How do we do this?" he said.

"I don't know."

A muted trumpet sobbed through the radio.

" 'Moonglow,' " he said. "I've heard this song from my bed. I've always wished I could dance to it."

Gently, she said, "You can, you know."

"I forget — it's a brave new life." When he held out his hands to dance, his voice was rich with affection. "Milady, would you care to?"

He took her by the waist, then cradled her hand and rested it against his chest. She looked up at him until tears, foreign to her, threatened to rise, and then she laid her head against him.

His heartbeat muffled the voice of the singer. *It must have been moon glow / Way up in the blue . . .*

Their feet barely moved on the wooden floor. He whispered, "I should have married you. I should have claimed you. But I was so damn proud. If you'd just said the word, if you'd just said that you'd leave Richard and come to me —"

"But, John. You didn't ask me to leave him."

"I told you that I loved you that day at the beach. What more did I have to say?"

"You went away, and you didn't come back."

"I thought you wanted me to go."

She felt his heart pounding under her cheek. If only he *had* claimed her. But he hadn't, so she'd stayed safely with Richard. And then she had heard that he was with

Ruth, and Ruth was pregnant.

The sob of muted trumpets swirled around them, enveloping them in sweet sorrow.

She burrowed back into him. Their feet scarcely moved as they swayed as one. This was all they had.

Remember this moment. Remember.

# THIRTY-NINE

*Indiana-Michigan Line, 1934*

Dorothy ran her thumb over the truculent lone hair under her chin. She could just make out the singer on the radio downstairs.

"No fair!" Irene shouted.

Dorothy started, then listened as the child's siblings calmed their sister. She had taken exception to Margaret buying something called "Park Place." Irene, prickly like her mother, Ruth, though not yet eight years old, would make noise about her disagreement. She was sturdy like that.

Well, all the girls needed to be sturdy now, now that their dad was awake. Dorothy suspected the girls were up here hiding from him. She should have made them go to bed, but she supposed that they were all stirred up from his awakening. She didn't blame them. He was a stranger to the twins, and all of a sudden he was supposed to be special to them. That would take some adjusting. To the older girls, he was something even scarier — a real dad now instead of the dream dad they would have created from the haze of their early experiences. Thinking of your parents as people was hard enough in any circumstance.

She pictured her own father when she was a little girl, up in their rooms, dressing to serve dinner to the Lambs. How handsome he was in his long black tails and with those bushy red side-whiskers! She saw his head tilted down in concentration as he poked a cuff link through its slot, his muttonchops glistening like chipmunk fur. She wanted to stroke them, but she never could, of course. She never touched him, nor he, her.

She'd been so proud of him! It never occurred to her when she was young that he was lower in rank than Mr. Lamb, even when her mother scolded him for drinking milk out of a cereal bowl, or for walking around their quarters in his undervest, or for sweating when serving a party of fifty, and other "ungentlemanly" offenses. Dorothy thought he was perfect. She loved to watch him read his newspaper in his chair under the floor lamp, his side-whiskers gleaming and his brown eyes frowning at the print.

One time while Dorothy was studying

him, he surprised her by grabbing her mother when she walked by — surprised her mother, too, by the sound of Mother's squawk. Father had pulled her into his lap and kissed her neck until they saw little Dorothy laughing, and then Mother had jumped up and fled and he had gone back to his reading. Dorothy had wished she'd been the one who'd been pulled onto his lap. But she never was.

No wonder she didn't know what to do when William was affectionate after they were married. She thought at first that it meant he needed male release, so she braced herself for relations. It was the least that she could do in repayment for his kindnesses, and sometimes he did make it feel rather fine. But to her surprise, often he just wanted to pat her shoulder, kiss her hair, or squeeze her hand, *just for the sake of doing it.* Once she understood that, she was grateful.

She never did know how to give him a little pat, though, just to pat him for the sake of patting him. She would have liked to. She even thought about it, hovering around him, wanting to reach out, coaxing herself to touch him.

But she was stopped by the fear that he'd want something more from her, more than relations, something that she didn't know how to give, and so she kept her hand to herself, even as another layer of loneliness poured over her heart like liquid rubber.

Something thudded against the side of the house. "What was that?" cried one of the girls.

Everyone paused to listen to a deep howling in the distance. An attic timber popped.

The girls shuffled in a herd to Dorothy's bedside.

"I miss Granddad," said Margaret.

Jeanne put a bedraggled hank of hair in her mouth. "Me, too. He'd make it go away."

All four nodded, a symphony of fresh skin, dirty bobs, and worried faces.

"How?" said Dorothy. "How could he make a storm go away?"

Quick to be the authority, little Irene, always her mother's daughter, spoke up. "He'd tell us a story."

"Like what?"

She raised her chin to recite. " 'Elgie met a bear. The bear was bulgy. The bulge was Elgie.' "

"That could make a storm go away?"

"If that didn't work, he held our hand."

Dorothy gazed out over this little crowd that shared her blood. They didn't ask her to tell stories. They didn't ask her to hold their hands. They didn't even consider it. She could lift her quilt now and invite them in, even as she peeled up a corner of her frightened old heart. But what if they refused to come?

The far-off roaring seemed to ease. Margaret pulled at Ilene's wrist. "Hey, it's your turn." She dropped to her knees over by the board game, as did her sisters. "Where's the other dice? Who's got the other dice?"

Ilene plunged under the bed then crawled back out. She opened her child's soft palm. "Here!"

The dice skittered across the floor. Dorothy lowered herself by degrees back down to her pillow, back into the bitter smell of feathers. They probably wouldn't have come to her, anyhow.

The wind banging her skirt against her legs, Ruth gave the crank a good yank with her left hand — never with her right unless she wanted that arm broken if the engine backfired — then jumped into the stuttering car. She had left Richard inside the Squibbs' tidy house with its lattice-skirted porch. Ethel Squibb was still stuffing him with oatmeal raisin cookies, payment, in general, for his finding the cure for sleeping sickness, and in particular, for opening an impromptu nighttime clinic for her family. He'd made his important call and now he promised to check on her little Alvin, sick in bed with a cough for two weeks now, and on her little Teddy with the leg that would not heal, and to lance a boil on Squibb's back. Even half-awake in gowns and night-caps, they worshipped him, which he gobbled up more greedily than the cookies. Anyhow, Ruth didn't have time to wait for him to finish, especially after they started grilling him about life with Betty Crocker. The storm was ugly and it hadn't even started raining yet. The Squibbs would take care of him. She had to get back home.

She wheeled the car in a circle, avoiding an empty bushel sent rolling across the yard and the wooden clothesline prop that had been knocked down into the grass. When she nosed the trembling flivver from the high hedge of privets onto the road, the wind seized on the car immediately, shaking it like a dog with a toy.

She nursed the old sedan along in the dark, hoping, all the while, that Nick had gotten the cows in. He'd be good with them, gentle with Boss as he led her in so as not to panic the herd. He was gentle with Ruth herself like that — to keep her from panicking, she thought with a laugh, and then frowned at the truth of it. Nick knew what a prickly pear she was, yet he was kind to her. It was a marvel. She hated to let him go.

But she had to. If John and she had any chance, he could not stay. She wouldn't wait to find out what John knew about them — she'd go right to John and beg for forgiveness. She'd been stupid and weak and out of her head with anger and fear. She loved John, had loved him since she had first laid eyes on him when June had brought him home. There *was* such a thing as love at first sight — she'd felt it. He was her sister's beau and yet Ruth knew that he would be her own husband the moment she saw him, as improbable as that seemed. No one took a man from June, especially not her star-crossed sister with the bad reputation and the even worse moods.

But Ruth had.

The headlights sifted over the weeds slapping around on the roadside and to a structure of logs — the cabin John's great-grandfather had built. How the house still stood after storms like this one was a mystery to her. What was keeping the logs stacked that some tough pioneer had wrestled there years ago, when much of the mud chinking had fallen away and the roof had bowed? Sheer memory of standing?

A gust swept dirt from the road, spraying it against the windshield in a gritty hiss.

The barn doors were bolted shut when Ruth wheeled into the yard; the chicken coop was sealed tight. She was aiming the car for the machine shed when she saw Nick, standing at the foundation of the house, peering into the parlor window.

That was peculiar. Surely he had the sense to go in during this kind of weather. He'd left his lantern on the back porch. Upstairs, a lamp was burning in the kids' room. They weren't in bed?

She parked the car then dashed to the house though it wasn't raining yet.

Nick snatched up the lantern and blocked the door.

"What's going on?" she panted.

The lantern light gave his face the look of one of those sad drama masks, all down-turned mouth and eyes. "It is probably nothing."

She couldn't seem to catch her breath. "What is nothing?"

He shook his head.

"Why are you out here?" She moved to get past him.

"Root, wait."

"You're scaring me!"

She brushed by his arm and pushed through the door.

By the light trickling in from the parlor, she could see that the kitchen was empty. Radio music drifted in from the parlor. She strode to it.

When she burst into the room, June lifted her head from John's shoulder. They were pressed together like lovers.

June felt John jolt. Ruth stormed into the room.

She hardly had time to lift her head before Ruth demanded, "What are you doing?"

June ironed the guilt from her voice. She had nothing to be guilty about. She was dancing with a lonely man before she went back to her own husband. "Where's Richard? Is everything all right?"

"Maybe I should be asking you that."

"It's all right, Ruth."

"If you must know the truth," said John lightly, "she's doing me the service of propping me up."

"Is that what you call it?"

John reached out to her. "Ruth, come on. Don't."

"Don't what? I kept the farm going for you. I kept this roof over your head. I kept your kids alive. I did everything — for you."

"I know you did. We all know you did."

Ruth turned on June. "You. You can't stand for me to have anything. Why is that?"

"That's not true."

"But you love to give to your poor little sister the charity case, don't you. I bet that makes you feel big. Miss Generosity."

"I wish you wouldn't do this, Ruth."

"I'm not pathetic, June. I may not be Betty Crocker, but there are people who respect me. There are people who know I will do whatever it takes. Some people lean on me, hard — your own bigwig husband, even. Do you know that he came to me just now with his tail between his legs? I don't know why he would expose himself like that." She hiccupped with a laugh, as if realizing she'd inadvertently said something funny.

"What are you talking about?"

"Oh, nothing. Go back to your dancing."

John steadied himself against the armchair then raised his head. "You don't have to make trouble like this, Ruth. It doesn't have to be this way."

"What way?"

"Just let people love you," he said wearily. "When you're not pushing us away, you are lovable, you know."

"Ha. If you actually believed that, you wouldn't have to say it."

"Ruth."

"Well, I have news for you — for all of you. People do love me." She paused as if searching for examples, and then sputtered, "Our kids do! Our kids are angels. They're the best thing that ever happened to me." She gave June a pointed look. "Too bad you can't have some of your own." She laughed humorlessly. "Funny, the one thing the girl who has everything wants, she can't have. It's a sad state of affairs, isn't it, when even if you're perfect, you can't get what you want."

"That's enough," said John.

"I do feel bad for you, Junie. I take less joy from your situation than you'd think. All this time, you blamed yourself. Turns out that you weren't the one who was at fault."

Something inside June went icy. "For what?"

Ruth shrugged. "Ask Richard."

Nick edged into the room. Seeing June's stricken face, he laid his hand on Ruth's shoulder. "Root, what are you doing?"

She looked up at him, then pulled back into herself.

"She has been so tired," Nick told them.

Ruth sagged against him. "Get me out of here."

"Where, Root? You are home."

Her voice had fallen to a whisper. "Just get me out."

"But, Root, a storm is coming."

John pushed off from the chair as if to go to her. "Ruth."

"No!" She clutched Nick's arm. "Please." Her voice was small. "Help me."

He bowed to June in apology. "I must help her. She is a good woman. She is only tired."

He led her away, as does a father guiding a child.

"I'll go get her." John took a step, then buckled against the chair. "I guess I'm losing steam."

June blinked at him through the silent screaming in her head. *She was not to blame. Ask Richard.*

# FORTY

*Indiana-Michigan line, 1934*

June could remember it like yesterday: she had just received a doll for her seventh birthday. It had a beautiful porcelain face and dainty dimpled porcelain arms and legs sewn to its stuffed cloth body; its white eyelet dress was as fine as a rich lady's. Best of all, and when June tipped it forward and back, its eyes opened and closed. She was doing just that, enjoying how it seemed to wake up and see her, when Ruth began to beat her own cloth doll (handed down to Ruth moments earlier), whacking it against the floorboards.

"They won't open! It won't open its eyes!"

Such a fierce little beast her sister was, June had thought, wild as a tiny kitten kicking and biting your hand in deadly play. It didn't know that you could kill it with a blow.

Now June stood at the window and listened to the wind battering the farmhouse. She heard snatches of Nick's voice as he led Ruth through the kitchen, and the muffled thumping of the kids upstairs. When the back door slammed, John pushed himself from the chair against which he'd been leaning then lumbered over to June. She felt his calming presence by her side. After a moment he gathered her to him, as would a friend who was helping a friend. They began rocking unselfconsciously to the music on the radio, like little children trying to comfort themselves.

After a while, she shook her head in wonder. "It's not me."

He kept rocking her as if they had all the time in the world.

"He let me take all those tests. Do you know the humiliation I felt? But that was nothing compared to the loss." She shuddered with a sigh. "I grieved each time I was told I was barren. I had to change my whole world order, rethink who I was, how I was going to spend the rest of my life. I had to think of myself as a lesser person —"

"But you weren't."

"Oh, I know that now. But that was how it felt." The wind moaned outside the windows. "Why would he tell Ruth that he was the cause? Why didn't he just tell me?

Big-mouth Ruth, of all people."

"Maybe that was the only way he knew how to tell you."

She pulled back to look at him.

"He must have wanted you to know, June, but had been afraid of losing you." He smiled ruefully. "Fear rarely brings out the best in people."

She drew in a long breath. "I think this might have done it. I think he's actually ruined us."

"Only if you want that."

He wiped under her eye, where tears would have been, then spoke as would a father to a beloved child. "Why are we so quick to probe the wound of what we don't have, when we should be marveling at what we've been given?"

She searched his face and, when she did not find refuge there for her anger, laid her head back against his chest. They resumed their wordless shuffle, dancing on as the wind scratched at the house.

Time had passed, June didn't know how much, when John faltered, stepping on her shoe. His voice rumbled in her ear against his chest. "Sorry. Did I hurt you?"

She shook her head, loath to put any distance between them, as if she'd glimpsed the future and letting him go would hasten it.

His words reverberated in her ear. "I guess I'm — I suppose I'm tired."

She pulled back and looked hard into his face. Exhaustion tinged his features with lilac.

She squeezed the alarm from her voice. "You've pushed it too hard. You can't expect to build Rome in a single day."

He smiled wearily. "How about a simple temple?"

"Not even a hut. Time for bed, young man."

Rubbing his back companionably, she walked him to the bedroom.

"Don't let me sleep too long," he said as she tucked him in.

"I won't."

"I'm serious. I've got to make up for lost time."

She kissed his forehead as if he were a boy. "All right."

He pulled her down to him. "I hate this bed. I'm so lonely, June. Don't let me be alone."

"I won't." She unwrapped his arms from her then slid in next to him.

He opened his eyes. "Thank you."

"I love you, John. I want you to know that."

A stinging filled her eyes, fueling the lump in her throat. A tear burned its way down her cheek, then plunked onto the pillow. So this was how it felt: it relieved even as it hurt.

"I've always loved you," she said.

"You don't know," he said, his voice slowing, "how happy that makes me."

Her bleary gaze fell upon the photograph by his bedside. Tinted by Mother, it was of Ruth, raw-boned and young in a yellow cotton dress and with a pink rose in her hair, a fierce smile on her awkwardly pretty face. She was trying so hard to look bold that instead she looked vulnerable. From the earliest age, June sensed that for all of her bluster, Ruth was the more fragile of the two of them. Yet in spite of it, she was the fighter, the rock. She was all of eighteen in the picture, June guessed. The year that she claimed John.

"June." John's voice was thick now. "You'll be here when I wake?"

He was beautiful when he rested, his face unclenching, the calm creature within the man unmasked. How dear he looked, patient and serene, his goodness purified by unfathomable suffering. She touched her lips to his cheek — he squeezed her in automatic response. Of course Ruth had fallen in love with him. He was so much like their dad.

"And Ruth will be here, too."

"I know," he murmured. His lips could barely move, his energy winding down. "I can always . . . count on Ruth."

Later, the wind was snatching at the house as she rose from John's side. She drifted out into the parlor, where the music was still playing, and then she slumped upon her sister's chair.

# FORTY-ONE

*Indiana-Michigan line, 1934*

What had she done?

The wind thrashed Ruth's hair and clothes as she threw open the door to the machine shed then stalked to the car, chased by the memory of her behavior. She groaned as she saw herself pulling at Nick's shirt, scrabbling for his pants, grabbing for his face, as the animals sheltering in the barn with them had stirred nervously.

Nick had fended her off. She had fallen back on his cot, the cot in the same corner in which John had curled the day their lives had stopped, and then Nick had stood over her. Even in the lantern light, in the pale blue glow that had robbed his eyes of their color, she had seen it all over his face as he looked upon her: sheer and utter pity.

She couldn't stay there. She couldn't stay anywhere on that farm, no matter if a tornado was hitting and smashing the place to pieces. She was going back to the Squibbs' to get Richard, the damn fool, her fellow fool.

She regretted it the instant she steered the T past the convulsing hedges and into the open. She should not have left the kids. Dirt, plucked from the road, browned the headlights and pinged against the fenders. A limb skidded across the hood. When something thudded behind the car, an animal sixth sense kicked in. It detected an unnameable vibration, far-off but nearing, like that of a distant stampede or the slithering of thousands of heavy-bodied snakes. Yet rain was not falling. Lightning did not strike. Save for her puny car lights, nothing dented a darkness so thick that it lived and breathed.

She railed into it like a child kicking the shins of a giant. "John! Damn you! You wake up and go for my sister the minute I turn my back. Couldn't you have waited *an hour*?"

As if in answer, a blast radiated up from the floorboards, bouncing the T on its springs.

"Great! *Great!* Well, I guess I deserve it."

She clung to the shaking wheel. A glance in the rearview mirror showed her hair reaching for the ceiling of the car, where it dragged along the upholstery like the trolley pole of an electric bus.

She shrieked then clubbed at her hair, and then she noticed a high-pitched hiss. She held her breath. Was the air leaking from a tire?

Her eye caught movement near her head: dust was seeping between the window frame and the glass. She shot glances around the compartment: it was sifting through the seam of the windshield onto the dash. She moved her foot. Little piles were heaping at her feet.

Just then, in the mealy glow of headlights waxing and waning through the dust, a wan blade caught a flash of white. A signpost. The crossroad. She could turn around.

Home!

She groaned with yearning even as, quietly, the failing beam was snuffed.

An acrid powder parched her nose. She sneezed, then sneezed. Her throat was closing up.

Unseen things banged against the idling car. In her mind's eye, she saw the newspaper photo of the black wall of dust boiling over the little town. She pictured cattle falling to their knees, their breath pinched off, people flailing, deer leaping, as the dust rained down.

Over this nightmare, another vision formed. She saw a pioneer axing a tree, then struggling to raise rough logs: John's family homestead. If only she could get there.

She nudged the T through the whirling darkness. Six more inches, ten. Keep going, keep going.

*THUD.*

Her nerves shot through her skin.

Every pore jangling, she gave the T gas. The wheels just spun. She threw the gear stick into reverse.

The tires screamed powerlessly — and she along with them. She rammed her shoulder to the door and shoved, bellowing in fury, until, like a cork from a jug, out she spilled.

Grit swarmed her instantly, needling her skin, stinging her eyes, invading her lungs. She snatched up the skirt of her dress, held it over her head, then staggered against the wind until it knocked her to her knees.

She crawled, hacking, as her mind floated from her suffocating body. *Why, your life really does flash before you when you are dying!* she marveled calmly, while, as if it were a movie, she watched Mother jump up, slender and beautiful, holding the finger that the toddler Ruth had just broken.

Now here was Dad, pinching together his lightly furred thumb and index finger to form a ring so that clever little Ruth could show that she could slip her hand right through it.

Oh, now there was John. So strong, lean, and young, smiling down on her from the tractor.

And there was she herself, poor her, bearing down under the gripping pain of her first childbirth. Nothing had prepared her for that agony. But nothing had prepared her for the miracle of that first gaze between a mother and the stranger coming from her own flesh.

An arm hooked her waist. She was being jerked into the present, forced unwillingly from her life-show, dragged back to join the living. A man choked and hacked in her ear as the wind pummeled them. She was still reuniting with her body, trying to make sense, striking out when the blow —

In spite of a distant grinding that Dorothy could not identify, her eyelids were sinking shut. She should be getting up to put Ruth's kids to bed, but she was being done in by the rhythmic bounce and snatch of one of them playing jacks while the child waited her turn at the Monopoly game. Rhythm or movement had a way of lulling Dorothy to sleep in minutes, the product of spending most of the first two years of her life being hauled along in a baby buggy as her mother worked in the Lambs' house. To this day, the twilight of Dorothy's consciousness before sleep was often accompanied by the sensation of being jiggled in a buggy and the image of her mother's annoyed scowl from under her frilly white maid's cap. Her mother's pretty face, twisted in an ugly frown, was gazing down on Dorothy now as she felt her arm being shaken.

She opened her eyes to little Jeanne. With her long chin, though softened with a child's creamy skin and brown calf eyes, she was the very image of William.

"Grandma! It's scary outside!"

Crunching a particle of grit between her teeth, Dorothy hoisted herself upright. Land sakes, the wind was beating on the house. How had she ever slept through such a commotion?

She slipped into her pumps and shuffled to the window, the girls huddling behind her. She couldn't see anything in the pitch dark.

She looked down. A little cone of dust was piling on the windowsill like sand in an hourglass.

"Down to the basement!" she roared. She shooed the girls. "VENUS!" Oh, where was that cat? "VENUS!"

She trundled after the kids as fast as her knees would take her. Arcane images came to her agitated mind: her paying the life insurance man last week, watching as he had rubber-banded her dollar to the cover of his book and then recorded her payment in it with a stubby pencil, putting her one step closer to allowing her daughters to bury her with a little nest egg leftover for the grandkids; her scrubbing the little girls' stockings over and over, to get them extra white; scouring the dishes after dinner as the rest of the family gathered in the parlor — the things she did for the ones she loved. It was all that she could offer them.

Bubbly clarinet music was bouncing from the radio as she herded the children through the front room. Their footsteps rattled the oil lamps on the tables. She heard her own fearful voice: "Ruth! June!" She remembered John was awake now. "Johnny!"

Where were they? Where was Richard? Even that Nick — where was he?

June came charging out of the back bedroom. "Mother! I can't wake John!"

The girls stopped in their tracks. Dorothy pushed them toward the basement. "Go! I'm coming! Hurry!"

Wiping her hands on her apron, she

turned to June. "Now what about John?"

June stared at her, a small smile on her face. Dorothy knew that look. She was frantic.

Dorothy bellowed at Jeanne, lingering at the top basement step. "Get down there!"

"Grandma, but what about —"

"Get!"

Jeanne trampled down the stairs.

"Let me see him," Dorothy demanded.

"I was out here letting him rest but when I went back to check on him, he wouldn't open his eyes."

"He does that sometimes."

"Yes, when he was ill!"

They entered the bedroom to a sound like hundreds of mice scratching at the windows.

"John!" Her voice was a wild warble. "Johnny! It's Dorothy and June. June is here! I know you want to see June."

The truth of that hit her. He did want to see June. More than anyone, and even Ruth knew it.

Groaning along with the house, Dorothy shook his arm. "John! Get up!"

Now June and she both shook him. He was warm and breathing and as heavy as a log.

"Johnny," she pleaded, "please wake up."

"Go!" June snapped. "Go be with the kids."

Dorothy nearly lost her grip. June had never yelled at her before.

"Get going, Mother! Why are you still there?"

June didn't know how much it killed Dorothy to leave her. She had sworn all those years ago that she would never leave her girl again. She inched down the dark hall toward a sinister hissing and whooping — the radio, its signal lost. Already disoriented by the thumping outside the house and by the banging of her heart, the alien keening unmoored her.

Strange visions welled up in the gloom. The flowered chair now held Father, waiting for her to bring her baby. The floor lamp with its branching arms was the infant June, reaching out: *Maa. Maa.*

For years, Dorothy had awakened in a sweat, thinking Mrs. Lamb had come. She'd race to little June's bed, her heart in her throat like it was now, to touch her. Only the warmth of little Junie's skin could calm her galloping heart.

But the child she had stolen back was not the one she had given away. Oh, she might have looked the same, with her honey-blond curls and those kitty-cat eyes, but *her* baby laughed and cooed and reached for things. This one was as expressionless as a china doll. No wonder she celebrated each of June's milestones after she got her back as if the child had won the Paris Olympics. Ruthie must have wondered why her own accomplishments were met with so much less enthusiasm.

Through the otherworldly whining and sobbing on the radio, cut a series of short bleats. Morse code?

Just like that, William was with her. He was standing over her at his desk in their bedroom back on Parnell Avenue, where she spun a dial on his crystal set — too roughly, and she knew it.

"I can't get it!" She rose with a scrape of chair legs, forcing him to stand back. "I don't have time to learn this. I need to pull those weeds in the moss roses while the babies are still sleeping."

His voice was as mild as ever. "That's fine, Dorothy. But before you do, give this one more try. I know you have an itch to travel. Well, here's how you can go around the world without ever leaving home."

She was envisioning herself satisfyingly plucking weeds from the dirt as he tapped on a call log penciled with entries. "I've talked with people in Pennsylvania, New

York, and Connecticut. Even some fellow in Florida. Once I get a little more money put aside, I can get equipment that will connect us with Europe. How do you like that?"

Her idea of connecting to Europe included eating spaghetti in Italy and clattering around in Dutch shoes, padding through English castles, and zipping around in gondolas. She wanted to see how the Old Masters lived, to have their paintings in the Cincinnati museum come excitingly to life. Edward would have understood this.

"How will you know their language," she scoffed, "once you connect with them?"

"We all speak the same language here, Dorothy — Morse code. It's universal. Know the code and you can talk to anybody on earth."

She had jumped up, nearly toppling the spindly chair. "Those weeds aren't going to pull themselves."

He never did buy that equipment. There were shoes to buy for the girls, the roof to patch, tires to be put on the truck, the rusted coal chute to the furnace to repair. Sometimes their belts were drawn so tight that she thought she should sell her music box. But she didn't.

And then William was gone.

She could feel his spirit now as she stood

in the darkened room. He reached out to her, a smile lengthening that chin. "We're not dead yet, Dorothy."

"Don't say that, William!" she bleated into the cacophony of wind and electric shrieking.

He drew her close, then smoothed her hair back from her temples, the way he knew to do. She inhaled his personal brew: pepper, soap, and whiskers. Comfort poured over her, filling her, warming her, radiating its light until it flowed through her eyes as tears.

A muffled yelp burst from the distance. "Mommy!"

Down the tunnel of time Dorothy plummeted, past her water breaking with June, past William leading her to his sister's, past the birth of squalling Ruth, past the long, bleak years in which she'd raised her children — the years during which she made herself survive, grimly as a soldier at war. Wasted years. The best years.

"Grandma!" The little girls were calling from the basement.

Her eyes burst open.

She trundled toward her grandkids as fast as her bum knees would take her. She patted her way into the kitchen, where she fumbled through the cupboard behind some

Ball jars for a flashlight. She switched it on then hobbled down the steps.

How had she never known how much she loved him?

# FORTY-TWO

*Indiana-Michigan Line, 1934*

Ruth awoke on her back. She beat the air, gasping for breath, as she fought to open her eyes — a mistake. Daggers of grit dug into their tissue.

She squeezed them shut and rolled to her side, where she barked until her lungs were raw. Eyes still closed, she reached up to gingerly probe the sore spot beaming from the back of her head. All she could smell was dirt.

A man said, "You're awake."

Her eyes flew open. Pale light swam through her watery vision. Dawn had come? She was digesting that fact when she found the stranger sitting across from her.

"Hello," he said.

She scrambled upright then crab-crawled away from him until she bumped into an obstacle. She patted its splintery surface — a log wall — then pushed herself against it.

She realized: it was quiet. The storm had passed.

"You've been out cold. I feared that you were going to stop breathing."

She flicked glances around the empty room, afraid to take her gaze from him. They were in the homestead. Her skin prickled: Had he hit her and dragged her in?

"That was certainly quite the tempest. One for the history books. I don't think anyone was safe."

Her children! She jumped up only to be whomped back down with a black mallet of pain. She held her breath as her sight gradually came together, and with it, pieces in her fractured mind: the big car tooling around the farm; headlines about the robbery in Auburn; someone vicious enough to strike a lone woman in a storm.

She blurted, "I know who you are!"

"You do?" He sounded surprised. He moved closer.

She shouldn't have told him that. She wasn't thinking straight — her head wasn't right. "Stay away!"

He began coughing into a handkerchief — starched linen with a monogram. She couldn't read the letters before he wiped his mouth and folded the square. "I guess your mother told you a few tales."

Not any more than anyone else talked about this killer.

Wait. How'd he know about Mother?

"I suppose you and I had the same idea," he said, "ducking in here."

Had he hurt her? Had he hurt the kids? Her heart raced as she calculated how to make a run for it.

"Well, I'm glad. It gives us a chance to chat. So what has Dorothy said about me?"

He knew her mother's name.

Her heart stopped.

She blinked to clear her vision. He looked far older than in his pictures in the paper. Jowlier. With a lion's golden eyes within a sunburst of wrinkles and a mane of white wavy hair. A life of crime must have aged him terribly.

"Look, whoever you are, I won't tell anybody I saw you. Just let me get back to my kids."

He cocked his head at her, tucking his handkerchief in his breast pocket. "Who is it that you think I am?"

"Never mind."

"I know who you are — Ruth."

The hair rose on her neck. She gritted her teeth to keep them from chattering. "What do you want?"

"You know." He started coughing again.

"I don't, Mr. Dillinger."

His cough rang higher. "Dillinger?"

"Just leave me alone. I'm not any trouble to you."

"I've been called a few things in my day, but a bank robber wasn't one of them."

She flicked a glance toward the open door.

He followed her glance. "I don't think you're in any condition to drive. For that matter, neither is your car. I'm afraid that you drove into a ditch."

Tears singed her throat, already raw from coughing. "Why are you doing this?"

"You know the saying, 'Better late than never'?" He gazed at her with those leonine eyes. "Has your mother ever mentioned Edward?"

# FORTY-THREE

*Indiana-Michigan line, 1934*

You could tell that this man named Edward was used to owning things, like his brewery and half of Cincinnati. He seemed to think he owned Ruth, too, that she should be grateful to hear the horrors he had been dropping into her ears over the past half hour. Her mind, already sideways from the blow, was bent further askew with each disorienting detail. Now he waited for her response with crossed arms and his thick chin up, aristocratic and arrogant in a crisp blue suit even while sitting on the cabin floor with his legs flung out like a toddler. Bad knees, he'd said.

"Are you sure your mother did not mention me?" he asked again. "I find that hard to believe."

She would have shaken her head but that hurt. How was it that this man wasn't covered with dust, propped up there on the floor, whereas Ruth felt like a human smudge, with her arms and hands and even the fabric of her dress coated with it.

"As you can imagine," he said, "I've been very anxious to get to know June."

"Is this before or after your mother took June from my mother and put her in the State School?"

His Adams's apple rippled the grainy skin under his chin. "I told you I had no control over that."

Rub her tongue over her teeth all she wanted, she couldn't get the dust out of her mouth. "I grew up across from that place."

"I know." He shuddered. "Nasty business, that. I've heard the residents wailing."

"You have? You were there?"

"Perhaps she told June about me, but didn't tell you. You would think she would want June to know so she might claim her heritage. I've been expecting June to look me up, although she has done remarkably well on her own. She's a Lamb through and through."

"You've been close enough to the State School to hear the kids?"

"What? Yes, I suppose so."

"Then you must not be okay with June having been committed to that place."

"As I said, that was my mother's doing,

428

not mine."

"If you've heard those kids, you must have seen them, too. You must have seen them clinging to the iron bars of the fence, or swinging all day, as shunned and forgotten as lepers. My neighborhood friends weren't allowed to talk to the 'tards' — their word, Mother wouldn't let us call them that. Kids were instructed to look away if they had to walk by the place. If a State School kid escaped, everyone hid, adults and children alike. Only my mother would go out to try to help them. The neighbors thought she was crazy." She gave a dry little laugh. "She let us believe it. She never defended herself."

He brushed at his sleeve. "That would be Dorothy, so refreshingly pure and simple. I like to think that her simplicity might have shielded her from some of the pain in her life. One can't feel what they don't know to feel."

Was that why Mother kept to herself? A lack of emotion? She was too naive to feel?

Ruth struggled to her feet, her head still swimmy. She had to get back to her kids. Thinking about their panic set her nerves on fire.

He looked up at her, his legs still splayed before him. "Well, endearing naïf that she is, Dorothy must be commended for figuring out a way to extract June in relatively short order. That took some cunning. I secretly cheered her on, even as my mother sent out Pinkerton detectives to find her and the child."

She put a hand to the wall for support. "You mean your child."

He ignored the comment. "They never thought to look under their noses, just across the street. Actually, that was clever of Dorothy. Dorothy was much more clever than Mother ever gave her credit for."

He rose with a groan and a crack of knees. "I would have never known where your Mother and June were, had she not written me. She trusted me." He brushed off his pants. "It was several years after the child was born. She signed it, 'Your Long Ago and Faraway Friend.' We never really got over each other, you understand."

Ruth grimaced. He really didn't see how she might find him to be objectionable.

"You wonder why I'm telling you this," he said.

No. She wondered why she was listening.

His thick chin went up a notch, nudging his lion's mane over his shirt collar. "Among other things, I've regretted my decisions. I'd like to tell your mother that. I'm man enough to admit my mistakes."

She muttered, "So you want to drag down June while you're at it."

He caught her gaze with an aggressive stare. "I hardly call acknowledging my paternity 'dragging her down.' " His smile was proud as a king's. "If she has not heard the good news already, I look forward to telling her that I'm her father. I imagine she'll find that she likes being a Lamb."

He glanced at Ruth as if waiting for her praise, then smiled in spite of not getting it. "I didn't expect her to be here when I came to see Dorothy — although I'm not surprised. It's the luck of the Lambs, you know."

"I really need to leave."

"I suppose you're critical of my letting her be admitted to the State School. Well, I had no choice in the matter, did I?"

Ruth murmured, "I thought we always had a choice."

"What? Speak up."

"I thought we always had a choice!"

"That's what I thought you said. Easy for you to say, my dear. Would you give up millions, if you were asked to? Would you give up your social standing, your whole way of life? June will understand, being a woman of means. Interesting that she married well, in spite of the environment in which she

was raised. It was instinctive, I suppose —
you know to which side I fall in the nature
versus nurture argument. Anyhow, I wasn't
worried about her. I knew I would always
make things right for her, eventually."

"Just when she needed you, after she got
rich and famous." Why now? she wondered.
"I suppose your mother died."

"You really needn't take that tone with
me. No, Mummy is still alive. See what I
am risking for your sister? Everything.
Mummy will be livid."

What about Mother? Would he publicly
acknowledge her? Did she want to be ac-
knowledged?

A single robin fluted in the distance, its
tootle muffled as by a heavy snowfall.

Dizzy or not, her kids needed her. "Goodbye, Mr. Lamb."

She took a few steps and then braced
herself in the doorway of the cabin and
looked out. A gauzy layer of dust topped
everything in sight, capping her car listing
in the dusty ditch, the fence posts, each
blade of grass, in taupe.

She stepped off the little porch. Pain flared
from her ankle. She must have twisted it
when she fell. There would be no quick
getaways on foot for her.

"Do you really think that . . . *vehicle* . . .

will start?" he called as she hop-limped to her car.

The attempts to crank the T proved him right. She slammed the tinny door and started hobbling down the road, her fury enflamed by fear. Please, let her family be safe.

From the porch, he announced, "I will give you a lift."

When she turned to him, he was strolling toward his limousine, fishing in his pocket for keys. The pleats in the wide legs of his expensive blue suit, though a little dusty, were still perfect.

He was the last person on earth that she wanted to share a car with. Yet a minute later she found herself on the plush upholstered seat next to him. His Cadillac had roared to life with a simple turn of the key. No arm-breaking cranking for him.

"Isn't this better, lass?"

*I didn't realize that Cincinnati was a part of England,* she thought irritably.

He turned to her after backing the vehicle out of the ditch. "I meant to ask, have you had people prospecting for oil or natural gas out here lately?"

"I don't know. Why?"

"I have wondered if there were still unexplored pockets of gas in this region, though the boom south of here in Gas City is getting played out. Oil's the better chance."

"Nobody has mentioned it to me."

"You don't say? While I was getting up the nerve to speak to your mother, I saw a car on your road that didn't look local, rather a big vehicle, seemed out of place." He glanced at her. "Well, let me know if they make you an offer. I'm always looking for ways to expand my holdings — diversification kept us Lambs afloat during Prohibition. And besides, what does it ever hurt to want just a little more?"

The Cadillac roared toward the sunrise.

"Stop the car."

"But we have a little ways."

"Stop. I can walk. And don't come up to the house. My husband's recuperating and we don't need company." She got out. Although, she thought, trudging toward the farm, they could use a dab of that good Lamb luck.

A voice bellowed from the top of the basement stairs. "Mother!"

Down in the basement, Dorothy lifted her head from the hot tangle of grubby limbs and bobbed haircuts clinging to her. Ruth?

The roaring, the awful scratching at the house, had stopped. The crow of Jeanne's rooster floated in its place. Dawn had come.

The wooden rafters of the basement ceiling creaked with the footsteps overhead. "Mother!" Ruth shouted. "John! June! *Girls!* Where are you?"

The girls raised faces sticky with sleep. "Mommy!"

Dorothy patted grimy heads. "Girls, you stay here. Let me make sure that everything's all right. I'll be right back."

They started to follow her.

"I mean it — stay!"

She left four sets of scowls.

Ruth wasn't in the kitchen when Dorothy got there. She ran her finger across the porcelain-topped worktable, then examined the tan powder coating her finger. Dust. It was everywhere, furring the draining board, the windowsill, the floor — even the glass of the kitchen lamp. When she rubbed her fingers on the swag of her collar, it was full of grit, too.

She banged at her dress, raising a small cloud, as she bustled toward John's bedroom. She spied her tinting on the desk in the hall. She paused just long enough to lift the wax paper she'd taped over the photo as she always did to protect it.

It was as if gauze had been pressed into the drying paint — the surface was as textured as the skin of an orange. A beautiful bride, ruined. How Mr. Cryder would yell.

Oh, to hell with him.

Her pulse lurched as she trundled down the hall. What had come over her? The language! What a mess we'd be in, if others could hear our thoughts.

Nick loped from John's bedroom, with the hunch of a swatted dog.

"What's wrong?" she cried. "Is it John?"

"Goodbye, Mrs. Dowdy."

"Where are you going?"

He paused. "She said to pack my bags."

"But you don't have any bags, do you?"

"I will go because she said to go. But Root is scared, Mrs. Dowdy."

"Ruth's allowed to be scared."

He studied her a moment, then nodded. "Goodbye, Mother." He shook her hand. "You are a good mama."

"Me?" She nestled his words to her heart as he strode away, precious treasure. If only that were true.

Her daughters were hovering over the bed when she entered John's room. Ruth looked up from wiping John's face with a corner of sheet and, seeing Dorothy, frowned as if she were trying to place something.

Dorothy sucked in her breath. "Is he up?"

"No," Ruth snapped.

June kept her face turned to John.

Dorothy's flesh prickled. "Maybe all he needs is another vitamin shot. Where's Richard?"

Ruth all but growled. "He's still at the Squibbs'." She glanced at June. "Don't blame me for leaving him there. He made me."

A knock came on the back door.

"There he is!" Dorothy exclaimed. Though why in the world would he knock? Was it Nick again — though surely he would have barged right back in.

The knock sounded once more, louder.

"I didn't think it was locked," said Dorothy.

"Just answer it!" Ruth cried.

"All right."

Dust scrunching underfoot, she trundled toward the door, making a quick jog out of the way, to the front room, to snap off the hissing radio.

The knocking rocked the outer door as she entered the kitchen. She grabbed her sweater hanging on a hook by the door — my, it had gotten chilly! The temperature must have plunged forty degrees overnight.

The sight of Richard's gray fedora through the back door window unleashed the irritability that comes after surviving something big. For crying out loud, why was he being such a nuisance?

"Coming!" She felt as cross as Venus when awakened from a nap. Her skin jumped: Venus! Where was she? Her agitation boosted by a fresh shot of fear, she paused on the landing to yell down the basement steps. "Girls, you can come up now!"

She flung open the door. "Family doesn't have to kn—"

The word died on her lips. Edward Lamb took off his hat.

"Hello, Dorothy."

# FORTY-FOUR

*Indiana-Michigan line, 1934*

The blood rushed from Dorothy's head, leaving her strangely aware of her skull. Its bony cap seemed to be the only thing holding her upright as she gaped out the kitchen door.

Thirty-three years had whitened Edward's majestic mane, swagged his leonine eyes with flesh, and bulged his middle against his watch chain, but she would have known him anywhere. Who wouldn't? With his chin up and shoulders back, albeit both a little meatier now, and that massive head, cushioned these days with a chin-strap of flesh, he was Lamb Pride personified.

"Dorothy?"

A kaleidoscope of Edwards spun before her: Little Edward in velvet shorts, darting after her in a game of tag; Edward the Youth, looking up from behind a forest of glass at the family table and winking at her

439

as she filled his mother's cup; Edward in his Prime, strolling through the Lambs' garden gate with a small amused smile. The girl in her reached for them with longing, even as the old woman recoiled from the lion peering through the farmhouse door.

"Looking as beautiful as ever." His voice was as rich and fruity as she remembered it, with his special hint of London fog. "You have not changed a bit."

Dorothy swallowed back some dust. "I don't know about that."

"It has been a long time."

She could not speak. How many years, decades, had she yearned for this moment? She had pined for this man, dreamed of him, had planned her escape with him when he came for her. And now he was standing on her doorstep.

Edward's smile dashed into a perturbed frown. Goodness, what'd she do? He was as changeable as Ruth. It struck Dorothy then that, though she had never dwelled on it, Ruth was his kin, too. They were all touched by Lamb blood. Except for William.

"Aren't you going to let me in?"

She could not make her hand move. Words popped from her mouth, words that she didn't know were there, they had been stuffed down so deep. "What would your mother say?"

"Pardon me?"

She cleared her throat. "How is your mother?"

He raised his eyebrows, then spoke cautiously. "Mother is Mother. Fine, for her age. I suppose she'll outlive us all."

She nodded.

They both glanced at the latch of the door. What was keeping her from the simple courtesy of letting him in? It wasn't like her to misbehave.

She sensed movement from below the basement landing: Ruth's girls were creeping up the steps.

He noticed her distraction. "Who's that?" He brightened. "June?"

"My grandkids."

He craned his neck to get a view of them. "Grandchildren," he marveled. "I have grandchildren. Both of my wives died before we had offspring."

The children gazed up from the stairwell like baby birds in the nest.

"Get!" Dorothy hissed. When they didn't move, she whisked them back, surprising herself. She usually relished an opportunity to show them off.

The girls stared at her, not sure what to make of the novelty of her bossing them when it wasn't an emergency. Reluctantly, they retreated down the steps, except for Irene, who couldn't be convinced, the very image of her doubting mother.

How precious this child — all of them — were to her! "Scoot!"

Dorothy could see the offense on the girl's face. But Edward's confident smile made her stamp her foot at the child. He was not getting her.

She inwardly sagged as Irene took one step at a time back down, holding the wooden rail. If she'd ever had this child's love, she had lost it now.

"Dorothy," Edward said. "I want to say I am sorry."

Dorothy shook her head.

"I should have said so long ago."

"Doesn't matter."

"It does. I know that. Actually, I did try to apologize, a number of years ago, after I got your greeting card. I came by your husband's store to find your house."

"You did?"

"The brute had the nerve to punch me."

Disbelief poked through her anxiety. "William? Socked you?"

"Right in the chin, he did. And I had told him that I came in peace!"

She stared at the man she had dreamed of

for decades. Rowdy Dowdy was actually rowdy?

"All I said to him was that you wrote to me."

Something cracked open in her chest; sorrow came rushing in. William had known that she loved Edward and yet he protected her. He had taken care of her and their children the whole of his adult life, knowing that her heart was not his, that June was not his, and yet he continued to give and give and give.

Dorothy felt movement just inside the house. Oh, that Irene! She whirled around to yell at her.

But it wasn't Irene. June was edging her way back deeper into the kitchen. She must have come out and heard them and was now retreating.

Dorothy's pulse jumped. She turned back around guiltily. Please don't let Edward have seen June.

Excitement animated Edward's lordly features. "June! It's your father!"

June froze by the worktable. She turned around slowly.

"Mother." Her voice was stiff. "Come in the house now."

"Come closer!" Edward put his face to the screen. "I want a look at you."

*Run!* Dorothy wanted to shout. But it wasn't her decision to make. Maybe June would want to be a Lamb. Heaven knows, she herself had wanted that for so many years.

Ruth dashed into the kitchen. "Mother, June, come quick. It's John! He's awake!" A glimpse toward the back door stopped her mid-stride.

The little girls were thumping up the stairs again. "Mommy! Mommy!"

Ruth came to the steps and flagged them back down as Dorothy blocked the door. In her side vision, she saw a child-sized blur. One of the girls had escaped.

Dorothy faced Edward rigidly so as not to give her away. Let her go up to her room, play that Monopoly game, stay out of sight.

He clapped on his hat. "For Christ's sake, what is wrong with you people? Isn't anyone going to open this door?"

Ruth drew up next to Dorothy and pulled back her chin, long like her father's. She looked to her mother for instructions, whom she had never consulted in her life.

Edward went red. "This is preposterous. Come, now, Dode, quit playing around. Tell June who I am, like the good girl that you are."

At that moment, little Jeanne, she of the

perpetual worries, ran up to the outer door and flung it open.

"Here!" Panting, she held out a shoebox. "Now leave us alone."

Edward crooked his mouth. "Thank you for the shoes, my child, but this is serious business."

"It's not shoes." She put the box in his hands then propped open the door with her bony body. She shoved grubby bangs from her eyes as he slipped off the box lid, plucked through the tissue, then drew out the small golden casket. The embossed cavorting cupids shone in the light of day.

"For the love of God."

"It's valuable. See, it's got a bird?" Jeanne stepped onto the porch to push the slender knob near its base. Out popped the feathered automaton, clacking its beak and twirling to the birdsong produced by the rotating metal cylinder hidden inside the box.

"Why are you giving him that?" Ruth said. "You must have spent every cent you had, buying that at the dime store."

Edward was red to the roots of his hair.

"You said it was your mother's," Dorothy said.

"It was." Edward glanced away. "Well, technically, it was my niece's. Mother bought it for her at a carnival when she came for a visit."

A blue haze fuzzed Dorothy's vision. Even as Edward grimaced at her through it, in her mind's eye mild-mannered William, fury flashing from his wire glasses, was rearing back and delivering him a wallop.

"Why don't you leave us alone?" Jeanne piped.

Edward squatted next to her with a grunt. "Who do you think I am, princess, that you want to chase me away so badly?"

She looked up at Dorothy.

She nodded.

The child glared. "Pretty Boy Floyd."

"Pretty Boy Floyd! You don't say. Well, I suppose that's a step up from Dillinger. No, princess, I own banks, not rob them."

Jeanne's face crumpled. She trampled down the stairs to the basement.

"You shouldn't have laughed at her," said Ruth. "It's not such a wild guess. I told you that there have been bank robbers crawling around the countryside." She touched Dorothy's arm. "Mother, about John . . ."

Gripping the open outer door for support, Edward straightened his knees. He sought out June, who'd drawn closer to the door. "June Marie. Dear. I did not want to do this so crudely, but have been given no choice. Have you ever heard of Lamb Brewing Company?" He gave her time to answer, then cleared his throat. "That's me. I'm Edward Lamb."

She glanced at her mother. Dorothy roasted with shame.

"I'm your father."

"I know."

*"You know?"*

"My dad told me, years ago."

"Is that a fact? I suppose he's done my work for me, then. Nice of him." He spread his hands. "Well, perhaps you'd like to chat. We've a lot of ground to cover." He stepped forward.

June pulled back. "I thought he was just telling me a fairy tale, to make me feel good after he'd driven us down Forest Park Boulevard once, and he saw that I was sad. He dropped the subject when he saw how it upset me, and never spoke of it again."

"Well, believe it, dear. You've got my blood."

"But, sir" — June smiled woodenly — "I don't want it."

"You don't want Lamb blood?"

One look at her sister and Ruth stepped in front of her. "Hey, I have Lamb blood. How about me?"

"How do you have Lamb blood?" asked June.

Edward stroked his cuff. "You do have darling children . . ."

Ruth pulled back with a repulsed laugh. "No!"

"Stop!" Dorothy cried. "Everyone, please, stop."

Her heart pounded when they did. She was not used to people listening to her. She rubbed her chin hair then expelled a long breath.

"I don't know who knows what, so here are the facts: I grew up with Edward. I loved Edward. I had Edward's baby. Edward is my half-brother. His mother took our baby. His mother put her in the State School when she was six months old." She turned to June, her gumption, her joy in life, draining from her fast. This might be the last time they ever spoke. "I let you stay in there for five months. For five months, Junie. I'm sorry. I'm really sorry. It's despicable. Now I will go."

Edward reached out to her as she turned.

Dorothy shied away from him. "But not with you."

Before she could react, June grabbed her arm and pulled her inside. Ruth went for the outer door.

"Wait!" Edward blocked it with his shoulder. "That was the past. This is now. Don't you think I could do a lot for that sick young fellow in there?"

"Look!" Ruth pointed. "Baby Face Nelson!"

When Edward glanced behind him, Ruth grabbed the door and slammed it.

June locked it quickly. "Goodbye, Mr. Lamb."

"Look at you," said Ruth. "All fierce."

June's hand remained firmly on Dorothy's arm as, through the glass, they watched Edward dab the back of his neck with his handkerchief while he wandered toward his automobile.

Just then, in the open car window, the cross face of a cat appeared. A lanky feline body followed, trailed by a remarkably long tail. Venus balanced on the window frame, her charmed-snake of an appendage swaying, before slowly, carefully, she eased herself down the side of the car, the prolonged *screeeech* of her nails against metal audible even in the house. She trotted off, the glory of her white nib bobbing over her head as Edward flung open the door and dropped into the vehicle.

"That's going to leave a mark," Dorothy said.

"Yep." Ruth let her approving smile fall. "Enough of this nonsense. I've got to get back to John."

Her entire being trained on June's touch, Dorothy raised fearful eyes to her daughter. She glanced away in embarrassment. "Junie, maybe we shouldn't misbehave like this."

But the girl was not letting go. By degrees, Dorothy let her gaze return to the face that she loved so intensely, into the eyes of the woman whose affection she had never had, nor deserved. And what she saw there was not fright, not fury, not repulsion nor disgust, not judgment, not scorn, nor even rejection, just cautious . . . wonder.

June drew a breath. "There's always a first time, Mother."

She left to follow Ruth.

Her old heart pumping, Dorothy pivoted slowly from the door. But as she did so, a glance toward the basement revealed her grand-girls, peering up from the stairwell like bunnies whose nest was about to be mowed over.

"Grandma!" Margaret pushed up her wire-rimmed glasses. "Please! Is it okay to come up now?"

Fear scraped Dorothy's chest as she gazed down at the next generation of her flesh and blood. What if she offered them her comfort and none of them chose to take it? What if none of them chose to come to her when she offered herself? She wasn't even sure if Junie would forgive her, once everything sunk in.

In her mind's eye, William raised his long chin to look up from his stack of bills. "Dorothy, dear. You're not dead yet."

Her hand went to the hair on her chin, bristly and recalcitrant, still growing in spite of everything, an upstart in old age, just like her. A salty lump threatened her throat as she let go of William. *I'm not, yet, am I, dear?*

She opened her arms to her granddaughters. "Come on up."

■ ■ ■ ■

# PART FIVE

■ ■ ■ ■

# FORTY-FIVE

*Minneapolis, 1950*

The clopping of two pairs of sturdy-heeled white shoes, as rhythmic as that of a team of matched horses, rang from the painted walls. Across the lobby, Mr. Gustafson held open the elevator door. The past sixteen years had further wizened him, elongating his withered upper lip, knobbing his cheeks, and shrinking his spry figure to truly elfin proportions, as if time had a way of concentrating a person.

His eyes shone like mercury under the crepe garlands of his lids as the sisters clattered on board. "Morning, Bettys! Mrs. Whiteleather — good to have you back! Where's your pearls?"

Funny, while June had given them up long ago, everyone was wearing pearls these days, although perhaps not the multiple strands she used to hide behind. "Thank you, Mr. Gustafson. It's good to be back."

"How are you, Mr. G?" Ruth brushed at her red swing coat — quite a fashionable coat, purchased at Dayton's. June was surprised at her sister's good taste, now that she had a little money.

Mr. Gustafson pulled the brass gate closed with knotty hands. "Oh, I can't complain, can't complain. Pretty flowers." He nodded at the bouquet of blush pink camellias dampening June's white gloves. "For the secret project?"

June aimed the downturned brim of her hat at him. "You are determined to get me to spill the beans yet, aren't you?"

"I'm trying!"

"Only a few more months until the unveiling in September, Mr. G." Ruth switched her black patent leather purse to her other arm. "You haven't long to wait."

He whistled. "September, 1950. Never thought I'd live that long. Never thought I'd be saying nineteen-anything for the date — where did the time go? Time's our most precious treasure, and here we run through it like a box of Red Hots."

On the fifth floor — the Betty Crocker Kitchens had moved a few blocks to 400 Second Avenue South, some time back — Mr. Gustafson folded back the gate like an accordion, then drew open the door. "Well, go on, girls. Go make someone happy."

"We will!" they said in unison, then, to one another, "Touch red."

Ruth rolled her eyes, feigning annoyance. June smiled to herself. *You were ever the child with your sister.*

In a blur of white gloves, bright hats, and black fedoras, visitors dressed in their Sunday best — mostly women and children but also a few men looking forward to the samples — were already gathering in the glassed-in reception area. Every day brought hundreds of them, which was only to be expected after Betty insisted her listeners come visit when she hosted *The George Burns and Gracie Allen Show* on the radio and in a cornucopia of current publications. There was talk of Betty taking her show to television, which seemed to be a promising new way of reaching a large audience, although perhaps not as effectively as Betty's soon-to-be-released secret project.

Already Betty's outreach was paying off. For several years running, Betty Crocker was the "Second Most Well-Known Woman in America," according to *Fortune* magazine. Only Mrs. Roosevelt beat her in popularity. As Ruth said, *Not bad for a real nobody.*

June could feel eager eyes scrutinizing her and Ruth as they passed by the plate-glass walls of Reception, the nearly audible turning of the guests' mental wheels ricocheting from the modern blond wood furniture: *Are you Betty? Are you?*

She held her breath until she had slipped into the dressing room area. She was still often mistaken for Betty, although Advertising had changed the official portrait of Betty Crocker in 1936 to that of a somber matron. In the wallows of the Depression, Advertising finally realized what June had always thought, that the nation needed a mother, not a blue-eyed girl next door. Regardless of what Betty's portrait looked like, however, all the girls were confused for her, even Ruth. Desperate to meet their hero, people saw what they wanted to see.

Disappointing Betty's fans when they found out that she wasn't real had never gotten any easier for June. For reasons she now understood, she still inwardly writhed during any confrontation, even after finding success as an illustrator (her drawings of children for Kool-Aid had launched her career, as had the ones for Heinz Tomato Ketchup); even after training other women how to think like Betty, including her independent-minded sister, before June had left the job thirteen years ago; even after core did not go away just because she knew its cause. But she was meeting the challenges of raising a son. The bleak insecurity at her working on it.

Ruth and she took off their coats, laid their hats and gloves in their cubbies, and got out aprons.

"Tie mine," said Ruth.

June tied her sister's apron in a bow, then turned for her sister to do hers.

The swish of nylons, laughter, and conversation filled the dressing room, rather like a cocktail party, June thought, though this one didn't make her as nervous as did those that she attended with Richard. Socializing would never come naturally to her, not like mothering had. She'd been astonished twelve years ago, when, after traveling across the country to Seattle after the adoption agency call, one look at her new little boy and love had billowed up and drowned out her usual inner clamor of inadequacy. This little soul trusted her, and she could not, would not, fail. Simple as that.

With forty-eight women now working as Bettys — forty-nine, if you included June, hired on for the Secret Project — all seven kitchens on the floor would soon brim with activity. Exchanging nods and chitchat, June scooped up her camellias and made her way toward what was called the "Kamera

Kitchen," where she was to work on the setup for "Baked Alaska — A Dessert of Beauty . . . and Mystery," a spread that was to be featured in the Secret Project. She parted with Ruth at the "Polka Dot Kitchen," so that Ruth could go on to the "Kitchen of Tomorrow," where, under the gaze of amusing Swedish figures spouting gay Swedish mottoes, Ruth would test new products, featuring flour, always flour.

Ruth had been on the staff since coming to live in the Twin Cities in the fall of '34. She'd been hired in a nod to the novice bakers of the world — a pity hire, in truth, although no one would say that aloud. At least they had better not say so in front of June. The bosses had heard the whispers that June's brother-in-law had relapsed into his slumber only hours after rousing from that first vitamin shot. Although Richard would administer more injections over the next few days — emptying in desperation all the vials that he'd brought with him on the trip — John could only wake for a few minutes at a time after that first burst of energy. It was as if the vitamin shot had been just a placebo, giving John the courage to rally every bit of his life force for that evening. Perhaps that push had been too much for his heart. He had died three weeks later. Heart failure.

June plunked the camellias in the vase on the table in Kamera Kitchen. It had turned out well for Ruth to work here. She was one of the loudest advocates for spelling out even the simplest cooking techniques in the Secret Project, like how to boil an egg, one of the aspects that made the project so different and special. It burst with pictures, menus, and foolproof recipes, a homemaker's helper for when one's mother couldn't teach them. Advertising would be pushing the idea that it was a cookbook for the modern woman, but June thought it might even be better than that: a tool for women to control their own world. Once they knew how to cook, to entertain, to manage the house, women didn't need Betty Crocker to tell them what they wanted. Given enough information, they could decide that for themselves.

June was directing the photography of a Baked Alaska with meringue peaks toasted into perfection by Janice from Milwaukee, when she heard a disturbance coming from behind the glass of the visitors' gallery. From old habit, she glanced around for a box of tissues — unnecessary, really, when the tour guides were such dab hands at substituting tears of disappointment and loss with a Kleenex and a brownie. But this time it wasn't a reader lamenting over her discovery of the truth. It was Richard, entertaining bystanders as he ushered Mother into the Tasting Kitchen.

Even though a frequent visitor to the Home Services kitchens, Mother stood shyly to the side. She'd never shed her awkwardness in a crowd, though she did find, as did her daughters, that her appearing in public was not the calamity for her or for them that they once feared. It was Richard who kept insisting that she go out.

Now Mother waited patiently, sidling up a hand to check on the smart hat that Richard had bought her. Being a stickler for plain speaking, June imagined that Mother did not enjoy his tall tales, with one of which he was no doubt charming his current audience. But Mother did appreciate how good he was to her — good to Ruth and the kids, too, insisting that the whole family come live with them on Summit Avenue (which prickly, proud Ruth only agreed to when he offered to rent their little carriage house). He brought up old JoJo, too, and stabled her in the garage for her last few years. Even Mother's beloved horse had the Summit Avenue life.

Still, Richard had not forgiven himself.

Though June and everyone told him otherwise, he blamed himself for John's relapse. He felt the injection had falsely encouraged John to do too much and he had taxed his nervous system from the exertion. Perhaps it truly had damaged him. That no other physicians would try the shots after John's case only confirmed Richard's fears and deepened his guilt.

But it was June who had felt guilty. Especially those first few months after Richie came into their lives, when Richard cuddled the child, sang him songs, brought home teddy bears, baseballs, and pogo sticks, trying desperately to make up for the years they'd lost when he'd been afraid to tell June he was infertile. Yet she knew that she was the one in the wrong. She had sold Richard short for far, far too long, wasting precious time in loving a man who was already well loved by someone else, when a good man was patiently waiting for her. If Richard could forgive her, she could forgive him.

They were reasonably happy now, as happy as anyone who has to live at the mercy of their life-time's and life-mate's quirks. The fact was, they were comfortable with each other's secrets. How many couples can honestly say that?

The photographer, Dale, popped the blown flashbulb from his camera.

"Say, isn't that your mother?"

June nodded as she took one more poke at the camellias.

Dale produced a fresh flashbulb from his pocket. "I can shoot the last of this film on my own." He fit the bulb into the reflector. "I think we've already got what we want."

"Thank you, Dale."

June clicked her way over the spotless tiles even as her sister emerged from the Kitchen of Tomorrow, as if it were nothing of consequence for them to go over and claim the elderly woman behind Richard, fidgeting with her new red hat.

# How the Story Begins

*1908*

Little Ruth felt herself being shaken. She opened an eye. Six-year-old June leaned over her, the sleeves of her red robe dragging against Ruth's covers.

"Get up! Santa's been here!"

Ruth sat up and rubbed her eyes, then blinked at the top of June's wavy gold hair as her big sister jammed slippers on her feet and buttoned her into her robe. She slid off the bed and let June lead her, slippers scuffing across the wood floor.

They crouched at the entrance to the front room. Empty pink sockets flashed where June's baby teeth had recently been.

Ruth tears the paper from the typewriter with a *rrrrip*!

In this revision, she needs to start the book in a different place, somewhere more exciting. Who cares about kids at Christmas?

Maybe she should start with Dorothy's recollections. Or with June being one of the Bettys. Ruth read somewhere that you should always throw out your first chapter and go with the second.

She feeds in another sheet, adjusts the gooseneck light on her desk, then sits back. Problem is, she likes little Ruth. Such a spirited sprite, just like her own girls had been. When she stares out the tulle-swagged windows over the garage, the venetian blinds open to the night, she can still see the girls gamboling on the lawn like they used to, making up stories, bossing each other around, disagreeing, then agreeing, laughing, shouting, singing. Such brassy, bold, outrageous things. Such tender and forgiving hearts.

She thinks maybe she should start with the little girls after all. She leans forward to type, then flops against the wooden harp of the chairback again. Who's she kidding, thinking this book will see the light of day? What publisher is going to take it? They say to write what you know, but who cares what she knows? She's no Dame Daphne du Maurier. She's no globe-trotting Michener. She is just a former farm wife from Indiana who is fool enough to write.

Secretly, she thinks she's got a bestseller.

She sighs heavily, listening to her mother scrubbing clothes in the kitchen sink, even at this hour, scrubbing to perfection with rickety old Venus chiseling at her ankles with her head. Well, don't we all want a little perfection, to do something best, to have a little something more than everyone else, even if it's just whiter underpants?

Ruth wants more, she'll admit it. She wants more than being a reasonably desirable widow (made even more desirable by turning all her suitors down), more than being a mother, more, even, than being America's Mother, although she is actually grateful for her daytime job and decent pay. She lives on Summit Avenue, for crying out loud! Why these aren't enough, she doesn't know. All she knows is that she has this constant craving, this itchiness in her chest, this longing that makes her despair of her daughters leaving home, of the white streak at her temples, of her mother's gnarled hands, of graying pets, of flowers fading, of leaves falling, of bare trees — anything that will not let her look away from the awareness that time is passing and will leave her behind.

She feels a little sick. But into her malaise floats the memory of her teenage self, bashing a broom over the head of the creep who'd threatened June. She sees teenage June, standing half-naked in a saggy swimsuit for all the town to see, mad as hell — for June. She sees herself traipsing alone to Chicago to become a genuine flapper.

Where are these brave girls now?

The mournful whistle of a train sounds far beyond the venetian blinds.

Well, she's not dead yet.

Laying her hands to the keyboard, she types.

# ACKNOWLEDGMENTS

While it might appear that you are holding a book or electronic reading device in your hands, you are actually holding a chunk of a life. Mine. For some inexplicable reason, several years back I felt compelled to take some of the elements that most haunted my childhood and fit them together in a completely fictitious story. The Fort Wayne State School (formerly known as the Indiana School for Feeble-Minded Youth), with the howls of its institutionalized residents audible to those of us living nearby; the tornados that periodically raked the Midwest; the damage wreaked on my mother's family when her farmer father was turned into a living dead man by *encephalitis lethargica,* or "sleeping sickness," in an epidemic that swept the world during the Great Depression; my mother's mysterious reclusiveness and my own fervent wish that she would be more like Betty Crocker: all these were bits that demanded to be part of a novel. It took four years of leaning on friends, family, and colleagues to put the pieces together and get the completed puzzle into your hands. I feel lucky to be able to thank them now.

From the start, my friend Jan Johnstone was instrumental in helping me to unify the disparate aspects. (She also introduced me to book clubs by starting ours thirty-some years ago, and took me to my first yoga class about ten years back — everyone needs a Jan Johnstone in their life!) When she learned that Betty Crocker was to play a role in my book and that I was traveling to Minneapolis/St. Paul to dig up what I could about America's Mother, she generously became my guide to the Twin Cities, as well to farming in the Midwest, educating me with a tour of her family farm in Hector, Minnesota. I thank her family in the Gopher State for so generously opening their homes and hearts to me during my visit: Geri and Joel Skogen, Sharon and Dan Marks, Chuck and Judy Gustafson, and Brian and Mary Gustafson, you are dear to me! Thank you, too, to Jan's childhood friend, DeeAnn Norskog Edlund, for rounding up some Betty Crocker information.

On top of the crucial grounding in Minnesota and farming lore Jan and her family gave me, it was Jan's sharing of her uncle Wallace F. Gustafson's memoir that actually organized the book. In it, I learned of the dust storm that terrorized the entire United States east of the Rockies on May 9, 1934. "Uncle Wally" wrote that he had been driving his mother to the Twin Cities on that day and had to pull the car off the road for a long time — the dust completely blinded him. As I read that, a chill went over me. I knew this was the event around which I could center my plot.

Only four years (!) and a lot of help from my friends later, and I had a book. Thank you to Karen Torghele, Ruth Berberich, Jani Taylor, Sue Edmonds, and again, Jan Johnstone, for hearing me out on long walks and over dinners, supporting me and "the Betty book" through thick and thin. Thank you, too, to Colleen Oakley, Stephanie Cowell, Alison Law, Suzanne Van Atten, Susan Rebecca White, Michael Martone, Amy Bonesteel, and Joshilyn Jackson for your writerly pep talks. A huge thank-you goes to dear family friend Mark Meyer for being my guide into the past in Fort Wayne, and to long-term pal and confidante Barb Bedwell McKee for giving me a home away from home and a lifetime of great memories.

(Thanks, too, Barb, for reminding me of the sound of those swings.) Thank you as well to Tom Murfield, Randy Harter, Monya Weissert, and Michael Martone, again, in your guidance of things Fort Wayne, and to Neal Butler, owner of Pio Market, for the tour of your grocery store which has remained much like it was when it was a cutting-edge self-serve Piggly Wiggly in the 1930s. Thanks so much, too, to Dan Wire, for the fantastic boat tour of the rivers of Fort Wayne, which are the lifeblood of those of us who grew up near them.

I'd like to thank my dear agent Emma Sweeney and the saintly Margaret Sutherland Brown at ESA for their readings of the book in its many forms and for their patient help in shaping it, as well as for their steadfast championing of my cause. I don't have enough words to thank my editor Jackie Cantor for giving me permission to write the story I really wanted to write, and then for coaxing the best out of me — I am beyond grateful. I'm indebted, too, to Karen Kosztolnyik, for shepherding the story through its early stages. A special thanks goes out to Michelle Podberezniak, my publicist, for her dauntless efforts. And without the valiant team members at Gallery Books — including Jennifer Bergstrom,

Aimee Bell, Lisa Litwack, Jen Long, Abby Zidle, Caroline Pallotta, and Sara Quaranta — you wouldn't be reading this.

Each of these individuals has blown life into the book you now hold. But *The Sisters of Summit Avenue* is foremost about families and sisters, both of which I have plenty. Thank you to my sisters, Margaret Edison, Jeanne Wensits, Carolyn Browning, and Arlene Eifrid. You, along with our brothers Howard and David Doughty, have made me who I am and greatly influenced this story. I'm lucky, too, to have three great daughters — Lauren Lynch, Megan Cayes, and Alison Stetler — to shape my thinking and to mother me as much as I mother them. Thank you, girls; thank you, Sean, Michael, and Jamil, my wonderful sons-in-law. Know that you and your children are everything to me. And thank you, Mike, for being the most supportive, wise, and steady husband humanly possible. But at the core of this book are my parents — my gentle dad, whom I worshipped, and my mother, whom I never understood. I'm trying, now, to know you as the girl you once were — Mother, this book is my love letter to you.

# ABOUT THE AUTHOR

**Lynn Cullen** grew up in Fort Wayne, Indiana and is the bestselling author of *The Sisters of Summit Avenue, Twain's End,* and *Mrs. Poe,* which was named an NPR 2013 Great Read and an Indie Next List selection. She lives in Atlanta.

The employees of Thorndike Press hope you have enjoyed this Large Print book. All our Thorndike, Wheeler, and Kennebec Large Print titles are designed for easy reading, and all our books are made to last. Other Thorndike Press Large Print books are available at your library, through selected bookstores, or directly from us.

For information about titles, please call:
(800) 223-1244

or visit our website at:
gale.co   horndike

To share you   omments, please write:
Publisher
Thorndike Press
10 Water St., Suite 310
Waterville, ME 04901